'A touch of Irvine Welsh... the narrative is electric.' *Guardian*

'Very original, with really credible characters and a great sense of time and place.' Ian Rankin

'Mesmerising. And kind of frightening that a female writer can crawl so far into the male psyche.' John Niven

'It is punk that is frequently described as nihilistic, but de la Mer shows that rave culture is far more deserving of that description... As vicariously thrilling in its portrayal of the hedonistic highs as it is honest in its depiction of how transient and empty those good times are.' Chris Brookmyre

'The depiction of a troubled masculinity in an urban setting is something we have long associated with male Scottish writers, and it's encouraging to see a woman take this subject on board.' *Scottish Review of Books*

'It's about time we had a female Irvine Welsh... It's a pill-popping, *autobahn*-speed book about dodgy soldiers, rave culture and Hamburg's red light district.' *Glasgow Herald*

'Individual voices resonate in a sparkling debut novel of friendship, love and betrayal. An anthem for the E generation.' Bookgroup.info

'A genre-defining tale of the early '90s rave scene... A Class A novel about a friendship under pressure during the early 1990s rave scene. *4 a.m.* captures [...] the perennial pressures of growing from carefree youth into responsible and rounded adulthood. Novel of the year? I've yet to read a better one.' *Brighton Magazine*

'Stunning. The talent of this novel is in its racy writing and flawless characterisation. The Glasgow dialect is perfection... This is a "must read" novel of British Army life in peacetime... Gripping, frightening, funny and sad, *4 a.m.* is a terrific read.'
NewBooks Magazine

'Original and well-executed... A remarkable book by an extra-ordinarily gifted writer, whose research into the psyche of the male persona explodes off every page.' Pamreader

'A fantastic new book with a distinctly musical flavour.'
Hit or Miss

'The novel is a hell of a read... it is an extraordinary debut and shows de la Mer to be a writer of both skill and aptitude... a gritty contemporary drama.' *The View From Here*

'An ambitious first novel [...that] hits some big philosophical issues. This book is about loyalty and betrayal, about friendship in adversity, about love and its shallow proxies.'
Caledonian Mercury

'The real success is how refreshingly de la Mer writes about growing up, what that means to friendships and relationships, and how that process is often, or always, a painful one... Some have called Nina de la Mer "the female Irvine Welsh", but that doesn't tell you enough about the quality of her writing.'
Dear Scotland

*To read an extract from 4 a.m.,
turn to p.277*

Layla

Nina de la Mer

Myriad Editions

Published in 2014 by

Myriad Editions
59 Lansdowne Place
Brighton BN3 1FL

www.myriadeditions.com

1 3 5 7 9 10 8 6 4 2

A CIP catalogue record for this book is available
from the British Library.

ISBN: 978-1-908434-29-6

Printed on FSC-accredited paper by
CPI Group (UK) Ltd, Croydon, CR0 4YY

For Sidney

Friday

1

You blink. Once. Twice. Double blink. The spotlights are dazzling today, an angry bright yellow. This deliberate, or what? It's not like you have to be tortured into getting your kit off: you're five minutes away from stark naked. Or is it a mind trick, a beacon from a guardian angel sent to put you off dancing and that?

What-*ever*, it's doing your head in.

You squint and turn to shield your eyes with the back of one hand, and at the same time the other – the left one – grabs hold of the pole. Now both hands come together as you swing, arse-first, away from the glare, and you grip the cold metal column, stalking around it best you can in towering new heels – and with a right cob on and all. One step. Two. And you stumble, nearly tripping over your long evening gown, false eyelashes flickering as you glance over at Derek. He's the floor manager, yeah, stood mouthing off at the bar as per usual, jammed in by a scrum of legs, thongs and too much eyeliner.

The other girls. Flies round shit.

Deep breath, and you decide the brightness ain't a warning sign. Guardian angel? You should be so lucky. Maybe ask Derek to dim the lights, then? A minute's hesitation to suss the situation while you slither down the pole. Nah, best not – be a bit like petting a pit bull. Not gonna happen.

Instead, it's bottom lip in, boobs out, as you bring one leg up through a split in the gown in a clumsy can-can kick,

3

your energy lifting as a new tune kicks in. Miles away, you hum along *la, la, la* to the music, your attention wandering off from the stage. Only Derek's staring you out, looking even greyer and grimmer than usual, so you tick yourself off, geeing yourself up to focus on the customers instead.

Customers? If only.

Only the odd one in this afternoon, everyone's getting warmed up down the pub: football on the box later, England playing. As for the non-footie fans, look at them, bunch of nobby no-mates, grazing the outskirts of the dance floor, peering into the depths of their drinks, shifty and nervous like they was throwing a party and nobody showed up. You smile, putting it right on, all white enamel and bright pink lips. A suit catches your eye and winks. Loser!

And to think at one point, not long ago even, you thought all this – the red leather booths, the leopard-print wallpaper, the pockets loaded with cash – was the business. 'Classiest spot Up West,' the boss, Jeremy, said. You snort. A tenner for a topless dance, fifteen for a private nude one, twenty for a 'lesbian show'. Very classy. But you're doing it for the baby, for Connor, yeah? It will all be worth it if you can rake in more cash for him.

You mull this over while snaking down the pole in an S-shape (not as easy as what people might think), totting up the dances you've done so far today. No: fat chance. You won't cover the house fee at this rate, never mind put something aside.

You sigh, close your eyes. Not cos of the lights this time but a pointless go at blocking it all out: the heavy blanket of smoke and sweat in the air; the repetitive beats; the fingers clutching at you; the four-letter words jabbing into your ears. Anyway. End of the day, it's only money. Not like Mum leaves Connor wanting, or that just money will be enough to get him back. Funny how he pops into your head whenever, wherever, your Little Man, as if he was lying swaddled right there on the dance floor, screwing up his eyes like he does just before he cries out, wanting you, needing you. Such a good baby, so sweet-natured – always quick and easy to settle.

You blink. Once. Twice. Double blink. Try to swallow a golf-ball-sized lump in your throat. Again, not the lights.

Christ, what's that? Out of nowhere, a commotion on the main floor. What the – ? Oh, OK, an argument, raised voices (the suit and one of the regulars) competing with the intro to a catchy tune.

'*La, la, la, la, la, la, la, la.*'

That's you dragged back to the here and now.

Worse luck.

You hesitate, freeze-framed in a sexy pose till you realise the song's that old one from Kylie, 'Can't Get You out of My Head', and those licks, that voice, are just enough to take the edge off the other stuff, to blot out the baby blues.

Yeah.

Sod it. Sod Mum.

You look good.

You feel good.

You're a movie star swishing down the red carpet, centre of attention, lapping it up: autograph-hunters swarming, paps snapping at you. Strike a pose. *Flash! Bam!* 'Over here, Layla! Smile for the camera.' The fancy designer gown on the Oscars Best-Dressed list. You picture the headline: 'ENGLISH ROSE IS BELLE OF THE BALL'.

But, as you hitch up the gown to show off some leg, a cramping in your stomach blows the fantasy sky-high. Oh, God, someone's having a laugh, ain't they? Not *that*? Second turn on the pole today with an audience and Aunt Flo pays a visit. First period since the –

You're a pop idol on stage at Wembley, choked up on the love of the crowd. Flushed and hoarse, the fans chant your name: *Layla, Layla, Layla…* hands clap in time to your latest hit… tickets sold out in minutes… a cover photo on *Heat* magazine.

Oh, what's the use? Your period's on the warpath now, making itself known with a savage ripping and roaring through your stomach. No choice but to skip out to the loos, even if it does mean a bollocking from Derek, not to mention a ten-quid fine. But – ah, good – there's Ivana, lurking on her own by the exit. You wave both hands wildly to tip her the wink – if anyone's going to steal your spot, it has to be her – and she flounces over, legs up to her perky Lithuanian boobs.

'Got to pee,' you say, hoping she'll read the urgency in your face.

'After all the trouble weev the boss this week? You taking the peess?'

You screw up your forehead. Wince. 'You know, pee…'

She doesn't seem to get it, but never mind. You help her jump up on stage and she gives your hand a squeeze. At least she's there for you, unlike the other hussies, out for themselves.

Even so, when she breathes a 'thank you' you can almost see the pound signs in her eyes.

It's OK – you understand. You're good mates, but when it comes to the hustle on the main floor it's dog eat dog, every girl for herself. So there are no hard feelings as you say, 'Thanks, babe,' though you're already scampering off by the time 'babe' has escaped your lips, rushing across the smoky main floor to the stairway, the hulking double doors marked 'Private' groaning as you push past them, your feet breathing a sigh of relief as you whip off the new shoes to take the stairs two at a time, and you arrive at the changing room puffing, panting, gasping for –

Whoah! Only, walking through the door, the breath is completely sucked out of you, and you sink like you was drugged into the *tss tss* of deodorant cans, into cackles and crackles of laughter; tripping out on lurid fairground colours and choking back a cough brought on by a fug of glitter, talc and smoke what barely covers a rank whiff of shit (the drains must need clearing again). For a second you dither, watching them, the night shift girls jostling and preening at the front of the mirrors – hell-bent on using up the world's supply of Rimmel Sunshimmer – before creeping past them to get to your locker where you root around for your handbag. And there, nestled at the back among your clothes, you find the scruffy bald toy chihuahua. You chuckle, in spite of yourself. But no time to say more about that right now cos your hand's on the cubicle doorknob; you're pretty desperate to sort yourself out, as it goes. But then – *grr!* – Celeste, your sort of friend-cum-arch-rival, holds you up, asking how you are: she's heard that Jeremy has given you a warning, put you on day shifts.

'You must be gutted,' she finishes, blocking your way.

God, you wish you was invisible sometimes.

'Nah, fine, long story,' you mumble, not bothering to ask how she is, sweat breaking out above your top lip.

And then, as you slip past her oiled-up, half-naked orange flesh, your stomach turns over, and you're gripped by a sense of panic what clings on till you've thrown the bolt across the cubicle door.

What the hell's wrong?

Are you going to puke?

You're sinking up down, up down, like you was on a rollercoaster, getting more spun out by the minute. With faint spots dancing in front of your eyes, you fish in the cavern of your handbag for a tammie. Four months since your last period – what are the chances? Ooh, lucky you, there's a Lil-let Super – 'Heavy Flow'. Perhaps you *do* have a guardian angel. Ha! But the tammie's plastic casing is ripped,

7

the tampon itself glittered with make-up, shredded slightly at the tip.

Whatever. It'll do.

And so you fold down the plastic loo seat what's speckled with cigarette burns, the loo bowl decorated with a dirty rainbow of reds, browns and yellows, in a right state and all – the kind of loo what, truth be told, screams 'This Is Your Life'. But you've no choice but to yank down your G-string and pee in it, screwing up your face at the heaviness of the flow – *gross!* – then wiping once… twice… inserting the tammie, careful to tuck the cord inside, far enough so that it don't hang outside the G-string, not so far that you'll wind up on your backside spreadeagled with a mirror and a pair of tweezers later on. Been there, done that.

And squatting there over that loo, against the backdrop of chitter-chatter in the changing room, you're stung by a feeling you've got to know only too well in the past twelve months (since all the problems began). And, even though time is money and you're missing your slot on the pole, you allow these thoughts to skim through your mind. Thought it'd be well easy to come up London and find a place to stay and a job, that life'd be one long party and you could blank out all thoughts of your Little Man. Thought – silly moo – that the streets of London would be paved with opportunities: office and PA work and that. Paved with wide boys and chancers and oxygen thieves, more like. Mugged yourself right off there, didn't you?

You clench your teeth. Slide your bottom jaw to the right. Take a little bite of cheek. Throw yourself a pity party, in other words. Only to immediately shake your head, try and fill it with some sense. And, pulling up your G-string, you force yourself to tune into a typical changing room conversation instead. 'And so I says, for a sit-down, darling, it's a hundred,' someone's mouthing off outside the cubicle.

An unfamiliar voice – a new girl. Sapphire maybe? 'Got a monkey out of him in the end.'

Yeah, Sapphire – nobody else's voice squeaks like that.

'Never!' somebody – Celeste, maybe – replies.

What bollocks! A hundred quid for a sit-down? In her dreams! And a weariness, an anxiety, an uneasiness washes over you, a new worry to add to the growing pile. Cos, recently, Sapphire and a group of new girls arrived, right? Gang of them from a club on some grubby industrial estate in the East End. Boss took them on 'to get in more of a crowd'. Dirty dancers, they are, grinding and groping their way through their shifts. *So* not playing by the rules! And that Sapphire, she loves herself, forever crowing that she's done Page Three (of the *Daily Star*, not the *Sun* – which speaks for itself) and swanning about like she was an old-timer, when she's only been here five minutes. You bet she wishes she was an ice cream so she could lick herself, the silly cow.

Damn it, what's wrong with you? You tell yourself to put the claws back in, to not let the period, the hormones, get the better of you.

Not wanting to miss an opportunity, the miniature bottle of JD at the bottom of your handbag calls out for you then, an old mate who'll see you through the next couple of hours of shaking your booty and treading carpet. You swig it back, do up the straps on the high heels, kick open the cubicle door… only to catch sight of Susie. Shit (pardon your French) – you didn't hear her arrive! She doesn't notice you at first, thank God, cos she's fussing over the girls, giving pep talks, handing out stockings and that. Susie, she's the house mother, yeah? Meaning that she's a housekeeper, mum, shrink, nurse; police, judge and jury – all those things at the same time. Though you couldn't do without her, getting on her wrong side ain't an option, so you swallow back the JD in one mouthful. To make the smell evaporate, right?

Her eyes narrow when finally she spots you, sneaking towards the door. She bristles.

'Thought you were on days this week.'

'Yeah, bang on, just…' And you scrabble about for an excuse for being away from the main floor, while she gives you the evil eye. Your thoughts spring back to her first rant at you all them months ago. *If you split up with your boyfriend, I want to know. If you have a cold, I want to know. If you get a drug habit, I want to know. If you forget to take your pill or to run it together, I want to know. And, worst of all, if you get your period…*

'Yeah, sorry, upset tummy.' No way you're being sent home now, after making, like, nada quid so far today.

A flash of worry flits over her face. OK, she might have a crap job, looking after us bitches, but she's alright really. For an old bird. What is she, like, forty or something? Same age as Mum, as it goes.

'Well, get back out there, then, and give it some welly,' she says, her knee bent across Celeste's back, pulling on her corset strings, 'Derek'll have a heart attack if he knows you're off the floor.'

You imagine flipping her the bird, your middle finger an inch from her crow's feet, the other girls egging you on.

Instead, knowing which side your bread's buttered, you channel meek and mild and say, 'Sure, sure, I'm on my way.'

She's blooming right, though, Christ knows how much Derek will fine you for being away this long, so you're out of there, gone, a ghost. Only halfway down the stairs the new stiletto heel spikes the carpet, and you're forced to look down while you dig it out, the threadbare once-floral pattern massacred by fag burns and an invasion of high heels, reminding you that Elegance is hardly the Harrods of lap-dancing establishments. Primark, more like. Yeah, forget the 'glamour' shots of ex-dancers what line the wall, prisoners banged up in fancy gold frames – a dive is what this place is, no matter how much the boss tries to sugar-coat it. It's a joke really, how you used to fancy your chances of joining the boss's pet girls here in his pathetic 'Hall of Fame'. Or 'the art gallery' as Derek calls it. You snort. Art? As if! Cos art makes people think, right, and not with their dicks...

But as you reach the bottom of the stairs you shrug off them negative thoughts, thanks to the JD mellowing you out and the muffled beats of an Ibiza classic vibrating through the walls. Gotta dance, might as well be to that – and you skip back through the double doors where there's a bit of a crowd now, the little round tables what surround the dance floor half-filled, the pole empty, Ivana squirming unrhythmically on some dude's lap. You snicker. Ivana the Terrible you call her (not to her face, natch), cos she can't dance for toffee. The boss keeps her on cos she's a dead ringer for Paris Hilton – and everyone's leched over that *One Night in Paris*, right?

Uh-oh, you've just realised who she's with: Halitosis Bob.

You lucked out with the loo trip.

Not quite ready to get back in the thick of it, you hover by the bar for a bit, watching her dance. She flexes back and forth on his lap. Flexes back and forth on his lap. Flexes... And, as you're silently urging her to put a bit of variety into it, Bob leans away and starts looking around the room. This ain't a good sign. She must have picked up on it, though, cos she's now trying to bend backwards over his knees, back arched, hands trailing the floor, only – uh-oh! – this makes her blonde Paris wig slip to one side. Blushing, she lifts one hand to secure it, and – *whoops!* – her entire body rocks and she nearly falls from his lap to the floor.

You cringe, hold back laughter. Bless poor Ivana – or should you say Paris? – a cardboard blooming cutout could do a better job.

God, look, can you just say something? You're not usually one of them snide gits who takes the piss out of their mates. But your period's bugging you and it's sort of like the boss's trap, playing you girls off against each other, trying to make you – whatchamacallit? – competitive and that. You shiver. Wrap your arms around yourself in a hug. Try and stop the raging hormones from getting one over on you.

And as Ivana/Paris gets her act together, stripping down to her perfect C-cups, you try to lighten up, your thoughts turning to the chihuahua. It was you who started it. Left the ugly toy dog with the googly eyes in Ivana's locker as a joke present, no gift tag, the perfect accessory for her Paris Hilton gimmick. Then the next time you was in the club you found it, without a word from Ivana, back in your own locker. Backwards and forwards it's gone between your lockers, ever since. Over your forced club expression you grin as you think of the laughs you and Ivana have enjoyed, a shared silliness what makes the club bearable, helps pass the time of day. So by the time you're back on the pole you've calmed it down a bit, the JD in full effect now and all, a warming light sending out little ripples of heat on your nearly naked skin...

You're sunbathing on a luxury private beach, getting lost, good lost, in the lazy reds, pinks and oranges of a tropical sunset... the yacht anchored not far out in the marina... champagne and oysters on ice...

Whoops...! You sway – make out like it was deliberate, try and get back into the groove.

From the crowd, a gob of bad language whistles through the air across the *thump, thump, thump* of a mighty rock anthem, and you raise one leg in a kick. The hormones rage and surge and make a nuisance of themselves. Spurred on, you decide to give the saddos what they came in for, and, belly sucked in, you:

clamber up the pole

wrap both legs around it boa-constrictor-tight

let your arms fall to your side, flipping your top half upside down.

And as you're dangling there, right, the aftertaste of one too many JDs racing down your throat, your long, dark hair sweeping the floor, a customer's face lines up with the silky rear-end of your evening gown, a randy dog panting its hot breath on your thighs. You squeeze your pelvic floor muscles, praying for it not to be obvious; a complaint about being on your period is the last thing you need. (It's happened – though not to you.)

More to the point: three metres away? As if!

Not like the bouncers give a monkey's. Light bounces off the shining billiard balls of their heads – they've seen it all before… too busy whining about the England manager's team choice, probably, to keep an eye on things. Besides, you lose out these days if you play by the rules. Oh. Don't matter – after turning upright, you see that the customer's backed off – phew! – and that he's beckoning you to a booth on the edge of the dance floor with a chipolata finger (the tight-arse, not paying for a private dance). You follow his denim jacket, flesh creeping for a split-second, sweat beading your top lip. A familiar niggle.

But you shrug it off cos he's saying, 'Come on, gorgeous, cat got your tongue?'

You gyrate towards him. He waves a tenner in your face. Your eyes glaze over. And, as you flick a switch on the edge of the booth to time his three-minute dance, your thoughts drift off to…

Covent Garden, The Royal Opera House. You're a prima ballerina, dancing Juliet, bending over the lap of your

Romeo; it's the finale – a last pirouette and the audience are in raptures, throwing endless bouquets on –

'Ow!'

'You alright, love. Got a problem?' the guy's piped up, turning your face around in line with his, squeezing your cheeks with thumb and forefinger – hard.

'Uh, sorry?' you say, the words muffled by hollowed-in cheeks.

'Gonna look me in the eye or what?' He squeezes harder.

'Oh, sure, right, of course, babe,' you soothe in a honey voice, wondering where the bouncers have got to. You go eyeball to eyeball.

'Good girl,' he says and lets go.

Then, with his mates cheering him on (not paying for nothing, though, are they?) you pull off your evening gown, sway your hips, your gusset brushing the zip of his jeans, all the while your eyes glued to his, the real world gatecrashing in on your fantasies.

You're a nobody. A nothing. Barely human. Nearly nineteen years old and down on your luck, all undressed and nowhere to go.

INBOX: 2 new messages

FROM: REBECCA
SENT: Friday 1 June, 15.25

Would you mind paying the leccy bill today, like you said? Don't want to get cut off!

Sure thing

Today Layla

FROM: DAD
SENT: Friday 1 June, 16.37

Will you remember me in a week?

Err, Dad, of course!!!!

Will you remember me in a month?

Mmm, same answer??

Will you remember me in a year?

Dad, not being rude, but have u been drinking?

Knock knock.

Err... u have been drinking, haven't u? But OK, who's there?

See, you've forgotten me already.

Groan

2

The late afternoon has turned weary and grey, morphed into a sad middle-aged bloke in the thick of a mid-life crisis – Derek maybe, sickly-looking, with liver spots and never-ending health issues. Or, to put it another, more honest way: the kick from the JD's worn off. Insult to injury, Derek's only gone and asked you to stay on for a bit – Kitten, the other brunette, is gonna be late. Cos, the club's got to provide someone for everyone, right, a flavour for every bloke's taste: a black girl, an Asian girl, a blonde, a brunette... Jez could shrink-wrap you and call you a variety pack.

Anyway. Don't know why he's worried. No customers in till later now, probably. The other girls bored and bitching, on the wind-up; Derek bashing the life out of a pocket calculator at one end of the bar, the bouncers huddled around a portable radio at the other. The boss has given them a free pass to listen to the pre-match build-up.

Bully for them.

Ivana sits opposite you at the middle of the bar, at a safe distance between Derek and the bouncers. You came up to keep her company a few minutes ago, cos the hussies were freezing her out: the old-timers in the club don't like her, see – too pretty for them, too natural – and the new girls, well, they don't like anyone, especially foreigners.

'But what do you think, darling?' Ivana's saying, putting her hand on your knee.

'What about?' you say.

16

'Modelling,' she says, 'Weren't you listening?'

No, you wasn't. But you know the spiel. Cos, Ivana's one of them thinks-she's-your-mum kind of people, right? Always got a little pep talk for you.

You're about to respond when at last the main doors open and a cold draught blows in around your ankles, bringing your skin out in goosebumps and making your nipples swell. Ivana's expression changes from good-hearted soul to Baltic bombshell (as she calls herself) and she purrs, 'Look, darling. Colin.'

'Do what?' you say, and your mood lifts for a second – like, only a split-second, you're not that sad – and you swivel round on the bar stool to take in the familiar baseball cap, white T-shirt and black leather jacket.

Always smells of soap, does Colin, pays for endless sit-downs with you, wants to chat, nothing more. The management don't give you grief so long as he keeps buying you drinks and that. And you don't give Colin grief so long as he keeps chucking you twenties… God, look, can you just say something? You know he's probably just as sad as the rest of the customers, but guys like Colin who only want a gossip and a drink, they're basically harmless, ain't they? Besides, he's a regular, comes in for most of your shifts, checks with the girls on reception to see when you're working. And sit-downs? Easy money. Right?

Wrong!

And you think back to one time when Colin lost it, got pissed and took advantage. Teasing you about your work name, he was, trying out one of the lines from the Clapton song… down on his knees, like he was about to propose… his breath boozy and fiery, his hands wandering… asking, again and again and again, *What's your real name? Come on, we're pals, you can tell me.* And you laughed it off, cos it's one of his favourite subjects, trying to guess your real name,

17

when he's not banging on about his ex-wife, that is. Only then he went hardcore, grabbing hold of your wrist, till you ended up telling him 'Beverly' – Mum's name, as it goes – cos your wrist was sore, a swollen red welt appearing on it, what lasted for hours.

And all the while you're going over this in your mind Ivana's gone off to find her own victim, and Mr Easy Money has jumped up on the stool opposite, asking, 'Hi, how are ya?', his little legs dangling in the air – he must be a few inches shorter than you, and you ain't exactly leggy. *Rumpelstiltskin in the flesh*, you chuckle to yourself. But out loud you just say, 'Hiya,' putting on them must-have wide eyes and licking your lips, while he settles himself on the stool.

Jenny, one of the waitresses, is all over you as soon as his arse hits leather, pen in mouth, waiting to take his order.

'The usual?' he asks, avoiding eye contact, attempting a grin, though it comes out more like a sneer.

And even though you don't like champagne, don't like the bubbles going up your nose to tell the truth, you know what's what, so you say, 'Yes, please,' as brightly as you can.

'So, what's new, pussycat?

You sneak a peek over at Ivana, who's now on stage, wishing you could sound off to her – she knows you hate Colin's stupid pet names for you. But you bite your tongue (them hormones ain't gone off on their holidays just yet) and smile your best toothpaste-advert smile. 'Um. Not a lot. Quiet.'

'Aw, poor Lay-lay,' he says, ruffling your hair, the mossy green graveyard of tattoos on his hands telling you he's much older than he lets on.

Then, silence. The grand sum of eff-all happening, apart from the usual comings and goings in the club, and at the same time you're aware of something uncomfortable, something dark hanging in the air between you and Colin.

18

One arse-clenching minute later and he breaks the silence.

'Noo shoes?' he asks in that annoying fake American accent of his.

'Er, yeah,' you say, following his gaze down to the glittery pink stilettos. 'Wow, you've got a beady eye, intya?' You're torn between appreciation that he noticed and freaking out that he did.

Little does he know why the new shoes. It was part of the row with Jeremy earlier in the week, right? That your other ones weren't 'glamorous' enough. You'd been trying to get away with three-inch heels, can't understand why other girls stick them agonising six-inch ones – might as well nail on horseshoes and be done with it. Of course that was only one part of the argument, but you're not in the mood to think about that now...

Instead you let your mind wander, and even though your head's filled with the racket from the hustle on the main floor, with the too-loud 'listen to me' voices of the other customers and the *thump, thump, thump* of the music, you feel the silence closing in. And a grim, grey loneliness, a loneliness what catches you off guard at moments like this – a loneliness you can't understand, being as you're surrounded by people – takes a hold of you, starts leading you into stony, shadowy thoughts. *Damn it!* If you wasn't so hormonal, and (let's be honest) so bored, you'd get the conversation going, buttering Colin up, massaging his ego and that. But your head's splitting, and you could do with a drink – a non-alcoholic one, you mean. God, are you getting a hangover already, at seven pm?

You gee yourself up to say something. Anything! 'So, what's new with you?' is all you can think of after a while. Dull as, you admit, but maybe it'll get Colin chatting. Or maybe he might even tell a funny story, like one from his lorry-driving days, when him and his mates used to neck speed and E to stay awake while they was transporting goods across Europe.

But no, worse luck.

All it takes is a small bone and he's off on one (Easy Money, like you said), starting up his usual moan about how his ex-wife's a 'stupid old cow'; and, sucking up his pint like a right old fart, he launches into it: how it was his daughter's eighteenth last week 'and I never even sin her'; how he misses his kids; how it's all that 'pardon my language – cunt of an ex-wife's fault... stealing my house, so I had to move up Tottenham, taking my kids away... ain't my fault, got picked up for speeding... lost my licence... lost my job...'

How the hell can he afford to come in here, then? you wonder, not for the first time, only to soon drift off...

You're out celeb-spotting at the Ivy. Colin Farrell passes your table and drops a napkin by your ankle, an excuse to get you talking. His brooding Irish eyes meet yours and you know something's going to happen between you. 'Claridge's or the Savoy?' he asks with a wink...

'... so I says to her, Sheila, you're just a gold-digging – pardon my language – cunt.'

'Yeah, that told her,' you chip in.

And then the hand's on your knee and he's going, 'You're such a good listener, pet. So nice to have someone who cares.'

'Mmm, yeah, lovely,' you murmur as Colin throws you over his shoulder and steps over the threshold into the penthouse suite.

Then Colin, the real one, lands a punch in the guts, asking, 'What about your dad? Did he come and visit in the end, then?'

'What? Never want to see that old git again,' you say, sucking your breath in, all thoughts of sunken baths and room service swallowed back with a you-probably-shouldn't-but-you're-going-to-anyway gulp of champagne.

'But I thought you told me how much you was missing him, how you'd hoped he'd come up and visit.'

Dur!

Dad's in a wheelchair after an accident a few years back, lives in a specially built bungalow with his new missus. He worked in a warehouse, Dad did, always playing the joker, then one day it went Bad and Wrong for him: a truck driver didn't see him messing about in front of the forklift. It pitched towards him and that was that. Both legs had to be amputated in the end, poor sod. Cos warehouses can be badly lit, yeah, and quiet...

But then, that ain't really what it's about, is it? Why you and Dad don't see each other no more, why your contact has boiled down to stupid knock-knock jokes by text, what with him saying nothing to Mum over –

And suddenly it seems stark raving mad: you sitting there in a spangly evening gown, Colin in his everyday clothes, talking about stuff you've packed away in a box at the back of your mind labelled *Do Not Open*.

You do that now. Take an imaginary box. Shove those thoughts in. Lock it. Change the subject. 'So, how come you're not watching the match then?' you ask, and that's an end to that.

Another glass or two of champagne, another forty-five minutes of boring chit-chat, one attempt, two, to stifle yawns... and at last a stag party turns up, six young lads up for a crack, and it's like the club's been plugged back in – *fizz, crack, pop* – to the National Grid. The girls' dresses seem silkier, brighter, the chatter livelier, sexier; the air is sparky, electric. You turn away, the green-eyed monster surging. Rather have fun with that lot than sit chatting with pea-brain here.

'Oy-oy, check that lot out,' Colin breaks into your thoughts, and you turn back round in slow motion, not that interested to tell the truth, only to cop an eyeful of the new girls, Sapphire and Bella. And you don't quite believe what you're seeing... cos they're dancing together, right, at the table of the rowdy lads who just come in? But not just dancing. Fondling, groping. Rubbing their plastic tits up against one another. You pull a face at Colin, but of course he doesn't notice cos he's all agog at...

lips tangling... tongues poking in each other's mouths, lapping at each other's boobs. OK, you've all done lesbian shows – guys, and the lesbian customers, love a bit of that – but on the main floor? In front of everyone? You frown, twist your neck around for a better view. Where's Derek? Jez? It seems to be one rule for the new girls these days, another for the old-timers. Anger snaps at you, a small dog at your heels, yappy and shrill.

So not fair!

And then, just as you're telling yourself to chill the hell out, it ain't that bad, Sapphire wraps her arm around Bella's waist. With the other arm, lifts Bella's dress. Thrusts her hand underneath the shiny pink fabric. You look at the lads, drooling, transfixed; you look at Sapphire, smirking, eyes glazed. And it's like someone's pressed *Pause* on the evening, the air overloaded and tense till she:

pulls out her hand from under the dress

puts her middle finger in her mouth

tosses a coy look at the lads and takes a long, exaggerated suck.

She never, did she?

Did she? Did Sapphire just – you feel yourself flush – finger Bella? Dirty dancing? And the rest!

You flick your hair, just for something to do. Pull at the hem of your skirt. Look around the room. Pray for the fire alarm to ring out. Then, after an hour-long minute, you lift your eyes to meet Colin's and he blushes, actually blushes!

'Well, that was, um, nice,' you say, trying to break the ice.

'Bloody slappers,' he mutters, rubbing his jeans with his hands.

Too right, you think – the tone of the club, it's gone right down! And, like, if these are the new rules, what hope is there for girls like you and Ivana? Girls who don't play dirty, who don't cross the line into – you gulp – damn near prostitution? You tip the rest of the bubbly down your throat. Excuse yourself from Colin for a quick word with Ivana, whose cage has also been rattled. Then, bottling up this aggravation, these worries, you paint a picture of whatchamacallit? – nonchalance on your face and sidle back over to him, managing a bit more chit-chat till at last – it's a minor miracle – Kitten shows up and Derek nods that, yes, you can push off. And so, with the mask of cool and calm slipping, you say your goodbyes to Colin, ignoring the puppydog eyes what trail after you as you peg it upstairs to the changing room.

A quick change of clothes (trainers, more like it!) and you light up a fag, sucking up a gluttonous lungful of smoke, and, though you're breathless and pale with exhaustion, you crack out the last simper of the day for the bouncers as you come out of the main doors of the club onto Dean Street.

Freedom at last!

And there you find Soho bombed out with the usual human debris of a Friday evening, all braying voices, the latest fashions and ears grafted to mobile phones. Ten months of pacing these streets and you're no closer to understanding what the hell it is about the place. Why do they come here, them trendies? you wonder, catching the smell of sweaty meat from a kebab shop, neighbour to the freshly painted black door and stuck-up brass plate of a private members' club. Two worlds side-by-side. And do you fit into either? Do you hell. Or into the next buildings on the block: an expensive café rubbing up next to the seedy doorway of a rent-a-room-by-the-hour joint, a grubby flyer Blu-Tacked to its wall promising a 'stairway to heaven'.

The words *sweaty meat* repeat on you like the garlic sauce on a kebab.

Christ's sake, what now? A worse-for-wear lad spilling out of a trendy new bar bumps your arm. He lurches, blurts, 'Sorry,' and you dodge out of the way just in time before he spews a Technicolor puke on the pavement, a loud 'ooh' of disappointment erupting from the bar what seems to echo across the whole of West London.

England missed a chance?

What. Ever.

1 MISSED CALL
INBOX: 1 new message

FROM: CATHLEEN
SENT: Friday 1 June, 18.05

Did you pay the electricity bill?

3

'*Are you a sinner or a winner?*'

You make out these words over a bad-tempered rabble of traffic noises as you go past the Nike shop on the corner of Oxford Circus. Ooh, not quite past, though. A pair of yellow and blue Nike Airs jump out at you from the window. You've been planning to buy them for a while now. Tomorrow, you'll get them tomorrow, as soon as the shop opens. Yeah, you'll be spunking near enough the day's earnings on them, but there's nothing wrong with a bit of retail therapy, is there? A girl's gotta cheer herself up somehow.

Rush hour's well over, but the streets are still hungry for people: hungry for the drinkers and clubbers, the tourists and the after-work crowd, hungry even for the winos and the beggars. Yeah, Oxford Street – it'd gobble up the whole of London if it could, the greedy bastard!

'*Are you a sinner or a winner?*'

Them words again, being spoken by a scraggy-looking bloke through a megaphone. You see him most days on your way to or from work. Somebody told you he's been doing this for years, preaching his evangelical crap on London's streets. Should be on a postcard, then, shouldn't he, sitting in a spinner outside one of them tourist shops, lined up next to the red phone boxes, the pigeons and the punks – all them London landmarks, half of which you don't even see any more.

What the – ? You shift sideways cos old Mr Sinner or Winner has budged up right next to you at the pelican crossing.

Well, him and all the others bustling north of Oxford Circus, anyway. You squeeze past, give him a wink and mutter, 'A sinner,' under your breath, and then you're gone, out of there, cowardy-cowardy custard as per usual, before he can launch into a sermon for your benefit.

Five minutes later and, as the ant-hill swarm gives way to the quieter streets of Fitzrovia, you try to remember how you came to live Up West. Not like you gave it much thought, really. Close to Elegance, probably. Near the shops and Oxford Street. The ad was one of them posh laminated ones in the newsagent's: 'Lovely bright room sharing with two other friendly female professionals. Near Charlotte Street. Call Cathleen', with the price and her number... Not exactly your thing, but you was desperate, thought you'd give it a bash.

The 'interview' was torture. End of. Cathleen sat there po-faced, perched on the sofa like she had a Cadbury's Creme Egg stuffed up her arse. Picture-perfect in her skinny jeans, Victoria Beckham bob and Ugg boots. Nerves getting the better of you... warm for autumn that day, you remember... overheating in your winter parka... not taking it off cos of the tarty dress you was wearing underneath... Sweating like a good 'un by the time you got to the front door, never mind when the interrogation started.

'Work as a receptionist in the day, as a croupier at night.'

She'd raised her eyebrows at that one. 'Work evenings, then, do you?'

'Yes,' you'd said, tugging at the cord to the parka's hood, 'that a problem?'

'No, no problem,' she'd replied quickly, the first musical notes of warmth coming into her voice.

The room was well nice – too good for you. You'd thought you could get a fancy office job, wear a suit to work every day. Your dream then was to work in a law firm or one of them banks in the City. Still is, as it goes, even if the closest you've come to an office job was receptionist at that fashion warehouse around the corner. That didn't last long. Too knackering, what with all the hours you put in at the club. As for being a croupier... God, look, can you just say something? It's not like you to tell porkies, but girls like that, you know what they think of you. *Slag, tart; how could she do it?*

Jealous, of course, cos you've got a better body.

But you fell in love with the room. It made you think of one of them sitting rooms from a browny-coloured photo in a history textbook, with its high ceilings, black iron fireplace and stripped floorboards. Besides, you was so effing tired of living out of a suitcase, of sofa-surfing, of overhearing the whispered conversations in the kitchens of your so-called nearest and dearest. Not to mention the disaster of your final pit-stop, kipping on Billy Rousseau's floor, cos look how that ended: your first line of coke, bed, the clinic. So, all that considered, when the interrogation ended, you'd put on your poshest voice and all but begged for the room.

And then it was all cups of tea and hugs and choccy-biccies – 'Well, you only live once,' as Cathleen said – and telling you how her last flatmate had done a bunk so she'd want references, and you were like, 'Oh, yes, I can supply references and that,' cringing at the telltale Peacehaven 'and that', though she didn't seem to notice or care.

'So, when can you move in, then?' she said.

Course, by the time you got your shit together and sorted out fake references, the other flatmate had left too, Rebecca had moved in to replace her, and Cathleen was in bits over it all. Made you feel as welcome as a rattlesnake at a kids' party that first day you lugged in your two suitcases.

But it was good to get away from Billy: to get away from his weird little flat decorated in fantasy art, the walls plastered with posters of bosomy women being strangled by giant snakes or captured by fierce-looking dragons; to get away from his fidgeting about, always with some new scam on the go; to get away from the little comments about your weight and your clothes, the huffiness when you came home late, the whatchamacallit? – possessiveness. Yeah, you suppose you should have basked in the attention, so why did it feel like being strangled, like he had his hands to your throat, choking the life out of you? Even tried to put his foot down when you told him you was getting your own place. Yeah, compared to him, you'd thought, living with Cathleen'd be a doddle.

If only.

Even so, it's a relief to round the corner to your street, cos you're fighting a losing battle with the pain in your feet and you've waved a white flag as far as them raging hormones go.

Hold up, though: you might have to get into battle mode again. There's the old pug-faced guy from the local Italian on the corner. You know what's coming. Yup, true to form, '*Buona sera, bella,*' he sings, from his usual position loitering outside his caff, smoking a fag. Reminds you of a tree what needs uprooting, he's that bent over, that fragile-looking. Anyway, him talking to you is a back-handed compliment or what have you, right? Cos it's done with a smirk and a look that travels up and down your body – resting on your boobs, of course. Dirty old perv.

Saying that, it's alright actually, the street where you live. Leafy and green and that. Quiet too. Oxford Street and Soho just around the corner; but it's like the fancy buildings here, the black and white marbled staircases, the shiny black railings are a world apart from the grotty Soho dive you've just left. Making the poky bungalow where you grew up – what? A galaxy away?

Jesus, Hayleigh, Peacehaven ain't that bad, you hear Mum say.

Yeah, sure, Mum, wrong again.

OK, you've got to admit you was chuffed when you first came home here each night, but the shine of the new's rubbed off. Only time you really feel at home is when the others do one and you get the place to yourself. Not being funny, but them two you live with, Rebecca and Cathleen, with their fancy media jobs and their degrees and that, they're so far up their own arses, they might choke on their own farts.

God, look, there you go, bitching again, but really, if they'd just be nice to you, you'd cut them some slack. Think the pair of them are in tonight, so it'll have to be a quick bath, *Big Brother* and then out East to hit the bars and clubs with your bezza, Ayesha. Less chance of bumping into any customers up that end of town. None of that *Don't I know you from somewhere?* crap. *One of them faces* is your usual reply.

You sigh, a deep black hole of a sigh, as if by breathing out you could destroy the furry blackness what seems to grow over your lungs in the club, a nasty memory of Sapphire and Bella's lezzer show flashing up in your mind. And that's how you enter the communal hallway of the flats, exhaling, catching sight of the strange oo-shape of your lips in the huge ornate antique mirror what looms in the hallway. It used to impress you, this mirror, made you think of money, of luxury. Now, you don't give it a second look. Had enough of your reflection for one day, of the other you's body haunting you from the black polished dance floor. Instead your eyes are drawn to the mat where the post piles up; last time you called, Mum said she'd written – at last.

Oh, terrific. It's been picked up already; the others are definitely home.

'*And in other news… blah, England friendly, blah.*'

Yup, the drone of the telly confirms this as you fiddle with your key in the lock: they're in.

Then it hits you. One minute boring stuff, everyday this and that, and then, out of nowhere, *bam!* – the missing of Connor smashes into you with the force of a battering ram. Sweat pours off your brow, like you've been caught in a sudden thunderstorm; knees shake, hands tremble. And you catch your breath as you push the door forward, winded and wounded from the agony of it… from the wishing, the hoping to hear a different sound than the telly as you walk into the flat, to hear instead the giggling, or even the crying, like what used to soar into your ears those first months when you got home after sixth-form college. And there you'd find Mum changing his nappy or tickling his toes, giving you evils as you raced in to scoop him up and be rewarded with a sweet, gummy smile…

But no, it's inevitable: it's the continued drone of the news you hear as you enter the flat. Worse luck. You support yourself on the door frame. Pulse stabilises, hands steady. And then your ears catch a more annoying buzz hovering in the air: gossip.

Creak! 'Ckin hell, there go the floorboards – talk about bringing attention to yourself. You was hoping to sneak past them straight to the bathroom.

'Hiya, I'm back,' you call out, ungritting your teeth.

'Yeah, hi.' A low raspy voice. Cathleen, then. 'Come in here a sec, will you?'

Creak, creak, creak… you stomp across the hallway, taking your impatience out on the floorboards, walking into the sitting room to find the flatmates thick as thieves on the sofa, the coffee table in front of them covered in nail polish

31

and remover, a bottle of Chardonnay, Pringles. Oh, OK, girls' night in. Nice of them to invite you…

'Listen, Layla, did you pay that bill?' Cathleen again, barely looking up from the telly.

A forest of tiny pine-needles prickles your skin.

'Yeah, course I did.' Then, quickly, 'Gonna have a bath now.'

'And Layla?' Rebecca this time, and you think, but can't be certain, that she sounds a bit sarky when she says your name.

'Yessss,' you say, almost haemorrhaging with irritation.

'There's another couple of letters for that Hayleigh Weeks. I was going to put "return to sender" on them but I thought – '

But your eyes are already fondling Mum's writing – *please let there be a photo, please let there be a photo* – and you snatch up the envelopes before she can finish. 'Uh – oh, it's OK, I'll do it – need to post something anyway,' and you're pretty sure that if looks could kill you'd be speared, stabbed, guillotined or garrotted, and lying dead as a dodo on the hall floor.

Cursing, you stomp towards the kitchen, wondering why Mum can't just get a Hotmail. Yeah, you should head straight for the bathroom, tear Mum's letter right open. You picture yourself doing it, brightly coloured photo after photo spilling out. Classic toddler shots: in a Noddy car on Brighton pier; or with the sun shining on him, too cute in his nappy playing with a bucket and spade; in a Winnie-the-Pooh high chair, mess splattered across his face. But instead you're gripped by a horrible deadening of your hopes: of seeing that button nose ever again… those big brown eyes a bit too close together… the nearly bald head with just a sprouting of black hair…

And what about this other letter, then? You thumb it briefly and then it hits you. God, yeah. That childish loopy writing – it's from him, ain't it? Michael. Connor's dad. That's weird. Wonder how he got hold of the address. Curiosity gets the better of you and you open it right away, eyes popping out your head as you read the four pages, scrawled over both sides of paper. No way. No sodding way! Too much to think about....

Eugh! Now a colony of fruit flies is trying to make a home up your nose. You bat them away with the letter then put it back in its envelope, leaning over the fruit bowl filled with black bananas to reach the kettle, what you stick on for a Pot Noodle. And you wonder if there's milk for a cup of tea, smirking as you read the neon Post-It stuck to the fridge: *Think Thin.* Silly cows. The fridge is empty except for another bottle of Chardonnay, a mouldy carrot and a half-eaten bar of Fruit and Nut. Never mind, the Pot Noodle'll do. Got to eat something, Jeremy's words from earlier in the week sticking in the back of your mind just as the Pot Noodle sticks in your throat: *Getting too thin – punters want to see curves, not some AIDS victim or a skag addict.*

After a couple of mouthfuls you bite down on your tongue – *ow!* – remembering the old sod's words only to be hit again by a familiar worry, about how things are going tits-up in the club. Great, just great, that's your appetite gone and ruined. You flick open the bin with one foot, ramming the Pot Noodle carton on top of a mini-mountain of rubbish, and all the while a voice inside you, getting louder all the time, is urging you to open the other letter, the more important one: Mum's. With a little huff you give in, give in to that voice, give in to the urge to hear about him, about the little baby, and you kick open the kitchen door to make your way towards the privacy of the bathroom, ignoring the giggles from the sitting room that echo down the hall where you think, but can't be certain, that you hear the whisper of your name.

Like you care. Got bigger fish to fry. Like Mum's letter. Mum's letter what you put on the basin now that you're in the bathroom. And then you:

Lock the door.

Put Michael's letter safely away in your handbag.

Start to get undressed, pull off the trainers, the socks.

Pick up Mum's letter again, now slightly soggy at the edges, put it down.

Only to decide that out of sight, out of mind's better and shove it in the bathroom cabinet for later. But, almost immediately, you're whipping the door open again in an eruption of anticipation, your fingers ripping at the envelope what seems to have been stuck down with superglue just to piss you off.

And, as you tip it upside down, just one single sheet of paper falls to the floor.

For fuck's sake! Oh, come on, can you just say something: it's not like you to drop the F-bomb, but one page? After all these months! And no photos! You flush, furious with the old cow. She's a mum, ain't she? She should know how it feels.

You skim-read the letter. She might as well not have bothered; there's nothing she ain't told you on the phone. Telling you more by what she's not telling you, in fact. Namely, she doesn't give a damn. About you. About Connor. About... About... you bite your lip... about any bloody thing, you rant to yourself, and, taking the cheap scraggy paper by its corner, you rip the letter into tiny pieces and chuck them in the bin.

What now? What now? What now?

With your head in your hands you sit on the edge of the bath, *What now?* the only words filling your head...

You consider re-reading Michael's letter. But no, you're in no mood for a guilt trip. Fag, that's what. You reach into your spilled-open handbag in the basin and pull one out, lighting it up, drawing on its stinky bad taste, forcing yourself to puff away on it to distract you from thoughts of Connor, from the letters, from the shit that went down in the club today.

Nothing doing.

Radio, instead? Yeah, switching on the little portable helps, channelling the ferris wheel of thoughts circling your head towards Pete Tong on Radio One. And, humming along to the remix of some tune what they play in the club, you continue to get undressed, peeling off the jeans, the G-string and the hot pink bra.

A fresh tammie and at last you're in a bubble bath, its flowery scent and a vigorous scrub rubbing out the cigarette smoke and sweat and JD what shroud your body from the club. You suck in some air. Drift off. Think of the letters again. But then – a bit of luck for a change – you spy a copy of *Heat* on the side of the bath. Just what you need: a trashy mag to take your mind off things. You grab a hold of it, raising it an inch above the bubbles – wouldn't want to piss off Cathleen by getting it wet.

Those birds on the cover – what a state! Right bunch of fatties and one so thin she wouldn't look out of place in a coffin. All that money they've got to spend on their bods, and you see better tit and arse every day down the club. Inside the mag, you feast your eyes on the headlines: 'WHOSE BABY IS IT ANYWAY?' 'DESPERATE JULIE HAS ANOTHER BAD DATE.' 'IS TERRY LOSING THE PLOT?' Ha! Moving on, you reach your favourite page, page three, where you gorge on celebs' cellulite, flab and other flaws highlighted in neon circles of shame, together with bitchy bright captions. Too fat. Too thin. Just right. (There's only one of those.)

Somehow, though, the pics don't lift your mood as expected. Besides, you're floating off somewhere else now, thinking again of Mum's letter, at the same time running your hand over your tummy, your boobs (God, are they sagging a bit?), your stubbly fanny. Should have booked a wax earlier this week. Never mind. Should get away with it for the next couple of days. And you sigh, wondering why the boss doesn't cut out the middle man and pay you in Brazilians.

After turning on the tap for more hot, you sink deeper into the bathwater and flick further through the magazine. On page ten a pretty celebrity in a bikini seems to be giving you a dirty look. It's that whatsherface, who Colin says you look like. As if! You'd need a lot of work to be as drop-dead gorgeous: boob job, collagen lip implants. Yeah, some of the girls in the club might make enough to get all that work done, but all your extra cash, it's for the baby, isn't it?

Jesus Christ.

The baby, the baby, the baby!

There he is again, chuntering into your thoughts. You want to yell. Just let it all out. Top of your lungs and break the sound barrier.

Sod this, sod the bath!

And you sit bolt upright, fling the mag out, spilling water and bubbles over the side. That's bathtime ruined. Usually the only half-hour in the day when you can unwind, but just now you feel like taking a garden spade to the back of someone's head. You yank out the bath plug and, as the water disappears down the hole, your feelings seem to be sinking down with it. You feel dizzy, acid, hot. Worried that you might faint, you grip the side of the bath and stagger out, lumber towards the small bathroom window and hoik it open. Phew, that's better: the room's less sauna-like now. And, with that small crisis over, you take the mood elevator up a floor as Pete Tong makes way for some cheesy Friday night trance. Before long the hormones have been kicked into touch, make-up has been applied, you've a fresh tammie in, and that's it: ready for action.

From the sitting room you can hear the synth of *Big Brother* starting up again after an ad break and you wander in to find the gruesome twosome have taken up all of the sofa, leaving you with the choice of a hard wooden chair or the floor.

'Chair, then, thanks,' you mumble to yourself.

Talk about the opposite of nice, pleasant atmos.

'So, can you tell them twins apart yet?' you blurt, making conversation, shifting about on the chair, trying to get comfy.

They both look at you sideways. Never mind thick as mud, you could cut the atmosphere into chunks and sell it down the market as blocks of concrete.

Things don't improve as the show trundles on. It's a new format, this series: no guys at this point, all girls – really pretty, the lot of them, great bodies and all – most of them could get away with working in the club. All got the right tone of fake tan and nails and hair and that, too. You snort hard. No wonder the club's getting less and less busy: everyone looks like a lap dancer these days. You wish you could share this little nugget with Rebecca and Cathleen but of course you can't mention Elegance, so instead you sit motionless, except when you're *pick, pick, picking* at your fingernails.

One more ad break later and the silence is broken. 'You should apply for the next series,' Rebecca says, flicking her long blonde hair out of her eyes.

'Shut up!' you say, but blushing, secretly pleased.

'Yeah, they love girls like you,' Cathleen pipes up, and you catch her winking over at Rebecca.

You frown, confusion sweeping over you – what's that wink about, then?

Then it's more deathly silence in the room, apart from the occasional ping of your mobile, as the contestants prance about performing senseless tasks.

Cathleen whispers something to Rebecca and they fall about laughing.

That's it! You've had enough! It's your favourite bit of the show, the first few days when everyone's showing off and that, but you decide it's time for a swift exit in case you're tempted to thump somebody.

'Laters,' you spit out as you collect up your jacket and handbag, and Cathleen chirps,

'Don't do anything we wouldn't do.'

'Yeah, same,' you reply, icy words spoken through fiery-hot lips, eyes welling up as you reach the front door.

You swear on your life, on Mum's life, on Con– no, never that, but you do swear, you'll show them. Show them who can have the most fun, the lightweights.

You think of Jeremy, Sapphire, Mum, Michael's offer, the letters, and you head out the door, Old Street a rattling tube ride away, a single mission chasing around your brain: tonight, for one night only (as if!), you are going to get well and truly mashed off your head.

INBOX: 2 new messages

FROM: BILLY
SENT: Friday 1 June, 20.55

Hi babes. Just checking ur all set 4 the big meet up 2morrow.

FROM: BILLY
SENT: Friday 1 June, 21.22

Babes???

> Yeah, soz. Was in bath.
> Yeah all set. What shall
> I wear?

Sexy sexy. Kenny's looking fwd 2 meet u.

> OK hon.

No kisses for Billy?

> Sure babe xxx

That's how I like you.

> Huh?

xxx

> Oh yeah, duh. Got
> to go. Going out with
> Ayesha now. xx

Don't do anything I wouldn't do. Mean it.

Saturday

4

'This'll do,' you shout through the gap in the screen as the cabbie takes the corner of Tottenham Court Road and Warren Street. 'I'll walk from here.'

This ain't the result of an unexpected urge to exercise more, or an impulse to get to know the local area better. No, it's much more simple: you've suddenly remembered there's a forty quid fine for puking in a black cab. Just what you need. So you leap out from the taxi, chucking two tens at the driver, vomit spilling up to your lips after you've mumbled, 'Keep the change.' His eyes become slits as you trip up on the kerb, and he burns rubber before driving off into the new day.

Then the retching begins.

It's one of them never-ending gut-wrenching pukes, as loud in sound and stink as it is in colour, the resulting splatter on the kerb a picture postcard of all you've snorted, sniffed or swallowed over the last few hours. Forget backpacking around Thailand – your druggy, boozy journey tonight has been much more enlightening.

Frightening!

Exciting!

What the – ? Not off your nut still, surely?

For now, you ignore that attempt at sussing yourself out cos your stomach lining's getting up close and personal with the gutter. Though they've already flirted with one another more than once or twice over the past few hours, to be fair.

At the same time, your handbag is clueless, no idea what's going on, swinging in a jolly way at your side, and before you know it you're laughing – 'ho, ho, ho' – out loud. What's that all about? Never mind, cos you're all done puking – good – and so you wipe the corners of your mouth with the back of your hand, deciding it's probably time to get to grips with a few things.

Like where you are exactly.

How to get home.

You know, the things you should have probably sussed before bailing out of the cab.

Only getting the lie of the land is tricky when Mr Ecstasy and Mrs Alcohol have ganged up in a drugged-up haze over your eyeballs. You lift your head from the sight of your own puke in the gutter. Squint. Blink. Squint again. OK, so there's a row of houses. You're in some sort of square off Warren Street. Can't quite make out where cos… eyes are rolling, stomach is turning over, skin prickling.

No way… coming up on something again?

You swear on your life that them perfect white buildings are having a right old dig: *look at her, a pikey from Peacehaven, thinks she's all that, but she's actually out of her depth, and possibly out of her mind.* And the white of the houses, so clean so pristine, takes you back home to Peacehaven… to the white cliffs, zigzagging down to the sea… across the main road from the cliff tops to the samey-samey streets of crap bungalows, *made of ticky-tacky, all the same…*

And you're trying to remember making your exit from the guy's flat (never did find out his name) and whether you took more drugs before he chucked you out (*sorry, love, my girlfriend's coming round in a bit*), only your eyelids are drooping, your lungs pushing in and out… the cold touch of a lamp-post proof that this is real life and you haven't drugged yourself into some sort of like alternate universe.

Timidly you turn your gaze on the sky, an upside-down ocean of blue – a beautiful day on the horizon...

... and there's no denying it, you're off your box, you're rushing, too far, too fast, on E or speed or coke or ket, you're not quite sure, but it's not like you haven't been here before, or that the feeling ain't nice.

The opposite, in fact.

You feel like running. Laughing! Dancing!

... onto the dance floor, throwing out shapes to the beat...

You are floating. No, flying. You are a beautiful sunset. You are hot chocolate and marshmallows on a cold afternoon. You are the shiny clean pages of a new magazine. OK, let's be honest, you're not in your right mind. Or even your wrong one. You don't know where you are at this point in time, but it's not like you care... if only you could feel like this forever...

But yeah, hang on. Let's think. Where exactly are you again?

A mini-panic; bit of a wobble.

You scan the neighbourhood for a street sign. That's it. Fitzroy Square. Not far from home. *Phew.* What's more, the coming up again, it's a comfort blanket to wrap yourself into as you pound the pavement –

God, you interrupt yourself, you wish there was someone to talk to. You feel chatty, speaky, talky. *La, la, la* – you want to sing, shout, dance about. No other option but to start a little conversation with yourself as you run your hands across railings and greeny moss-stained front walls, try and place one foot in front of the other, to dawdle steady and smooth...

Did you really cane more MDMA?

Dunno.

Where d'ya get it from?

Who cares?

Which direction home?

That's right. You can cross Fitzroy Square.

But the white buildings look down on you as you walk further along, stuck up and cliquey like the prefects at school: a reminder of who you are, that it's 'them and us'.

No, no, no, don't put yourself on a downer, don't think about school. About home...

You're losing it.

Maybe a lie-down would help?

Shuffling forward, you come to the little fenced-off lawned garden in the middle of the square. Here, maybe? Chill out for a bit, then make your way the few streets home?. But – *rattle, rattle, rattle* – the bulky black metal chain on the gate is locked; the grass, so lush, inviting and green, is on the other side. The thought of a crisp, leafy salad makes your mouth water. You think of the countryside. Of emerald fields and open spaces. Of that one time Dad took you up to the Downs with your bike, a red Raleigh. He'd given you a Girls' World for your eighth birthday and you'd sobbed your heart out till he'd taken it back to the shop and got you this bike, this brilliant lovely bike, that you zoomed about on everywhere.

Rattle, rattle, rattle – you try the chain again. Glance around. Good, nobody about. Too early for that. You hesitate. But no, it's OK, you've jumped higher fences. The handbag gets flung over first. Then you've no choice, your keys and mobile are on the other side, so you put one foot on the rail and hoik yourself up, fling yourself over – *wheee!* – landing with a thump in the gardens. And then, scooping up your handbag, you flop onto the blanket of grass, ignoring the damp, the litter and the mud, burrowing your fingers into the soft carpet of green, dew jewelling the grass and now your fingers, so tempting and soft...

... as soft as the green shag-pile carpet at home, its touch smooth against the avalanche of plastic toys and baby clothes, the food and baby puke and God knows what else trampled in it. Mum was a child-minder for a while. Always did have a funny thing for babies, the 'tragedy' she calls it cos she only had you, only had one of her own. And lying on the grass, it's like you was there on that carpet, Mum having a right go, telling you to tidy up, the pong of the terry nappy bin funnelling up your nose –

no, not that! Not nappies, not battles, not Con–

You roll over as the sun peeks out from behind the clouds and a sliver of sunlight stabs into you, a sliver so determined and sharp that it almost pierces right through your heart. And you think back again to that room at home. Did your head in how hot it was, especially when you was being suffocated half to death by the squeals and wails of the child-minded kids and the telly and the arguments with stepdad three. No wonder you'd hung out so much at Michael's; no wonder his house became a sanctuary away from Mum... your only escape hatch at home being the bathroom where you'd cram yourself in with your school books, stripped down to your bra and pants: 'totally tropical', Mum liked to keep the house...

... a gentle finger-stroke of sun on your face now, the E – yeah, it must have been E what you took – whirring and stirring life into your fingertips, your toes, sending a spasm of pleasure through your body. You squeeze your eyes closed. Stretch out your arms. Flap them up and down like a kid making angels in the snow. The world begins at your head and ends at your toes; you're safe now in a rose-pink bubble, drifting along... floating... everything else closed off, shut out.

The sun's rays beat stronger. Are you ready, maybe, to reach out into the big wide world? Your fingers grub about in the shag-pile carpet – no, the grass. A different texture now: feathery.

You jolt back.

What the – ?

Puffed-up and stupid-looking, a grossly fat pigeon sits next to you, looking like a great overstuffed toy. Thing is, this toy belongs in the doll's hospital: one leg missing, spots of red blood accessorising the Christmassy silver-white pattern of its neck, one of its wings scraggy and broken-looking, its black pinprick eyes winking at you.

Poor little thing…

…and that terrible day when it all got too much and you was having a zizz in Mum's room, ignoring her yells to wake up the baby and you thought (what a bitch you were!), *Christ's sake, why me?* But you forced yourself to crawl out of bed and the minute you shuffled into the bedroom you knew that something was Bad and Wrong, cos, even though the room was hot, an icy feather of cold was touching your face…

You open your eyes and the pigeon is nestling there, next to your handbag and you're gaping at it… no, gaping into the cot, staring into the cot, at your Little Man, his face, mottled and blue… and the pigeon must be dying, you think, and you pick it up, stick your finger under its beak, try and feel for a breath…

…a siren wailing in the distance. Mum rocking back and forth. The ambulance taking a lifetime and more. Poor little thing. Mum chucking you out not long after. 'Not fit to bring up a kid,' she told you. She should know.

Suddenly, footsteps.

'You alright, dear?'

A posh git in lairy red trousers is peering at you through the railings, a glossy dog on a lead in one hand, bundle of Saturday papers in the other. You stare him out, but then you're drawn to something soft and welcoming in his eyes and, overwhelmed by a loneliness what has brewed up inside of you, you decide to speak with him, to have a little chat. He's another human being, after all, to be fair.

'Lovely day, ain't it?'

He steps closer to the railings, his dog eyeing you like you was a tasty piece of meat. Him doing similar.

'Mmm – ' he looks up at the sky ' – should be. And what finds you here at this ungodly hour on a Saturday? Everything alright?'

Well, that's enough to get your goat. Listen to him! Who does he think he is, your knight in shining armour? The other girls at Elegance might have that Cinderella way of thinking, but not you! Yeah, what makes him so different from the guys in the club, trying to 'take you away from all this'?

Now what?

He's never? Is he? Is he ogling you?

Hang on a sec... or is he looking past you? At the pigeon maybe? Either way, you're not having it. You pick up your jacket. Sling it over your chest. Answer, 'Yeah, fine.'

Only now you're gripped by the thought that he's all the blokes in your life who've done you wrong: he's Dad, Jez, Billy, Michael, the stepdads (all three of them). You see them in your mind's eye, talking their crap, making their promises, letting you down, giving you grief, and you can't help it: it's like you was possessed and there's no choice but to hurt him, to put in the screws.

You tell him to leave you alone. What does he think he's doing? Is he some sort of perv? You saw him looking. He ought to be ashamed.

He steps back, eyes narrowing, one eyebrow raised; his dog growls and he tugs on its lead. 'Really, I'd like to help.'

But there's no stopping you now. Trying to chat up a young girl – what would his wife think? Shouldn't he know better?

And, even though his skin has become flushed and he ain't got a clue what's going on, he says, 'Come on, let me help you. You do seem in a bit of a state.'

Bit of a state? Really?

You touch your face, surprised to find it wet, and manage, 'No, no, I'm fine,' and after he backs off a little you spit out, 'Just get lost, will you?' till you hear footsteps echo around the square after his 'Well, if you're sure…'

… and sure you're sure, cos you was the one who was cool, calm and collected, who dialled 999, who comforted Mum, only later realising that you'd wet yourself. You comforting her! What was that all about?

Shaking with the memory of it, with the unbearable cruelty of it, you try and drag your mind to the present.

It's in a bad way, the pigeon.

There's nothing else for it. You sweep it up, eaten up by a sense of dread, a terror for its future what's gnawing at you, and you feel imaginary fists knocking at your head to do the right thing, and you think this time you will do – do the right thing – and in a mad rush of love – or is it E? – you decide you'll protect it: protect the pigeon.

The handbag and the hankies will do for a nest. The first aid kit at home should help. And that biology GCSE might come in handy.

Poor little thing.

Your eyes flick open first, then your lips – no, not yet: they're glued together, gacky, moist. Hello, hangover and hello, Saturday morning. Only it isn't morning, is it? The Hello Kitty alarm clock (a present from Dad), or more exactly the small hand pointing to Kitty's middle-right whisker, tells you what you didn't want to know: three o'clock. There's a message on your phone. You're meant to be meeting Billy in a bit. A strange tugging in your gut, then, and your tummy sort of rumbles, a low, groaning rumble like digestive thunder. A warning? A reminder? Something about last night?

Oh, shit, yeah. Last night.

The pigeon...

Bloody hell. What was you thinking? For a split-second you wonder whether bringing it home only took place in your imagination, the secret, seedy part usually home to death wishes, weird sex fantasies and the J-Lo obsession – that kind of shit. You strain your ears. Try to get a whiff of any pigeon smells. Have you finally lost it, letting a pigeon live – hopefully live, anyway – under your bed? On the other hand, why worry? End of the day, it's only a bird. A pet. Yeah, a pet like a cockatiel or a parrot. Or a budgie! Yeah, a budgie. Your nanna, she had one of them. Charlie, she called it, after her little brother who died in a car crash. Loved that little fella, she did.

No time to chew that one over, though, cos a hungover giddiness and nausea have come into your head, as well as a nicotine craving. You reach across the bedside table for a fag and a lighter. Course, nicotine's the last thing you need to take the edge off, but the desperate from-your-head-to-your-toes urge for a fag outweighs the queasiness of lugging the smoke down.

Bleurgh. Now a whiff of something more sinister is carried through the air over the woody, dry nicotine – a cruddy animal smell.

Double bleurgh. Right, time to face the music.

Stubbing out the half-smoked cigarette in an empty Coke can on the bedside table, you steel yourself. Lean over the edge of the bed, your head dangling over its side. Whip up the duvet in a sudden burst of confidence, to check on the box. And yup, it exists, it's real, still there, next to the rucksack containing your life savings, the fruit of ten months' hard labour. Now, with both hands, you reach under the bed and drag the box along the floor till it's slap-bang in front of you, a wild scritching and scratching sounding from inside it. Instinct tells you to jump back. Well, instinct or a fear of flapping and swooping and clawing. Cos what if it flies out, soars above the room and shits on the floor, all over your clothes, over the new bumper sex edition of *Cosmo* and all?

But soon you're telling yourself not to be such a big wally, and you heave yourself out of bed, grabbing an old-fashioned umbrella what you bought in that fancy brolly shop on Tottenham Court Road in a recent spending splurge. Then you:

poke at the box

push it across the floor

edge slightly nearer

lift the top cardboard flap, and peer, still umbrella-armed, into the makeshift nest. And there he is, flapping his one good wing – cos it is a he, of course – winking at you one-eyed. You dither. Twirl a length of your hair around your finger. And soon he's trying to flap the other wing. Failing. Then both eyes close, plunging him into darkness, into whatever place pigeons go when they're not staring out beady-eyed at the world, and you'd think he was dead if it wasn't for a weird little noise coming from inside the box. You peer further in. He looks right at you again. You're sure of it. Right in the eye. Coos.

Aw, he's kind of cute actually. 'Hello,' you say.

The two tiny ebony points of his eyes blink as if he understands the greeting. And it comes back to you with an intense whooshing, a tugging at each tightly strung cord of your heartstrings – the promise to look after him, you mean. Besides, you've wanted a pet since moving up London – a companion, something warm to cuddle, something what wants you, needs you. And this pigeon – well, he might not be warm and cuddly, but he definitely needs you, don't he?

So, first things first. What should he eat? You pull on a pair of jammie bottoms and pad down the hallway to the kitchen, filled with a smug sense of your own do-goodliness as you pull out boxes of cereal, sunflower seed packets and crisps from the cupboard. Sunflower seeds – perfect! Then you fill up an eggcup with water and, after a small tussle with the box, a bit of – whatchamacallit? – tentative edging closer, and though it takes, like, forever, you manage to feed him some seeds, and with a proud nod of his head he dips his hooded-claw beak into the water.

When he's done, you stagger to the loo then crawl back into bed, twitching with nerves. You know that Billy will be peed off that you're late, but instead of getting ready you put things off some more. Gaze at the one picture on your wall, the *Breakfast at Tiffany's* poster, pick at a spot what's flaring up on your chin, all the while listening to his coos, the bed sinking beneath you like it's wise to the tiredness, the heaviness what's tugging you, unavoidably, inevitably, towards sleep. And as you turn your face into your pillow, away from the stream of sunlight coming in from the window, you doze off, your thoughts becoming muddled, scattered...

Should you give the pigeon a name? No, no names... Cos when you give them names, that's when you care for them, that's when the trouble starts... No names, no names, no names...

3 MISSED CALLS
INBOX: 3 new messages

FROM: BILLY
SENT: Saturday 2 June, 14.59

Be on time later hun. You feeling sexy today? Wear a dress ☺

FROM: BILLY
SENT: Saturday 2 June, 16.10

Where r u? U trying to embarrass me?

FROM: BILLY
SENT: Saturday 2 June, 16.35

WTF? Get ur arse over here right now.

5

A little later, you wake up, your forehead damp with worry. Damp with worry for the pigeon, damp with worry that you're now late to meet Billy. But it's not just your forehead. Your pits are also damp. Between your legs is damp, damp with the sticky leftovers of sex with a stranger as well as a gory reminder that you forgot to put in a new tammie when you got up and fed the pigeon. Good-looking, he was, this latest 'conquest' (as Ayesha would put it), although he reckoned himself. Media bore in square black-rimmed specs. A twitch of dissatisfaction between your thighs reminds you that he was a disappointment in the sack and all. You squirm at the dampness down there. It don't feel too bad actually, dreamy and soft.

Your mind drifts. To last night at first. To drugged-up hardcore shagging. Sexy? As if! Better to be carried off elsewhere, somewhere softer and gentler instead: to Michael and naughty afternoons skipping school to do it in his mum and dad's bed. And yeah, that's better: something's stirring now. You glance at the clock. Time for a quick one, surely? And so you keep on stroking, the heel of your hand pressing down, a delicious weight at the top of your pelvis. Sweating now, hot, you roll over onto your front.

And suddenly Michael has been kicked into touch as dodgy images of Sapphire and Bella burst out before your eyes.

Oh, God, leave it out! Not them!

You try to change the dirty moving pictures in your mind to a different fantasy. Boys. Three of them, Michael at the front of the queue. Only – damn it! – there they are again. The girls. Tits like torpedoes, nipples like bullets, landing strip Velcroed to pubic landing strip.

Girl on girl, a twisted voice inside you pipes up, and the moving pictures flash quicker, filthier. Your body responds to: tongues. Everywhere. Flicking in mouths, lapping at slippery wet thighs. Bella's head disappearing between Sapphire's big plastic orange boobs. Christ's sake, not them, not Silicon Valley! But it's no use, you're nearly there, your breath fast and hot... Sapphire's fingers parting Bella's wet pubic hair, her tongue long and licky, pushing in deep... *Girl on girl*, your mind heckles again and – *pant, pant, pant* – that's it:

A short. Sharp. Cum.

Terrific. Even a good wank's not satisfying these days.

You snuggle back down under the duvet. Dead inside. Yuk, yuk, yuk. Why them? What are you, some sort of les–

Damn it, this room needs an airing! You kick off the duvet with sticky, hot legs, jump out of bed, and stagger the three steps across the room towards the big sash window what you hoik open, only to be greeted by an eff-you fog of pollution and the sounds of London in the daytime drifting in – a crotchety clanging and banging, taxis tooting, raised voices (angry or sad, you can't tell). A world of life in full colour what you wish would absorb you, suck you up, to put off the inevitable, and a worry kicking in: what's with the sometimes thinking about girls when you're turned on? You catch sight of yourself in the wardrobe mirror as you lumber back into bed. *Eugh*. What a moose. Mucky pyjama bottoms, sweaty hangdog face. Can't bear to look at yourself. What a start to the day. How, you think, did you get here? Well, that's one's easy. The usual vicious circle: worrying about Connor, booze, boys, more booze, hangover...

And now, what the heck: you've gone and added the pigeon to the shit-list.

When you finally leave the house, after a freezing cold shower and another struggle with the dodgy front door lock, the worries crank up a gear, a grumpy mood taking root what's not helped by the acid brightness of the high summer sun. Fifteen minutes to the Soho pub where you're to meet Billy. Fifteen minutes? Might as well be fifteen years, what with the pain jabbing and poking behind your eyes. If only you had a Valium to take the edge off the comedown.

Then, a flash of guilt. What if you'd had a dodgy pill last night, slipped into a coma... got in trouble with the police? Never get your Little Man back then, would you?

Every day, you swear on your life you'll do it: turn your back on everything and everyone – Billy, the overdue bills, Jeremy and the club – and run back to get him, even if you haven't reached the magic ten grand you want to put by before heading home. But something always happens. A drink, usually. Two. Three. Four.

And you snort, remembering your original aim to make fifty grand in a year. Believing the hype from people like Ayesha that lap dancing would be a fast route to easy money, your fastest route to getting Connor back.

The snort becomes a full-on grunt. Jesus Christ, for one day could you just not think about him?

Not an option, though, is it? So you heave yourself and your hangover down the street, head-space taken up by thoughts of his first word ('car'), his first steps (at fourteen months – or so Mum told you). Ooh, the Italian restaurant's busy today, you notice as you head towards Soho. Probably the spillover of the weekend Oxford Street shoppers. *Urgh.* You prefer the area on weekdays when it's graveyard-quiet, only the odd suit about to offer some clue that you're in the centre of town. People, right? Can't stand them at the best of times, never mind on a comedown. What you need now is to get a move on, eyes down on the sizzling hot pavement, to ignore the floods of people, ignore the dappy tourists outside Pizza Express, the loud-mouthed families and the sappy-looking couples shopping on Regent Street.

Hold up, though: that baseball cap and white T-shirt on the other side of the street... they're familiar... could it be?... only they've whizzed away in a blur before you can be sure. Nah, couldn't have been. What would he be doing away from Soho or where he said he lives, up Tottenham?

Talk about seeing things!

Still, the last thing you need is to bump into a customer. Or anyone really, so, aware of the clock ticking, you break into a run, ignoring the hangover jiggling about in your gut, barging past the people walking at a chilled-out Saturday pace, nearly tripping up over a *Big Issue*-seller's feet; trying to empty your mind, to make it blank and Connor-free, your feet pounding in your head as you run faster across Oxford Circus, your strides focused and long, so that by the time you've reached the pub to meet Billy you're sweating, heavy-breathing, your ponytail sticking to the back of your neck, sweat patches coating the armpits of your previously crisp white T-shirt.

Not a good look.

Inside the pub the air's smoky, beery and stale, and you wrinkle your nose at the hotchpotch of smells. This ain't your favourite Soho pub (for obvious reasons, you tell yourself) but Madonna's 'Vogue' is playing on the jukebox, a favourite: reminds you of dancing around the living room with Dad. Before he lost his legs, natch...

A deep breath and you scan the room, catching sight of Billy who's sitting at his usual table in a corner with his mate,

The Bloke (*Got a Great Bloke who I think you should meet*, he's been banging on for weeks). Gulp. With your teeth biting down on your lip you fish in your handbag for a smoke, only for your fingers to brush against Michael's letter.

You snatch your hand away. Swallow back a guilt-flavoured taste of saliva. Focus on Billy instead.

Christ, don't he ever change out of that cruddy shiny grey suit and white trainers? A sprout of chest hair creeps out the top of his white T-shirt. You can hardly blame it: you'd try and escape if you was stuck down there, and all. And you wonder for a minute why he didn't want to meet at his office, what he says is just around the corner. Come to think of it, in the year that you've known him, you've never seen this 'office', and you're starting to wonder if it really exists. Like, why come here if it's a sort of like job interview, to this packed pub, rammed with sad old blokes with grizzly hangover faces, who've been on the lash since opening time.

Billy, when he spots you, curls his top lip, scowls. Channelling Elvis, bringing off Del Boy. Why, why, why did you ever fancy him? That ridiculous bum chin. Chinless, that's what he is. Spineless, too.

'You're late,' he says when you've finally pushed your way within earshot, then he's looking you up and down. 'And didn't you get all my texts?'

Christ, even his voice gets your back up these days.

'Oh,' you lie, plonking your arse on the seat opposite him, 'my phone needed charging.'

He glares at you – well, a lame Billy glare anyway – and you add, 'Sorry,' making eye contact with The Bloke so that Billy knows you ain't apologising for his benefit. You change the subject. 'Mmm, that looks good.'

Your mouth is watering at the sight of his burger. You ain't eaten since that mouthful of Pot Noodle, like, three million years ago, BP. Before Pigeon.

'Veggie burger.'

'Oh, yeah? They run out of beef?' you say, aware of The Bloke out of the corner of your eye. Isn't Billy going to introduce you?

'Nah, I've decided to go vegetarian,' he replies, and takes a bite.

One thing you can say about Billy is, he's full of surprises.

'Oh, right. No more KFC, then?' About the only thing the unadventurous bastard'll usually eat.

'Nah, I'm still eating chicken.'

And this, you think, is why you don't fancy the guy no more.

You try and catch the eye of The Bloke again. Surely you're not the only one who thinks Billy's a dickhead? Only The Bloke's face is a brick wall. Good-looking actually, in a James Bond sort of way. Suited and booted.

'So,' Billy says at last, wiping mayo from his chin, 'Kenny, meet Hayleigh…' Kenny McVeigh. Some sort of talent scout for the porn industry – apparently.

'Hi, Kenny,' you coo, using a well-practised you're-clearly-a-shady-sleazy-git-but-I'm-pretending-you're-Mr-Respectability tone of voice.

At first, you think he's alright. Quite charming, in a bit-of-rough kind of way. When the hellos and chit-chat and whatnot are over, though, he shows his true colours. Speaks to you through Billy, like you wasn't there. *So she's drop-dead gorgeous, grant you that, but can she act? Has she got the bottle to do it on screen?*

What are you – invisible? Sod this!

'Just going to order some food,' you say. 'Want anything?'

You're only half out of your chair when Kenny leaps up. 'I'll get it for you, princess. Burger?'

You judder at the 'princess' but nod in what you hope is a grateful yet sexy way. Shout after him, 'A real one, though, please!'

'So, what do you think? Top Bloke, ain't he?' Billy's saying as you watch Kenny push to the front of the queue in the crowded bar.

A new song bellows out from the jukebox, 'Patience' by Take That, a sad melody to match your fading mood. Cos you're not sure about all this, to be fair. It was his idea. Billy's. You'd been moaning about the new girls, how they've been bringing down the tone, how it's getting harder and harder to make a decent wedge cos of them. And you was pissed As Per Usual on V&Ts and Billy was like, *Well, I know how you can make some money fast, get your baby – what's his name, Curtis – back quick*. Seemed like a good idea when your belly had a litre of vodka in it, but now?

You share this worry with Billy.

'Well,' he snaps, 'bit late for a change of heart, ain't it? You're not going to show me up, are you, girlie?'

It might almost sound threatening if Billy wasn't about as threatening as a dried lentil. Only a thought springs into your mind then. A warning from your cousin, who introduced you to Billy, when you first moved in with him way back when. What was it? Something creepy he did to an ex-girlfriend?

But no time for chewing that one over, cos Kenny's back with a 'Food won't be long,' and he smiles for the first time. Gold teeth. Oh, terrific, a gangster. You should have recognised the look a mile off. Sure, some girls at Elegance think the whole gangster thing's glamorous. Yeah, baseball bats to the kneecaps, that's glamorous. Being humped and dumped – that too.

But you put a twinkle into your eye and return the smile. Cos, gangster or not, Billy might be right, his Bloke might

61

have the solution to getting the baby back quicker. As for Billy, well, he's like a smell under your nose what won't go away. Not that you're sort of like ungrateful, what with him coming to the rescue when you was homeless and jobless and that, but you won't ever forgive how he acted around the time of the termination. End of.

Oh, yeah, the termination. That's a shocker, right?

Well, it was for you anyway. *Once upon a time there was a girl*, you'd start if you was writing it down, *and she had a baby who she adored more than life itself, who was taken away from her, not by a witch or an evil stepmother but by her own real-life mother, and all she could think of was returning to him. Only then she met a big bad wolf who told her that taking her clothes off could make her fast money and that would solve all of her problems. But this big bad wolf didn't just want to help, he wanted to take the little girl away and hold her captive in his castle (shit flat, more like), and he huffed and puffed till she had sex with him and she did, and, even though she wouldn't call it rape, to be fair it weren't exactly what you'd call making love, and, what do you know, the girl got pregnant again. And there wasn't a happy ending...*

'Layla,' Billy's saying.

'Yeah, I like it,' Kenny replies, fiddling with the clunking great Tag Heuer on his wrist. 'Need a last name, though. Something eggs-ott-ick.'

'What about my surname?' Billy asks. 'Rousseau?'

Layla Rousseau, porn star – it does have a ring to it, you admit. And then they're cheersing each other, looking pretty wrecked now, as it goes, little trips to the loo and Billy's constant nose-blowing giving away what they're up to. Nice of them to offer you some. But who cares? You'd rather zone out to the tunes on the jukebox, be plied with one V&T after another, munch away on the burger what's just arrived.

As for the termination, you wish that was the end to that story, but it's like one of them magical books with no ending, the Never-Ending flipping Story in fact, a nightmare what's chased around your thoughts since it happened four months ago. Right from the start Billy was – well, not a shit, just predictable. *Well, you ain't keeping it, are you?*

Well, yeah, you remember it flashing before your mind. *A little sister or brother for Connor.* But how? Not like you could even be a mum to him. And what would Michael say? Mum? Dad? Never mind what another baby would do to your body: it hasn't recovered from Connor's birth (sixteen stitches from the episiotomy what still need to be covered with make-up in the club). As for how having even one baby's messed with your mind... Not that the termination did your head in any less, or that you was any less scared beforehand either. But did Dickhead give a shit about those fears? If only. In bed, the night before it happened, you had to shake him awake, let all them worries spew out. 'I'm scared of dying,' you told him. 'The leaflet says you've got a one in a hundred thousand chance of death after the operation.'

'Come on, love. Don't be stupid,' he replied, 'That's like one in a million or something,' and he rolled over back to sleep.

And he was the one calling *you* stupid?

And so the next day you ended up laid out on a trolley in a manky old hospital gown, your knees trembling, the anaesthetist telling you to count back, 10, 9, 8, 7...

... and the next thing you knew you was awake, groggy, but awake, listening to women moaning and groaning in the beds next to you, some bird on a right trip when she come to from the anaesthetic: *Horses... can I still ride my horses?* she was saying. It was so, well, weird, the contrast. The starch-clean uniforms, the sterile metal equipment, the nurses' kind expressions and gentle questions compared to the real part:

the agonising cramps in your tummy… the fainting when you tried to leave… the blood, unstoppable rivers of that. And the guilt. The guilt of murdering your baby.

Murdering your baby!

This murderer's guilt washing over you as you got dressed. *An outrage, a scandal,* you thought, viewing it like a newspaper headline: 'BRITAIN'S WORST MOTHER KILLS BABY AFTER DESERTING FIRST-BORN CHILD'. Hanging around for Billy in the waiting room, them words catapulting to the front of your brain. *I've just had an abortion.* An hour passing. Two. It dawning on you that Billy wasn't going to pick you up, take you home, after all. Walking out of the clinic in a dream, in shock maybe. Everyday thoughts, hopes, memories, snatches of songs, the cogs and wheels of the brain going round – *need to remember nappies; the wheels on the bus go round and round; clank, brr, whoosh; where's my keys, my shoes, my purse…?* – all of that usual background slush gone, your mind invaded by that one thought.

I've just had an abortion.

Sitting on the Tube, rattling across London, aware of the clots of blood soaking through the sanitary pad (*I've just had an abortion*). Would you make it to the loo in time to change the pad? A man looking up at you over the top of his book (*I've just had an abortion*). Sitting on the bus, too weak to walk from the tube station to the pub, your legs shaky, your stomach raw (*I've just had an abortion*). The bus conductor asking for your ticket (*I've just had an abortion*).

Sitting in this same pub you're in now, hoping that Billy would be around. Yeah, believe it or not, despite his crapitude, wanting him to be there for you…

… and you look up, take a bite of burger, send Billy a dirty look, wanting to be anywhere, anywhere but here.

'Ain't that right, Hayleigh?' he's saying.

You start at the sound of your name, so used to Layla these days. God, you wish Billy didn't know the real one.

'Uh, sorry, what?'

'Come on, Dolly Daydream.'

Dolly Daydream. Billy's pet name for you. *That's right, you're a dolly bird, a dreamer. Thinking about bunnies and rainbows and everything pink.* Not that you're Brain of Britain, but look, can you just say something? You're not so stupid that you don't know when to look stupid. Not so dumb as to want Billy and Kenny to see past the fake tan, the make-up and the bimbo act. Like, what man wants to listen to a girl with her own opinions, speaking her mind? No, if the club's taught you anything, it's that nothing works better than playing Little Miss Nice Girl and coming over the doormat.

And that's exactly what you do now, smarming, 'How can I help?'

And then Kenny starts with the buttering-up, saying you look like her off the telly (like you don't hear that a million times a day), that he's sure that he can get you Top Dollar if you pass the audition. *Whatever, mate*, you want to say, only to bite it back down, clam up, let them get on with the numbers and that, so that you can get back to your burger, get back into your thoughts and the past...

... so you came here looking for Billy that afternoon, surprised when the words that came out your mouth to the pub landlord was, 'Seen Billy about?' and not, 'I've just had an abortion.' You found a seat (*I've just had an abortion*); drank a Coke (*I've just had an abortion*); when you was less dizzy, hit the bar again (*I've just had an abortion*); ordered a drink, alcohol this time (*I've just had an abortion*); ordered and snorted back another (*I've just had an abortion*); till that thought became bored of squishing out all the others in your brain, and it clawed its way up your throat, and it was sort of like you was being forced to try it out loud – 'I've just had an abortion,' the words coming out chewed-up and weird as if your mouth was stuffed with cotton wool.

'Eh?' An old fella who'd been sitting next to you, turned away. Then turned back. 'Look like you could do with a drink, pet.'

And that was the start of a drinking session what went on into the night. A drinking session what, truth be told, hasn't yet stopped four months later. But, no matter how much you drink, you're losing weight, right? It's empty, your belly, so empty you still can't quite believe it. You put your hand across it now, hoping to feel the skin itch and prickle, to feel those first alien butterflies flitting across it, to feel a bump grow and stretch under your T-shirt, like before…

'Thursday it is, then.'

You rejoin the land of the living, snatch your hand away from your stomach in case Billy can read your mind. (As if!)

'Thursday?' you say, looking out the window at a pigeon eating a puddle of sick outside on the sill. *Eugh.* You think of your own pet pigeon under the bed at home, and push the last of your burger to the side of the plate.

'Dozy mare. Thursday morning, eleven sharp, your audition.'

And Billy's beaming smugly as though he's just handed you an amazing gift, a black velvet Bond Street jewellery box. Bow on top. When in actual fact, you think, your hand outstretched to shake Kenny's, it feels like he's dolloped a pile of steaming dog shit into your palm, same as all the others you've met since moving up London have done: Jeremy, your flatmates, Sapphire.

You've had it with them! Had it up to the back teeth with the shitstorm life's been chucking at you the last few months, as a matter of fact. And recently it's like that shitstorm's

66

gone berserk, spraying you with all its strength and power, covering you from head to foot with its muck. Trickling inside all the openings of your body: getting to your brain through your nose and ears, even into your – pardon if TMI – lady bits and all.

And if you want to dump shit on me, folks, you think, *I'll just fling it back, and double. Just wait.*

Yeah, forget keeping things in, not speaking your mind, forget nice.

Just you lot shitting wait.

SENT MESSAGES

TO: DAD
SENT: Saturday 2 June, 19.48

U know, would b nice 2 hear
something other than knock-
knock jokes some time x

Sunday

6

Though it ain't your usual style, you sneak past Jeremy's office. Buggered if you're paying the house fee tonight. His office door's open but he's yabbering away on the phone – usually keeps it open unless he's hoovering up lines with Derek, or some desperado's playing his skin flute. OK, you're making that up, but it wouldn't surprise you.

Anyway, look, can you just say something? It's not like you to duck out of the house fee. Really. You're a good girl, don't like to get on the wrong side of the managers, not sure what's got into you, getting a bit partial to risk-taking these days. You pass further along the corridor, mulling this over, but soon with a shrug you've let yourself off. Like, what's the harm? Not like anyone's going to get hurt. Besides, the fees Jez is charging these days, they're criminal! And, satisfied with yourself, with coming over all judge and jury on Jez, you find your eyes drawn to the paint flaking off the lime-green walls, and you reach the changing room door, wondering why the club's so quiet today, none of the usual buzz in the air. Sunday, you suppose, and you're in early for a change.

No hangover today, see – had an early night last night for once. You escaped Billy and Kenny before things got out of hand. It was obvious from the industrial quantities of rum and Cokes they was necking that they was settling in for a session: Billy starting up on his – probably tall – tales of being in the SAS... of how he plans to retire a millionaire at fifty... how his big break's just around the corner, he can feel it… No way you wanted to get sucked into all that BS. Instead, you've had twelve hours' beauty sleep, done a bit of shopping in Oxford Street and got here in good time for the night shift – at last: your first one since Jez put you on days. Cos sometimes it's worth spending more time getting ready, right? Taking more care over the rituals of putting on your make-up, pulling on your stockings, putting a sensual touch into the routine. Don't know why. Some days you just feel like kicking the arse out of it – maybe you could even go on the hunt for a new regular or two? Colin's getting on your tits these days and Dev, your other regular, ain't been in for a while.

You swing open the changing room door. Wow, Katrina's in already. Not that she notices you; she's posing in her undies under the only section of mirror with working light bulbs, her gaze fixed straight ahead on her own reflection. You let your eyes run over her body for a minute. Just looking. Not perving or nothing, honest. Anyway, Katrina, she's black, yeah, and sometimes you envy her her skin colour. No arseing around with fake tan required, saving herself a quid or two, and the time… All that time what you spend in the spray tan booth trying to turn your skin a perfect Midas gold and not a Man from Del Monte orange. Still, at least you've never gone as far as Sapphire – aka Little Miss Oompa-Loompa.

With a guilty twinge about the wank, you tell yourself not to dwell on that, not to work yourself up by thinking of her. Instead you focus on getting ready, slumping your handbag on the ledge under the mirror to the right of a cluster of lotions and potions, powders and bottles what are spilled out from Katrina's Louis Vuitton handbag. She still doesn't look at you. What is this? The cold shoulder?

'Hi, honey,' you say, waving your hand across the mirror.

'Oh, Hayleigh, hi,' she says.

Cor, what a cheek! Acting like she's only just spotted you, but then she's air-kissing both sides of your face, all matey and that, saying, 'How's you?'

Katrina's alright, can sometimes be a bit of a bitch, to the new girls and that. But you like her; she can be wickedly funny. Anyway, more to the point, you trust her, and it don't take much for you to have a moan up these days.

'Well, if you must know... bloody Jeremy won't get off my back recently. It's like I told you, I was gonna have a word, about pay and that...' And you go on, telling her about your recent disagreements, all the while lining up a selection of different coloured pots on the ledge above the sink, whipping off your clothes. Only you break off before you get into the juicy stuff, cos you've caught sight of Katrina in the mirror, her bottom lip curled to one side, frowning, hand on hip.

'Oh, erm, sorry,' you say, thinking, have you said the wrong thing? Has she changed her mind about complaining about the house fees? 'It's just I thought you agreed, that we should try...' And you trail off, not sure where this is going.

She stays tight-lipped, continuing to frown as she fluffs up her afro with a metal comb, her eyes glued to the mirror. *Au naturel* she likes to keep her hair. Then, after a few minutes of awkward silence, she seems to make up her mind about something, strutting across the changing room in her six-inch heels to close the door.

You pull your stomach in, fill your lungs with air; got a feeling something bad's coming. 'You alright, hon?'

'Yeah, *I*'m fine, babe,' she says, stressing the 'I'.

Oh, OK. You stop what you're doing – dabbing a constellation of glitter across your chest – and turn towards her, mouth set in a grim straight line, chin jutting. 'Go on, then, spit it out.'

'Look, I've wanted to tell you this for a few days,' she's saying in her South London twang, still fixing her hair in the mirror, 'but we ain't been alone.'

'Oh, yeah?'

'I been hearing rumours about you.'

Your heart skips a beat. Do they know? About Connor? The termination? The porn offer? 'Rumours?'

'Yeah,' she says, and she's all like multi-tasking and that as she tells you this, curling her long, thick eyelashes with eyelash curlers, her fingernails painted so black it looks like she's used ink instead of nail polish. 'Little bird told me you've been getting into the brown stuff.'

Never mind skipping a beat – you wonder if your heart's gonna stop.

'Of course,' she continues, setting the eyelash curlers to one side, working on her lips now, building up layers of greasy pink, 'I dittn't believe them.'

'Heroin.' It's a question, you suppose, but it's all you can do to say it, as if you was learning a new word.

'That's why you've lost all the weight?'

'Heroin.' You try it again.

'Well?' she asks, replacing the cap on the lip gloss, turning towards you, both hands on hips now.

Anger hits you racing-car-fast; no time for a slow gear-change from a brooding red crossness – it's there all at once, an overpowering and white-hot fury, what makes you flustered, murderous, speechless at the same time.

You turn to the mirror. Dab more glitter on your chest. Short, sharp, bullet-speed dabs. Then, seeing the expectation of an answer in her face, you reply, although, 'Don't be bloody daft,' is all you manage to chuck from your lips.

'Look, babe, don't be angry. Like I said, *I* dittn't believe them.'

There she goes, stressing that 'I' again.

You make a wish, that the ground would swallow you whole. Like, what are you meant to say? Talk about embarrassing! Cos it's cobblers, of course. All cobblers! You lean over the sink, balling your fingers into fists. God, look, you swear on your life you ain't usually such a head case, so quick to fly off the handle, but when people make up stuff... Your chest tightens then, a sickly feeling gurgling up in your tummy. You wheeze. Cough. Bloody hell, not an asthma attack. And you wonder if you've brought your inhaler, only to picture it on top of your bedside table.

What about practising them labour breathing exercises instead? Yeah, that could work. You make your out-breaths and in-breaths loooooong and slooooooow, matching in rhythm. 'RE...' you think on the in-breath '...LAX,' on the out, and after a few of them, Katrina looking on in silence, your heart rate's coming back down to normal and you make a second wish: that the ground would spit you back out so that you can deal with all this BS. And now that your tongue's no longer on fire, your lips no longer burning with rage, you do just that, asking the question, 'Who's "them"?'

Katrina goes back to the mirror, putting the finishing touches to her hair with a storm cloud of hairspray. 'Well, you should ask Sapphire if you wanna know more.'

Sapphire. You knew it was all a front, that mateyness, the sucky-uppiness.

'Oh, right,' you say, 'Course.'

But is Katrina throwing you a banana skin? Can you trust her, after all? You look her square in the eyes and she smiles, a dippy, doleful smile, and somehow you know in your heart it must be true. Think how off with you Jez has been recently – Susie too. Sapphire must have been bad-mouthing you.

Your anger bites again, showing in a clenching of your jaw, a grinding of teeth, and you get on with the rest of your preparations with zipped-up lips, cursing the light bulb what blinks on and off above your section of mirror, cursing the trembles in your fingers what are stopping you twisting the lid off a body lotion bottle, all the while waiting for Katrina to leave the room so you can let it all out.

Then, just when you don't think you can hold it in for much longer, she finally gets lost and you let out a sob, blink back the hot tears what are puddling your eyes, your imagination sparking, going off on one, and you conjure the idea that you've been poisoned, poisoned by a hatred from someone else, from Sapphire, a hatred what you ain't been the victim of since all that gossip what was spread about you by the bullies at school.

The words *mud sticks* flash before your mind. Huh! Never mind mud, cos in the bullies' case they was right at least – you *was* pregnant – but here? Heroin? Bullshit. Utter bullshit. And what's bullshit like? Sticks worse than mud and stinks more and all. No wonder Jeremy's been giving you the cold shoulder. You put your head in your hands, drop it down, and spread out your elbows on the sink. Close your eyes. *Think, woman, think! Think what you can do to sort this.*

If only Susie was here. She'd smooth things over with Jeremy, wouldn't she? Only she's got tonight off, you remember. Visiting a 'gentleman friend' she's been knocking off once a month for donkey's years. You flick your eyes to the rota what hangs on the changing room wall above the skanky old washing machine. Look up and down the list to see if Ivana's name's on it – she's the only one around here who talks sense – and, after making a quick note that you're due on the pole in five minutes, you read something what makes you half relieved, half see red.

Sapphire won't be in today. Typical. Jez gives you Saturday off, the best money-making night of the week, and gives Sapphire Sunday. Thought he was doing you a favour by putting you back on nights, but not now. Talk about playing favourites.

And then you realise what's got to be done: you have to get her back – and double. So, as you pull a black leather thong over your black-stockinged legs in quick, jerky movements, you make a plan. A plan for revenge, you mean. Now for an outfit. Got to look your best if you're going to pick up a new regular. Your black Karen Millen dress? The one posh dress you've bought since working here. It's your eff-off–and-die-I'm-Queen-Bee-in-this-club dress. Gets the girls cooing over it, asking to borrow it and that, and, more to the point, gets the guys hot under the collar. You step across to your locker, grinning in spite of your bad mood as you root around, wondering if Ivana was in yesterday, i.e., if it's your turn for the chihuahua. The dress should be folded up at the back somewhere; maybe the little dog's –

No way. No. Sodding. Way.

It's in there alright, the dress. In there, ripped to pieces and scattered around the locker, looking like black ash after a fire. She might as well have burned it. That's how it makes you feel: as if she'd set fire to the dress. Or punched you in the head, beaten you, assaulted you.

You stamp your foot. Kick the locker below yours, leaving a dent. And you wonder, not for the first time, why you and other girls can't be friends. Why can't they – you pick up the shreds of fabric and let them fall through your fingers to the ground – well, be... be – you root around for a word – be NICE to you?

It must have been Sapphire what done this, Sapphire with her fake smile, fake boobs and fake everything else.

With a tight frown and muttering to yourself, you scrabble in the locker to check on the rest of the clothes, check that the little toy dog's not been butchered. Breathe a sigh of relief that no, it's only the black dress what's been ruined, and you reach in to grab a slutty red one instead, pulling it over your undies in a trance, doing everything that happens next in a blur of confusion: kicking open the scuffed door that leads backstage with staccato kicks... strutting onto the main stage to throw out a medley of shapes for your two-song turn on the pole... hopping down from the stage, nearly twisting your ankle cos your movements are so violent, when they should be the opposite – everything done in soft focus, Vaseline-smeared.

Soon though, in comparison to the bright lights on stage, the darkness of the main floor is a release, a den of earthy shadows and whispered conversations, perfect for hiding away in. Only then – typical! – just when you think you're safe, ultraviolet lasers from the new light show ricochet across the room, spinning you out, and these lights, this darkness push you into confusion, into anger again – cos it's a sort of like reflection of where you are now, caught between dark and light, between letting Sapphire off and getting her back, between being the bigger person and plotting your revenge. But, even as these thoughts hare through your mind, you're shelving them, deciding to focus on the customers, to get back to your plan of having a good earner tonight, yeah, of raking it in? And, squinting to make out the shifting shapes of the huddled groups and the single black silhouettes of the loners on the main floor, you smile: good, a few more customers in now.

Time passes; nothing much happens. A flock of other night shift girls arrives; the harmless customers of the day shift leave, gradually replaced by the needy drunks of the evening session. The air turns bluer, more competitive. And it's almost like you can taste the change in atmosphere with the night drawing in, a veil of heaviness, of seediness, coming down over the club. And somehow this change in atmosphere, the long journey into the night what stretches before you, makes you lose interest in going on the hustle, stops you from being arsed about getting a new regular. Like all the competition. Being a try-hard. So not worth it, you think, as you watch Katrina and her mate Pam prance about in their 'coffee and cream' knickers, their gimmick being a black-and-white double act what the guys seem to love. It's… you scrabble around for the word. Degrading, that's what it is.

You feel your spirits sink down, your heart sag. If only Ivana was here. You could do with someone to goof around with, someone who don't take the whole thing so seriously.

She's not down to work tonight, though, of course. So, who can you rant to? You've got to get it all out somehow. To someone! You kick out at the empty stool next to you, stubbing your toe. *Ow!* Right, you think, jumping down from your stool and then hopping about on one foot (not easy in five-inch heels) – that's a sign. A sign to forget it. To let your shoulders come down, to move on. You wave over at the barman and order another drink, your, like, gazillionth one of the night, only to sense a movement behind you.

An interested customer at last?

'Hi, Lay-lay.'

Colin. Surprise, and something else you can't quite put your finger on, seizes you. Maybe that you're running out of things to say to him, fed up with his pity pleas and bitching off his wife.

'I've… I've missed you,' he says, his black leather jacket making static as it brushes against the red polyester dress.

You shrink back, your nostrils twitching, cos his breath, a mixture of a sour milk and beer, is getting you right up the nose. And what's all this *missed you* crap? It's only been, what? Not more than a couple of days? Casting your eyes about the room, you hope that someone might be kind and save your life by joining the conversation. But when that idea falls flat and he leans across you, his breath hot on your cheeks, you down the last of your vodka-tonic, pushing your glass to one side of the bar...

sick of the booze
sick of the customers
sick of it all!

You give him the once-over, try and suss him out. Like, is he going to lose it? Turn on you again like that one time a few months back? No chance. He's too stupid with drink to do anything – well, stupid. You could push him over with one finger, he's that far gone. But – ever conscious of the CCTV cameras – you rein in this fantasy and light a cigarette instead, your eyes burning into his stupid, lolling, drunken head, watching his eyelids droop and flicker, flicker and droop as he tries to act sober, spouting garbage. And then, when the conversation, for what it's worth, dries up, you wonder, should you tell him? Spill the proverbial about what went on earlier with Katrina? He's a shoulder to cry on, after all, ain't he? On your side?

A new round of drinks arrives and, with a bit of Dutch courage inside you, you decide yes, why not go for it? After all, he's bent your ear enough times. Payback time!

And so, as he sits cradling his beer, you go heart on sleeve, mouthing off about everything what's bothering you: Connor and Michael, Billy, the flatmates, Sapphire. And to be fair to the chap he turns out to be a good listener, his neck nodding down-up, down-up in agreement, like one of them toy dogs – even butting in at one point to say that Michael sounds like a decent lad. As if! Besides, who'd have thought it? Colin being that person you've been looking for, that person to hear you out.

Only, after a while, you're forced to say 'Colin!' cos he's propped his head on your shoulder (heavier than what it looks), his baseball cap falling in sort of like slow motion to the floor. He don't try to pick it up, though, cos his eyes are rolling in the back of his head, and now – *whoosh!* – they're closing, like shutters. Of course. Of course he was never listening. He's been falling asleep this whole time.

Jesus Christ! Why is nobody there for you at the minute? Mum! Dad! Billy! Now even the man who pays to spend time with you can't be arsed to cheer you up. Derek walks past, arm in arm with one of the old-timer girls, and she laughs, making the L-shaped *loser* sign on her forehead. And, as she and a few other dancers drift away towards the private rooms with big money types, you can't help yourself, can't help feeling a spare part. Tears well up in your eyes, hot tears what then splash down on to Colin's bald head (so that's why the baseball cap).

Only now you see he ain't asleep after all, cos he's going, 'Hayleigh,' and he's reaching across to stroke your face. 'Don't cry.'

What. The?

'What d'you say?'

He bolts upright. Eyes flick wide open. Don't seem so pissed all of a sudden.

'Layla,' he says, saying your stage name a bit too loud. 'Don't cry. Don't cry, Lay-lay.'

'No, you didn't. You said – ' and you stop there. Is your mind playing tricks? You losing it or what? Besides, what's that expression? About biting the hand what feeds? You ought to let it go, so what if he knows your na–

but you ain't got time to think about it, cos he's lunging at you… fingers gripping the tops of your arms, burning into your triceps… his tongue, slippery, sea-weed slimy, licking at your lips. 'There, there, love, I'll make it better.'

What a loser! You push him away, sort of like not all that bothered – you've handled worse – but then his hand, yeah, it's under your dress, crawling its way up your leg, on your knee, your thigh, groping at knicker elastic –

'Colin!' you shout, pushing with all your strength against his chest. 'Get. Off. Me!' And you lean back, nearly falling from the stool. At the clatter, Celia, the waitress, looks over, only to turn back to a customer without doing nothing. Cheers, love. And so you shout, louder this time, 'Derek! Iain!'

Within seconds the bouncers are on you, Colin's eyes still roaming over your body, though his arms are pinned down by his sides. And he's looking – what is that expression – hurt? Hurt! He's the one who's hurt? You wipe snot from under your nose, fuming; wipe the wet from your cheeks. Like you thought, stupid little cow that you are, that he was OK. And as Iain, the head bouncer, starts giving it all his ex-Army bollocks, bawling Colin out, another thought pops up in your mind: that Colin was your friend.

As if, you think, as Colin's hauled out his chair by Iain and Derek.

As if, you go on, as he twists back and looks at you, his face erupting in a purple-red madness.

And then all at once you're jerking backwards cos he's pulling away from Derek and Iain, lunging again – and this time you don't think it's a kiss he wants. Unless it's the Glasgow variety.

Friends? you think, for the last time, as you jump three more steps back and Iain gets him in a headlock.

As if.

INBOX: 2 new messages

FROM: DAD
SENT: Sunday 3 June, 17.32

*Bit harsh love. Trying my
best*

FROM: BILLY
SENT: Sunday 3 June, 18.07

*You done great! He
thought you was brill.
You shd b dead chuffed.*

7

Hot and sweet, like you, Jeremy's saying, and though you don't laugh at his joke you show your appreciation with a thumbs-up, cos you've never been so glad for a cup of tea, not ever, and it's like you're a little girl again as you sit, dwarfed by his big swingy-around office chair, your hands gripping the way-too-hot mug, your tongue slurping at the still-too-hot tea, and Jeremy's wrapped his suit jacket over your knees, cos you don't know why but your legs are trembling – still, half an hour since Colin was ejected from the club! – and it's like you can't stop them thoughts and fears whizzing and whirring in your –

And then you're deep-breathing. Deep, from-the-bottom-of-your-lungs breaths, trying to chill out, to calm down.

Jeremy's sitting on his desk, the usual random towers of paper shifted out the way, and – *whoops!* – as he shunts his body further left, his arse slips on a copy of *Which Car?* magazine. Nobody speaks: not you, not Jeremy, not Derek, who's followed you in from the main floor. Just the *blink, blink, blink* of the CCTV monitor showing any signs of life, the rest of the room clammed up in awkward silence. Both hands cradling the mug, you wonder why you've not noticed the prison-cell feel of this room before. Just one high window with bars on it, drab light green walls. Yeah, a prison cell or a headmaster's office. Only with more porno mags and Pirelli calendars, obviously.

Phew, a joke – you must be feeling better. Your hands relax around the mug; your forehead and pinched cheeks soften.

Maybe sensing the change, Jeremy speaks up. 'Well, that's another good customer down the drain.'

You smart at *good customer*. Easy money, yeah. Harmless, maybe. But good? Your hands clench around the mug again. Christ, he's an old woman, Jeremy, the way he bores on about his supposed problems: about them feminists who protest outside the club, about the council checking up that the girls are playing by the rules. And now this: moaning that he's losing *good customers*. Not him who has to put up with the shit these *good customers* fling, is it? Not him who gets poked, prodded, and... and... and feeling like you're about to break down, you think back to Colin's lips sliming on you.

Derek, who's been brooding in the corner, now pipes up. Waiting for Jeremy's reaction, you suppose, before daring to wade in himself. He clears his throat – can't usually speak without first hawking up a sticky gobful of phlegm.

'Yeah, and we've little Layla here to thank for that, eh?'

You half spin around on the chair to face him. You what? Blaming you for Colin stepping out of line – way out of line! – is he? But as ever you bite your tongue, hold back, say the opposite of what your mind, body and soul are begging for you to scream out at the top of your lungs.

'Sorry,' you mouth in a whisper, dipping your head down towards the steaming mug of tea, looking at your chest still rising and falling in pathetic little huffs. And what's with him using your stage name and all, like... like you wasn't a real person or something? You smirk as he erupts into one of his coughing fits. Serves him blooming well right.

But for once Jeremy seems reasonable. Kind, even. He leans over and rubs your arm. 'Not your fault, love.'

'Jeremy, look, can I have a word?' Your eyes drift over to Derek. 'In private? Think we need to clear the air.'

He nods at Derek who backs out of the room, almost bowing, the brown-nose, closing the door behind him with a gentleness you're sure he isn't feeling, the sound of his coughing following him out of the room. Like, what's it going to take for him to quit smoking? A death certificate?

Anyway, screw him: now he's out the way, the main aim is to get Jez on side. You clear your throat. Come out with it, vanilla-style, no sugar-coating.

'Them new girls, Jez…' and you make your voice breathy and light as if he was one of the customers '… they're making a bad scene.'

He arches his eyebrows but keeps schtum, and you steal a peek at the TV monitor, where you briefly watch Katrina spinning down the pole. Spurred on by the memory of her weasel words, you go on.

'Them… them… rumours what you've been hearing about me. I swear on my life, they're just that…'

Standing up now, he lifts both palms in the air, his body language telling you that everything's cool. 'It's OK, it's OK, I believe you,' he's saying, and all the while he's pulling you out of his chair, gesturing you towards the little wooden flip-up chair at the other side of the desk and settling back into his own chair, elbows splayed out behind his head. 'But they're here to stay. Basically, love, I like you, always have – you're my little grafter, ain't you? – but you're going to have to play nice with the new girls, decide if you want to do things my way.'

Or the highway, your mind ticks.

And then he goes all businessman on you. 'I've got my bottom line to think about.'

Anger flashes into your eyes but you try and keep it locked down.

'Yeah, course,' you snivel.

'Keep your nose clean and you'll be alright, Hayleigh,' he says, sifting through a pile of papers on the desk.

'Yeah, sure, of course,' you mumble, again.

And then he's running his fingers through his Fifties-throwback greasy quiff, saying, 'Look, love, let me give you a piece of friendly advice...' and he goes off on one of his favourite rants. About his girls start off grafting, innocent, but then it's inevitable (he says it *in-erv-atable*) how after a while, like some sort of witchy black magic, they get lazy, drink too much, or turn into sluts.

He continues, 'But then – ' and he's saying it almost like a threat ' – I know that you're different, that you'll stay white as snow, that you'll do anything to bring in some new guys – to make up for Colin.'

OK, he's saying that you're different, that he likes you... so why do you feel like you've just had a bollocking? *Another* bollocking! You used come in here to see Jez and have a laugh; it was blurred – like, his office and the changing room, you couldn't slide a cigarette paper between them. Now, it's all preaching and headmaster voice and stuff. Christ, you've had enough for one day.

So when he finally pauses for breath you say, 'Look, Jez, can I go home? Kitten's in, and Star.'

'Yeah,' he says, all po-faced and arsey, 'that's fine.'

You're out of your chair before he's finished the last word.

'But Hayleigh, aren't you forgetting something?'

You spin back around, hand on the door handle. 'Oh, uh – yeah, thanks for the tea.'

He stares you out.

'Uh... er...?' You fish around in your mind for what he wants.

'House fee?'

'Oh, God, yeah, right,' you go, scrabbling in your purse and pulling out a couple of the notes what Colin shoved in there earlier, before he went off on one. 'Thanks.'

Outside, the heatwave's behaving like it might finally be in the mood for a rest, a cluster of rainclouds looming over you and an electric feeling charging the air. The words *doom and gloom* run through your mind, chasing out all other thoughts as you dredge your feet along Soho's empty streets. Sunday, early evening. People having a night off from the sauce, you suppose – always dead around here Sundays. Funny that, cos Sundays used to be one of your best nights to go out clubbing. Down Oriana's in Brighton, happy hour all night on a Sunday. It was at Oriana's, in fact, the night you'd been out before Connor – no, you don't want to think about that night out with Michael. His attempt at getting you back together. His attempt to show you he'd grown up in the year since you'd binned him.

No, you really don't want to think about him – you've got enough on your plate – and so you try to zone out, instead dreaming up the best way you can get back at Sapphire as you *stomp stomp stomp* down the street, the first big splashes of rain dropping onto the pavement, quite a relief after the sultriness of the past week. And at last you turn off Regent Street; always good to get away from the temptation of the shops, the bars, the pubs. On the corner the Italian's still open, and a rowdy group have made a home at the big round table under the burgundy awning, half-empty bottles and side plates scattered over the red and white checked tablecloths. They're so boisterous that you don't notice him at first, a customer on his own, at the corner table, something familiar about... you strain your eyes at the black leather jacket, the baseball cap... no way... but, yes, as you walk nearer to the table, you see that your suspicions have been right all along...

Colin.

You knew it!

Knew you'd seen that baseball cap in the street earlier this week!

You'd got hot, bothered, walking back from the club, but now your blood runs cold; in fact all of you freezes: face, legs, hands, arms, toes, fingers, unable to move, frozen in a feeling you ain't felt since you walked in on the baby, quiet and blue in his cot.

What should you do?

You could run, run the other way, back towards… but too late: he's swinging around as if he'd smelled you out, and now he's rising out of his seat with a sudden pounce, his hands plucking at you, his lips contorting into a grimace. You stand face to face for what seems like minutes, him half out of his seat, just that between him and you, the table in front of him littered with empty beer bottles, a bowl of untouched soup.

You freeze.

Make like a statue.

Hardly dare breathe.

A waiter bumps past you, holding a tray piled high with pasta and pizza what he puts on the rowdy people's table. You sense they have one eye on their dinners, the other on you.

And after serving them the waiter turns to you with a 'Would you like a menu, madam?' – one eyebrow raised.

And it's a relief, a relief to be spoken to, a relief to know that you're surrounded by other people. You start to thaw, to relax, to melt into the security of the crowd, of the other people around you. And then you smile, a club smile, a cracking I'm-pretty-remember-me smile.

In case you're on *Crimewatch* later on, right?

And then you're telling yourself not to be daft, it's only Colin, and you say out loud, 'No, no, I'm not staying,' for Colin's ears more than anything.

A quick glance his way.

'Bye, Colin.'

One step down the street. Two. Don't turn back! Don't turn back! Your body's still frozen and you want to be her: to be Layla, confident-on-the-dance-floor Layla, who can move her arms, her legs, bend them into whatever shape she likes, deal with whatever the customers chuck at her. But instead, as cars flash by, and the tall buildings either side of the street cast shadows hemming you in, you're the other you: Hayleigh, your legs leaden and plodding and not doing what you tell them, your heart pumping, nerves shot to bits.

It's a hundred metres from the restaurant to the flat. You take the first ten metres slow and sure, a couple of people overtaking you on the pavement... thirty and there's more bounce in your step and you mouth a silent thank-you to your new Nike Airs... fifty and you hear footsteps, a *clip clip clip* of feet behind you, not overtaking... seventy-five and you know that it's him, beside – no, in front of you now, blocking your way.

'Hayleigh,' he's saying, not pretending any more. 'I just want to talk.'

You crane your neck to view the front steps of your block. What should you do? Knock him to the ground and run up the steps? Cry out? Yeah, right. What would you say? Besides, who'd give a toss about a lap dancer being followed by one of her customers? You know what people think: *Asking for it, isn't she, working in a place like that?*

'Honest,' he says, reaching both hands up, palms out, very easygoing. 'Just talk.'

For the first time since the restaurant you take a good look at his face. It's puckered up, red. Christ. Has the stupid ugly chump been crying?

God, he's just a lonely old soul who's latched on to you, ain't he, really? Ain't got nobody else. You look towards the building twenty-five metres away – so close to home now. Besides, you think, feeling in your jeans pocket for your mobile, you can always call the police if you have to.

'OK, five minutes,' you say, walking on a bit further, him hanging at your side, till you arrive at the flat, where you sit down on the front steps of your building. No point pretending you live anywhere else now.

'So,' you go, your voice low, steady. 'What is it? What do you want to say?'

He crouches down beside you on the steps, his bum plonked one step below yours. But he's still close, too close, the black leather jacket oozing a fusty dead animal smell – funny how you ain't noticed that before.

'Well...' he starts, and, fingering his baseball cap, he launches into it: how things went wrong at home... how he was chucked out by his missus... how you're his mate, one of a few. Turns out he's a gambler. So that's how come he can afford to come into the club. But how he's had a run of bad luck... can't afford to pay his rent... spends all his money on you...

You glower out at the street, the sky above the rooftops glowering back at you. Darker now, the pinks and blues of earlier bruised by more sinister blood reds and purples, occasional drops of rain splashing on to you. Why you, why you, why you? Why did you end up with the nutter as your regular? Just your rotten luck! But shoudn't you care about him? He's made of flesh and blood, worries and problems too, ain't he? Even so... all them worries he has, they ain't nothing compared to yours. Aggravation fixes around your eyes then. Yeah, it's not your fault that he's been tempted by you, by the club. That's what you're there for, ain't it? You've had enough of buttering him up, making him feel better, when it's you, you're the one who's down on your luck. You're the one with the real problem! With the baby to get back to!

'Look, Colin...' you start when you think he's done with his sob story, and you search about for how to put it, a hardness coming into your mind, your voice. 'I'll tell you this once.' You take a deep breath, collect your thoughts, think of the best way to put it. 'It's a job.' He looks at you, blankly. 'Them pity pleas, the bimbo act what I put on... Look, I, er, told you about Connor, yeah?' Another blank look. 'About my baby. I do it all for him. You're OK, right, but you're just a customer to me. Like the others – '

'But all them sit-downs we had together...' he interrupts.

Irritation swirls in your belly then. What, does he think he owns you, cos of the money he's shelled out in the club? And you spit it out, wanting to put the screws in now. 'No one special.'

Oh, what now? He's started boo-hooing, really sobbing his little heart out. You feel your neck flush red, embarrassed for the old sod. Then he stops fingering the baseball cap, looks up at you, an expression you can't quite read on his face.

'You're all the same, you and all the other girls.'

'Sorry?'

'All soft and gentle and butter-wouldn't-melt at first, then you turn different. You turn cold. Cold and... and,' he's saying, between sobs, 'cruel.'

And with that last word he flings his baseball cap to one side, and grips the metal bar of the railings by the steps.

A tug of guilt tinged with embarrassment pulls at you, and you step down from your pedestal. You think of the money he's given you, of how he's helped you – in a roundabout way – with Connor. Besides, you ain't some

92

kind of cold-hearted bitch, are you? You reach out, the tips of your fingers touching his arm, surprised at the coolness of the black leather jacket against the heat in your fingers.

And that one bit of kindness is just enough for him to try it on again.

He raises his chin towards you. 'Just a kiss. That's all I want. A kiss.'

What is he like? 'One kiss and you swear on your life you'll leave me alone?'

A nod and he's already leaning in, his lips brushing yours... and you think again of the money, all the cash he's given you... and it's like you're warped by confusion over what to do, how you should be with him, but it's OK... it's OK, you tell yourself, you're in control, you're the one with the sort of like power over the sad old git as he continues to kiss you, no tongue this time, and you keep your lips tight shut, only then...

no way!

his hand, the right one, is clutching between your legs, his fingers like a claw at your crotch. You lean back, your neck cricking. You yelp – *woof!* – like a dog. Claw wildly at his face. A scratch appears, blood. But you don't care, you'd do anything to get him off you and so now you push back against his chest and you can't believe he's doing this, can't believe he's tugging at the button of your jeans and then you remember what he's just said – *other girls* – Christ, he doesn't even think you're special, and that's it, you're not having this, not being relegated to his bottom division, so with all your strength you bring up your knee and slam it into his balls, putting into that slam the weight of all the worries and problems and issues of the last few months...

His reaction's different from what you expect. He holds on to the railings. 'I love you,' is what you think he's trying to say between hopeless-sounding coughs and splutters.

You curl your face into a mask of obvious disgust. Picture yourself spitting on him. Smacking him across the head with your handbag. Poking him in the eye with razor-sharp fingernails.

But instead, without looking back, you race up the stairs, slipping on the wet marble of the top step, flustered as you scrabble to find the right key on your key ring. What? Even your keys are against you? And then, after a stumble, you bound into the communal hallway, where your fingers are too trembly to fight with the lock, and you hammer on the flat's front door.

Hammer, hammer, hammer. Beating out a rhythm with your fists. Straining your neck behind you. Expecting him to be right there, in close-up, horror-film-style. You've just locked the main door, but, even so, the distance between it and you seems so small, so terrifying, so real.

The next-door neighbour, a posh bird, sticks her beak out of the other ground floor flat.

Hammer, hammer, hammer. You turn your back on her.

Then it's a blur: Rebecca opening the door… you pushing past her, pelting down the hallway… tears flowing so fast they're probably forming a little river behind you as you run… the floorboards creaking. And Rebecca's face. Is that concern you read in it? Kindness? No. Course not. It's wouldn't-piss-on-you-if-you-was-on-fire annoyance, that's what you read, and you run into your bedroom and throw yourself on the bed, your hands bashing the pillow what, to be fair, has got used to this kind of attack in recent weeks.

And then you hear it – the pigeon. Comforting coos what pluck at the very core of you, what make your heart keep from thumping, and you reach under the bed to pull out the b–

Outside, a car door slams and you jump, drop the box. A high-pitched voice rises up from under the window. *Jump.*

Rebecca pushes the bedroom door open. *Jump*. You kick the box back under the bed and throw her a laid-back look, a quick nothing-going-on-here-guv'nor kind of look.

And then she surprises you by saying, 'Fancy a cup of tea?'

'Yes,' you say loudly to cover up any pigeon sounds. 'That'd be nice.'

And you mean it – that would be nice.

4 MISSED CALLS
1 VOICEMAIL
INBOX: 2 new messages

FROM: AYESHA
SENT: Monday 4 June, 04.02

*OMG, have just met
the most amazing bloke.
PICK UP UR PHONE!*

FROM: AYESHA
SENT: Monday 4 June, 13.01

*Soz about calling last night.
C u later xxx*

No worries babes. Had
a terrible nite. Still on 4
8pm@OldSt?

Yeah, cool c u soon x

Monday

8

Come on, Ayesha! Silly cow's always late. Five more minutes
and you'll call her mobile. But will she bother to pick up?

You're standing at the mouth of the tunnel outside Old
Street tube station. Passing the time by chain-smoking and
counting the number of Hoxton fins what swim past you
out the entrance. One, two. Nah, that's not one. This lad's
got more of a classic punk mohawk than a trendy haircut.
You prefer his style. You make eye contact, flash your pearly
whites, and he looks away, too cool for school. Typical! Like
a congregation of fashion victims, this lot, worshipping the
latest show-offy styles. What's wrong with a pair of jeans, a
nice top and heels? An outfit what don't scream 'look at me'?
And then you're asking yourself, *Bitter much, Hayleigh*?
Up to them what they wear, after all. Still, you can't believe
how mobbed it is for a Monday night. Wish you could have
stayed Up West where –

BANG! A car backfires and you jump, lose your train of
thought. Or at least you hope it was a car. You're often on
edge in crowded places in London: on the Tube or in town,
what with them bombings and all; don't get nothing like that
down south – well, not since them nutters tried to blow up
Mrs Thatcher before you was born. You shift your eyes left
to right but nobody else is in a flap. OK, just a car, then.
Must be your nerves, what are grating after the night you
spent tossing and turning like a princess with a pea under
her mattress. You tried to sleep with one eye open, half

expecting Colin to make a dramatic appearance from inside the wardrobe or from under the bed. Exhausted, at two am you even ended up lugging forward your chest of drawers and heaving it across the bedroom door in case somebody – well, Colin, to be exact – tried to barge in. Only then there was the window to worry about…

So yeah, you're twitchy, wired, nervous, your brain in worst-case-scenario mode, running wild with visions of sirens, grisly slasher-movie scenes, *Crimewatch* reconstructions and that. And those five brews you drank before leaving the house only add to your jitters.

Anyway, where was you? Oh, yeah. Wishing you could have gone out clubbing Up West. None of that up-your-own-arse attitude there. Just dancing round your handbag, cocktail menus, kebab at the end of the night. Only there's that problem you've mentioned before – the customers. No way you want to be seen around Soho, or run into one of them on your night off. See, it's like them empty promises you make, of meeting them some time for a drink outside work; or the opposite, when you lie: *If only you wasn't a customer, you know I can't date customers* – all them tactics blow up in your face if you meet a customer in the real world. What happened last night proves that. Shame, though, cos you find the West End more honest, more sort of like, *Give us your money and we'll show you a good time.*

Whereas Out East. Well. It's so – whatchamacallit? – *preten-shuss*: covered markets filled with 'boutique' shops; butchers selling organic hand-reared donkey meat or whatever; organic vegetables, organic cotton – organic toys, you even seen once down Spitalfields market. Yeah, bollocks to all that: you're a West End girl every time.

You take a last drag of your cigarette, pleased to have west and east sorted. Be here all day if we tried to sort out north and south of the river and all.

So yeah, what you need's a night out, a proper old-school, cheer-yourself-up night out like what you used to have with your mates back home. None of this deep house, guest-list Shoreditch crap. OK, so you was out on Friday as well up Old Street. Maybe that makes you a hypocrite. So what? You're young, you're carefree, you're single. Kind of, if you don't include Billy.

Carefree?

As if!

And your mind chases back to hands clutching at you... tongue lapping at your lips... Look, can you just say something? Nobody's expecting the violins to come out over what happened yesterday, but it's got to you, it really has. You're not made of stone, believe it or not.

At last. A new lot of people are coming out the tunnel and you peer over their heads, hoping to catch a glimpse of Ayesha's jet-black hair. Instead, a slippery, youngish guy swaggers up to you. You flinch; your heart pumps faster. Like, what does he want?

But, nudging his mate as they cock-walk past, all he says is, 'Cheer up love, might never happen.'

You feel your cheeks flush. Why do you always get that? Did your face set in a sulk one day when the wind changed, or what? You imagine kicking him in the shins – *crack!* – but instead you turn your back to the tunnel wall, pull out your lighter to spark up another fag when – *wham!* – somebody slams into you.

'Evening, luvver.'

Ayesha. You give her a mini-hug, enjoying the light, flowery smell of her perfume. 'Hiya,' you say, and, with a playful slap to her arse, 'You're late.'

A quick chat and then you're setting off arm in arm up Old Street, nipping into the newsagent's for fags and a can of Red Bull, bit of energy to get you going for the night ahead. And of course Ayesha can't resist – blatantly in front of the newsagent guy – nicking a grab-bag-sized packet of cheesy Wotsits, which has you both chasing up the street in hysterics, hands slapping thighs, clutching your tummies. You don't know why she does it, steal stuff and that... but she always does.

And then, when you've got your breath back and you're as far up Old Street as the 333 Club, Ayesha makes you stop on the pavement, and between stuffing cheesy Wotsits in her gob starts up a right moan about how sore her feet are from dancing all day and, like, convinces you to hit a few bars before the club, to take the weight off. 'Besides,' she's adding, her eyes twinkling, 'there's something I want to discuss.'

Before you know it, you've queued up for a drink in some random bar and are pushing your way through the crowd to find a table, cos it's hectic for a Monday, what with Ayesha always insisting on hanging out in the latest cool place. And at last, having squeezed past a dishy bouncer who gives you a wink, you find a table for two.

The minute your arse hits wooden chair, Ayesha launches into what she wanted to chat about – her new job at Stringfellows. 'You should audition,' she's saying, bigging it up. 'The girls are friendly; the money's really, really good.'

Stringfellows! What Ayesha's forgetting is, she's a right stunner, while you're... well, you've got a good body, a nice face, but you're just an average dancer, really. Besides, the competition and the cat-fighting's bad enough at Elegance these days, never mind somewhere classy like Stringfellows.

You put this into words. 'To be honest, babe, I can't be doing with the whole thing no more, no matter where I'm working.'

You take a sip of your drink through a straw, trying to ignore a urinal smell what's stuffing up your nose. (Course – that's why the table was free, you're by the blokes' toilets.)

'Eh?' Ayesha says, her eyes wandering around the room. 'Thought you loved your job.'

Shows how well she knows you. 'Nah. I've had enough, if you want to know the truth.'

Ayesha's eyes glaze over – she's never one for a deep and meaningful – but you persist. 'Yeah, babe, I've had enough of the hustle, the naff-all support from the management, the tiffs with the other girls.'

'Is that what your text was about, then?'

'Eh?'

'Said you had a terrible night.'

'Well, yeah, actually.' (So she did pay attention to your text. You had the hump, to be honest, that she didn't reply.) 'Something pretty bad happened.'

That gets her attention: nothing Ayesha likes more than a bit of juicy gossip. And so you go into yesterday, fill her in about Colin, finishing up with '… and it looks like Jeremy wants me out and all.'

'See, then,' she goes, her eyes twinkling all the more, 'even more reason to audition for my place.'

You drop your eyes to the floor. 'No, babe, I mean it.'

'Besides,' she says, making light of it, putting on an American accent, 'Hayleigh, honey, you don't earn your lap dancing stripes till you've had a stalker.'

Is she joking? Will she ever take your side over anything? You glare at her, and, spurred on by her crapitude, you jab your straw in your glass and come out with what you're really feeling. 'I'm sick of it, actually. The pawing, the gawping.' The straw's all bent out of shape now, like you, and you add, looking her right in the eye, 'Like, don't you ever feel… used?'

'Oh, yeah. Somebody's paying me to hang out with the girls, have a laugh and fleece some idiot who's not getting any. I feel sooo used.'

You don't get it. She's meant to be your mate. What's more, she's clever, studying for a degree and that. Can't she see the dodgy side of the business?

With a flick of her hair, she goes on. 'Anyway, sounds like you're jealous of those new dancers to me.'

Cobblers! Just cobblers! You stop drinking and swizzle the straw around in the glass. Jab. Jab. Jab. It's more than likely she'll get into one of her sulks now, but you're too het-up to care. On a roll now, right? Want to get this all out. 'But don't you think that's just what the bosses want? Us to be jealous of one another? Like, to make it better for business?' She rolls her eyes. You persist. 'Yeah, and it's like the blokes hold all the power, anyway. Cos we're, like, just giving the money back to blokes, different blokes, the managers, in our house fees and that. It's…' and you fish around for the right word '… it's degrading.'

She goes for the jugular then. 'Don't try to be clever, Hayleigh, it doesn't suit you.'

You feel a blotch of deep red flush up your neck. Who does she think she is? Just cos she went to some fancy grammar school, done her A-levels, is studying at uni, don't mean she's always right.

'I'm getting a drink,' she says, and flounces off, leaving you to your thoughts. Good riddance.

Ayesha's a weird one. Her birth family were dead poor, couldn't look after her and, reading between the lines, you think they might even have beaten her. Lucky for her (not that she thinks so), she was adopted by a posh white couple. She's always moaning about them. They sound lovely to you. Encouraging her to go to college, giving her whatever she wants, not bawling her out, even when they found out she was dancing to pay her way through uni. Like, you couldn't even *tell* your own family about the dancing, never mind expect them to stick by you.

What she was just saying about the club, though, about having a laugh – can she really mean it? When both of you – the dancers and the customers – look down on each other? Like the guy, the customer, right, he thinks he deserves better than his wife or girlfriend, and that getting out his wallet's a quick fix to that problem, while at the same time you think he's a saddo who can't get attention from a good-looking girl unless he pays for it. You see that now. How it's – whatchamacallit? – demeaning for both sides. But Ayesha… Well, it's her hard cheese if she don't see it that way.

And now she's back, sitting opposite, putting a fresh drink down in front of you, saying, 'Look, sorry, hit a nerve, I suppose. Can we change the subject? What about your mum? Did you hear from her?'

Mmm, funny, that beer mat's interesting. You fixate on the dirty brown picture of an old brewery on the back. Flick it up, Ayesha snatching it from you, saying, 'Nice trick,' as it flies – *wheee!* – through the air.

'Come on, tell me.'

You lean half back on your chair, and stretch out your legs under the table.

Then she comes in with the killer. 'Get a picture like you hoped?'

You're suddenly very thirsty, and turn to Ayesha with a 'Fancy a shot?'

And then she's grabbing your wrist, going, 'What's up with you? Don't bottle it.'

'I don't want to talk about it.'

Which isn't how you're feeling inside. Inside, your heart is torn into a million tiny pieces as if it had gone through a shredder, negative thoughts, what have been hunting it down for weeks, butting into your brain:

Mum didn't send a picture of Connor and it's killing you!

You had an abortion and it's killing you!

You can't take your job any more, and it's killing you!

You want your baby back and it's blinking well killing you!

Instead, you do the usual. You hold your tongue, bite your lip – do all the things cowards do – and say, 'Think I'll join you on that mission tonight.'

Four double vodka-lemonades later and you're milling around outside a new club on Curtain Road, in the queue on the wrong side of the rope with about thirty others, only a couple of smug-looking bastards on the VIP side. Ayesha's fault. Always has to be the latest club, even when it means spending precious drinking time standing like dorks in a queue.

'Come on, let's just go somewhere else,' you say. It's a warm night but you ain't got a cardigan and your skin's breaking out in gooosebumps.

'Alright, alright, keep your knickers on.'

She's a cheeky minx, though. Walks up to the bouncer, goes up on tippy-toes and whispers something in his ear, and before you know it he's pulling the rope to one side and the rest of the queue are bitching you out. Got to love that girl. She'd do anything to get into the right places. No shame, no gain, that's her motto.

And the next thing you know, thanks to her you're standing in an over-air-conditioned room, crammed with people who look like they daren't move in case their way of walking or talking or smoking has suddenly gone out of fashion. Worse still, a ploddy and dirgy beat is booming out of the enormous speakers. Dub? Get me out of here! You grab a hold of Ayesha, only to end up doing circuits arm in arm through endless draughty corridors, wondering with every step if this was really worth the twenty-quid entry.

You say this to Ayesha, who tells you, 'Oh, shut up, I'm sick of your moaning,' and she wanders off, leaving you to half dance, half stand next to a speaker in the house music room.

Maybe you should just have a good dance? But your heart's not in it. That's the most heartbreaking thing about the job. Before you started at Elegance, dancing was fun. No, more than that: it was your life; it was sort of like, if they cut you open, them red and white blood cells would be doing a salsa, a rumba, a disco or a rave. And you enjoy a rush of pleasure as you think of your first love – ballet. Even the smell of your pink leather ballet shoes used to make your heart sing (Tchaikovsky, natch)... You think of dancing on stage in a tutu, winning a medal for your Grade 6... then, later, when you was offered a job as a podium dancer at those rave nights on the pier, even though you was paid in white powder... even that seemed innocent, pure. But as the DJ drops a house classic, which would usually get you up and dancing, you sink into a red leather sofa at the edge of the dance floor. Cos dancing, now that it's lumped together in your mind with the club, has a black tinge to it; it's tainted, gone off. What's more – and your throat wobbles at the honesty and disappointment of it – there's always someone better than you. A new girl at Elegance whose moves are sexier, more sensual than yours, whose body's more supple, bendier. And you look out at the people throwing out shapes on the floor, and dancing's the last thing you feel like doing.

There's a boy, though, who's been giving you a look since you came in this house music room – the glad-eye look, right? There he is again, weaving his way gradually closer to you through the dry ice, checking you out. Quite handsome: tall, pink V-neck jumper, hairs sprouting out the top. You see yourself stroking that chest, twirling his chest hair around your fingers, making you feel better. Yeah, if in doubt, you think as you knock back your drink, if you're bored, if you're hating yourself, if you're thinking about the baby, Mum, your stupid life, there's always some boy who can make you feel better.

He waves his glass at you and mouths, 'Drink?' and you stand up and step forward, a hazy look of pleasure sweeping over your face, in no doubt as to where this drink might lead. Before he walks off he touches your arse, and for a split-second a graphic picture of Colin cuts into your mind, but you shake it away, getting giddy at the thought of more booze, drugs (he looks like a coke type) and shagging (they all look like that type).

And as the bloke saunters back, drinks in hand, Colin does a vanishing act – *piff paff poof – gone!* – and you're doing the own-worst-enemy thing: smirking, sticking your chest out, dancing slowly towards the pink-jumpered hottie, thinking, here you go, yet again.

INBOX: 1 new message

FROM: MICHAEL
SENT: Monday 4 June, 23.12

*So did you get my letter Fox?
YOUR mum gave me ur
address. Hope u don't mind.
My mum said I should right
so u had time to think it over.
But not this long. Drivin me
crazy. What do u say? xx*

Tuesday

9

Everything's still. All you can hear is Ayesha's breath what snuffles from her lips in little animal mewls and moans. The pair of you are lying back to back, stiff as two sentries guarding the bed. A wave of neediness flows over you; you could really do with a cuddle.

Should you? Dare you?

Trying hard not to make the bedsprings creak, you do a mini-roll onto your other side, the left one, your nipples now a feather's width away from the points of Ayesha's shoulderblades. She doesn't move. You millimetre forward. Still no movement. Why not try spoons? you ask yourself, and reply by all at once lifting your knees to curl them inside Ayesha's, laying your arm across her pierced belly button. This makes her shift a little in her sleep, and you cuddle in.

For the last ten minutes you ain't dared to breathe out, sort of like wallowing in the memory of last night, hardly daring to think what might still be to come, but now a tightness in your chest means you have to exhale – *phwoo* – and you think of that breath, that *phwoo*, sappy cow that you are, stroking the soft downy nape of Ayesha's neck, her long dark hair piled on top of her head like some sort of black velvet crown. How did it manage to stay so neat? Like, last night's fumbles. You were rolling around all over the place, you, her and the lad you brought back and who, you're glad to see, has now done a runner. (Mr Pink V-Neck, right?)

113

Last night's fumbles. They come back to you with a quiver and you squeeze your thighs to hold in the memory.

It just seems so... so... well, so normal, lying next to her after all that went on in the dark... in this bed... A lightness floats into you, a sense that this is how everything is meant to be. Yeah, like a weight has been lifted, now that *it*'s happened. And this makes you happy, giddy. Like laughing, even. And you snigger, almost out loud.

'Ha!' Yeah, definitely out loud this time, cos Ayesha's waking up, with a start.

With slits for eyes, she stretches her arms in the air, the covers falling away, exposing her large brown boobs what flop over the top of the duvet.

'Man, I feel like shit,' she says, yawns, then looks down and snatches your hand away from her belly.

'Oh?' Disappointment tugs at you. 'I feel alright, really.'

She yanks the duvet back up. 'And what were you doing just now anyway?' Her eyes widen again. 'With your hand?'

What else is there to say? 'I, er, I... well, spoons,' you go.

'Well, don't, yeah?' Ayesha's saying, bending her entire upper half out of the bed, picking up a T-shirt off the floor what she then pulls over her head.

'Oh... OK, then,' you say, making a face. She's teasing you, isn't she?

'And what's that face mean? Bloody hell, you're getting on my nerves.'

Jesus. Someone got out of bed the wrong side.

She goes on. 'I hope you don't think that after last night...'

'What?'

'That we were going to...' She doesn't finish her sentence and instead pulls the covers up around herself again in a sort of like exaggerated way, making a point.

'Oh, get over yourself,' you bite back, grabbing your own T-shirt from the back of an armchair, trying to blot out what played out on there last night... Ayesha, legs spread... you and the guy either side, taking turns...

'You do, don't you? Want more?'

'Yeah, right,' you say, a mosaic of blotchy reds making a pattern across your chest. 'And anyway, you wasn't complaining last night.'

You're pulling on your knickers now, fumbling, fingers twitching. And then a wave of nausea hits you. A jittery feeling, a violent thumping in your head. Great. The hangover's kicking in.

At the same time, Ayesha replies, matching your jerky movements, her croaky morning voice going up a key. 'Well, that was just the booze, wasn't it?'

What's eating her? Well, not you anyway. The redness spreads to your cheeks, your forehead. Could you be any more flushed? 'Oh, whatever, babe,' you spit out, reaching over to turn on a lamp, cos the curtains are still drawn in the small, showy bedroom. 'Where are my socks?'

But she don't let up. That's Ayesha for you: can't let anything go. 'Bloody hell, you liked it, did you? It was just a laugh, to turn that bloke on.'

Oh, wait. You *can* turn redder.

'You did, didn't you? It turned *you* on!'

You rummage under Ayesha's furry designer bedclothes for your socks, wondering why she's still having a go. But then it's Ayesha we're talking about. Taurus. Say no more.

And now – insult to injury – she's coming up behind you, jabbing you with her index finger in the back, singing, 'Hayleigh's g-a-ay, Hayleigh's g-a-ay.'

Cranky and prickly after days of not enough sleep and doing lines and never-ending problems, you forget yourself, forget for a second – a split-second too long – that there's

115

some things you should think in your head, not say out loud.

'Well?' you say, pulling on one heart-print sock. 'So what if I was?'

Ayesha's eyes are two big pupils, owl-wide. 'Whut?'

'So what if I was?'

'Well, are you?' she asks, sitting back down on the bed, fully dressed now, lighting a fag.

'Yes?' you say, like a question, your voice rising.

Her eyebrows arch up to the ceiling then, and stay there as if suspended by some sort of like invisible thread.

'No,' you say, not a question this time.

Her hands bunch into angry claws and she gives you a look, cigarette hanging from her lips.

'Maybe so?'

'Oh, very funny – you had me there for a minute.' She chucks a pillow at you and a feather dances through the air, making you think of the pigeon.

Even so, you laugh, a weak one, and then mutter, 'Yeah, very funny.'

And while Ayesha nips out the room for a shower, them words – *yes no maybe so, yes no maybe so, yes no maybe so* – start tapping out a beat in your head. You've only slept with a few blokes (small fry compared to Ayesha's dirty dozen); does that make you gay? *Yes no maybe so...* But some girls' bodies, they get to you... *yes no maybe so...* Christ, you're confused... *yes no maybe so...* And last night, so horny and sweet... *yes no maybe so...*

Distractingly, depressingly, this head-scratching, this worrying, goes on till Ayesha walks back in the room, sunglasses on, saying, 'Shall we nip out to the café in Victoria Park for some brekkie?' and it's like a lever's been pulled back to mateyness, and the conversation's been swept so far under the carpet that it's been collected up in a dustpan and brush, put in a carrier and chucked out with the rubbish.

Not only that, but now she's all chipper and full of never-drinking-agains and she's even – drumroll, please – apologising for not being a morning person.

You don't point out that it's after lunchtime.

God, you wish that you could mirror her mood, put what happened yesterday to one side. On the outside you try, all like smiling and nodding and that, and yet beneath the surface that beat – *yes no maybe so, yes no maybe so* – won't give up, nearly driving you to distraction.

You just don't get Ayesha. All you've been through together at the club, and you've no idea what makes her tick. Not for the first time recently you wish you was closer to Ivana. She don't mind getting deep, talking stuff through. And she'd do it with a laugh and a joke, and all.

'Come on,' Ayesha says, though you ain't agreed to go along yet. 'I'm starving.'

'Alright, then,' you say.

But, while she's getting her last bits and pieces together before you leave the flat, you text Ivana to see if she can join you. Like, Ivana, you're pretty sure she wouldn't give a tinker's toot what way you swing. Unlike Madame Ayesha. You glare at her while she locks her front door. Grit your teeth. Clench your fists into weapons of mass destruction (you wish). Cos, like, Ayesha, yeah – on the one hand she's all Ms Leftie Liberal about empowerment and lap dancing and that, and on the other... Well, not being funny, but she's as bloody open-minded as your nanna, and that's saying something.

It takes the walk to Victoria Park to chill you out. A walk through Ayesha's estate. Past a group of young black lads bouncing a parking cone off a car bonnet (like, shouldn't they be in school?), past a couple of mums with their buggies, their heads thrown back in laughter, past a couple of fit older guys who wolf-whistle at you. By the time you reach the café your head is exploding with tension. All this schlepping over East blooming London: you'd have been more than happy with the greasy spoon around the corner. But, no, it has to be *haute cuisine* for her ladyship, even for breakfast, and so you've ended up here, shelling out a tenner for an 'Eggs Benedict' ('Try it,' Ayesha said, when you turned your nose up at the idea, 'don't be such a chav') in an overcrowded café where a group of yummy mummies next to you squawk over a wait for their food.

Now, as if she's a mind-reader, Ayesha licks a dollop of yellow sauce from her lips from her Eggs Fancy-What-Not and makes obvious evils at the group of skinny women. Not wanting to get sucked into one of her cat-fights, you shift your eyes to the café counter, and your brain sort of like starts to hiccup to that *yes no maybe so* once again.

Like. Are you? And you hold your breath, feel your stomach muscles tense. Are you gay?

And as Ayesha waffles on about this boyfriend she's going to ditch, and this new lad she's going to hook up with, you can't help yourself: you think back to when them thoughts about girls first started. School, probably. Didn't get on with the other girls at school – to be honest you was bullied for most of year 10 and 11. Had to hide when you did well in English, or history, your favourite. *Boffin*, the other girls called you. Then, later, at sixth form college, when they found out you was pregnant, *Margarine*. Bamboozled by that one, you was, till Michael explained: spreads easily.

Nice.

So you'd hung out with him and the boys. Does that make you gay? No, course not. But it was like you shared the boys' fascination for the girls, only you had the luck of a bird's eye view – of the (sometimes optimistic) bras when you was changing for PE, of the lip gloss slathered on blossoming lips in the cloudy, dirt-speckled school bog mirrors. Yeah, you was one of them, a girl, but it was like they was a different breed from you; they made you goggle-eyed, like the lads.

'I'm bloody serious.' Ayesha's saying, and you try to find a suitable expression in response, though you've no clue what she's on about. 'I think he's fallen in love with me.'

You pull a sucky-lemon face. Not that you're jealous. Just that Ayesha and her oh-my-God-he-fancies-me attitude doesn't wash with you. You fork over the uneaten eggs as she bores on about how hot she is. Like she needs to tell you.

Then she's saying, 'Listen, you're taking ages over that,' and she pokes at your plate with a knife. 'Not getting anorexic on me, are you?'

'Shut up!' you say, looking over at the door in the hope that Ivana might walk in by way of distraction, cos suddenly that sorrowful feeling of fullness in your tummy has returned, a familiar metallic taste filling your mouth.

With a chill of apprehension you recognise this feeling, this taste: this feeling what's grown inside you since the termination, this feeling of your stomach being filled to capacity as a sort of like replacement for the baby who should be growing inside it; this metallic taste what flavours your mouth as if you'd shovelled down a meal made up of thumbtacks and nails. And it's like, no amount of scrubbing your tongue and your teeth can take away this taste; no amount of starvation, in the end, can stop the sensation that the baby should be developing inside you.

You push the plate away, and eye Ayesha, who is munching away on her own food. Only then she surprises you by saying, 'Shouldn't be eating this, really; I'm trying to be good. Even then, I put on a pound last week.'

You look her up and down. She don't look any different, to you. 'Oh, yeah?'

'Mmm…. Wondering about giving up booze as well. I mean, it's just empty calories, isn't it?'

You roll your eyes. You're grateful for the distraction, but you can't bear it when she goes on about her weight. And she doesn't let up there. 'Yeah, and also I'm worried that my Depo-provera injection is making me fat.'

Now that's a bit more interesting.

'Oh, you went for it, did you?' you ask. It's been one of her favourite subjects recently: whether to have the contraceptive injection, to stop her periods and that. Cos it makes working in clubs easier, right, if you don't have periods?

'Well, yeah, I had to – no way I'm gonna risk messing up that Stringfellows job.'

'When did you get it done?' you ask, but no reply, cos Ayesha's mobile's ringing. Kanye West, 'Gold Digger', the ring tone. She jumps out her seat.

'Sorry, babe, got to take this. It's Andrew.'

'Andrew?'

'Jesus, Hayleigh – Andrew I was just telling you about… Hi, Andrew,' and she's pushing the table away, mouthing 'two mins' at you, before shoving past the squeezed-in tables to stand outside the busy café, her head thrown back in laughter.

Like you care. You've already drifted off. Trying to sift through a whole heap of distractions what are clogging up your thoughts. School. All the bullying, the bitching, the cat-calling. Like you say, horrible in year 10 and 11, the cusses of *cradle snatcher* echoing after you down the school corridors, what with Michael being a year younger than you. Bloody jealous they were. Him being, like, the heart-throb of year 10. Being a heart-throb didn't make him a good dad, though, did it? You snort. Yeah, he came to visit after the birth, but you knew it was you who was keeping him interested; it was you he was coming to see. He didn't cuddle the baby, or kiss him. And you knew it was his mum who'd bought the gifts when they came to visit two days after Connor was born. Not one single little trinket or nothing from Michael himself. And, when you'd tried to breastfeed, Michael had looked away. Huffy and that. Jealous. And so you'd binned him not long after. Had little to do with him, apart from through his mum and that one night near your eighteenth. And look where that got you!

But now, with the letter... No, it's a headspin: too much like hard work to think that one through...

Yeah, so painful, you'd even prefer to think about the bullying. Worse still, it got in year 12, especially as the pregnancy went on. Yeah, that's right: even in sixth form college you was bullied by girls who should have known better. It was like they got an energy from the baby growing inside you, an energy what fed the nasty black slime of their cruel words, fed it up into a monster what grew as the baby grew. And them pregnancy hormones weren't on your side either – you was a gibbering wreck, on the verge of tears at anything and everything: blubbing during history at a picture of disabled kids going to the gas chambers, being excused from the lesson cos you was crying so hard. And the morning sickness. It was crippling, damn it... Like the time you was lining up for a plate of chips at lunch, and that greasy chippy smell set you off... had you running out of the canteen... never forget the sound of your tray clattering to the ground. Fed the bully monster for a week, that one did. *Sickbag Hayleigh*, they'd taunted you.

No wonder you spent breaktimes with Michael, scurrying back across the campus to the high school, clinging on to him with all the neediness and staying power of a leech. So yeah, going back to that gay thing – you've had boyfriends. Loved Michael, even. Whatever that means. And now, with him getting in touch, with what he's saying in the letter – wanting to try and make up, to be there for Connor and you… huh! Too little, too late, you think. Like, you've made your own way for twelve months without any man's help, thank you very much. You thump your fist on the table, the muffin and egg bouncing up on the plate.

But no time to dwell on that, anyway, cos Ayesha's walking back in, shimmying through the crowded café, smiling and glowing – yeah, glowing – and you do feel a twinge of bitterness now.

She grabs the leftover muffin from your plate, wolfing it down in three bites, and then says, 'Come on, hurry up.'

'Alright, alright,' you reply, knowing this means you've been bitch-ditched for her new fella.

There's a welcome cool breeze on your neck (it's boiling in here) just then, as yet another customer comes into the café. You turn around. Oops. Another customer stumbles into the café, you mean. Yup, it could only be…

'Hey, Ivana, over here!' you say, flapping your arms about in sort of like over-enthusiastic waves as you watch her compose herself and set her sunglasses right after tripping up over the step. She blushes and shambles over, a little boy, a toddler, to one side of her, an older girl to the other.

'Hello, Hayleigh,' she says, and then falters as she looks over at Ayesha. 'Ay… Ayesha.'

Ouch! You're suddenly aware of a burning sensation. Ayesha's hand twisting the skin on your wrist under the table. You grab the hand doing the burning and give it a little pinch of your own.

But you don't let on to Ivana – don't want to make her uncomfortable – and so you keep the pain out of your face as you say, 'Hi, Ivana, hi, kids,' in a light voice.

And as the pain subsides you have a sort of like little chuckle to yourself, cos you knew that Ayesha would get all handbags-at-dawn if Ivana turned up. They was ships that passed in the night at Elegance. Battleships, that is. Ayesha bitching Ivana out cos apparently she doesn't take her *performances* seriously, isn't a *professional* – as Ayesha put it. A professional what? you wonder. A professional tit-and-arse peddler? A professional dry-humper? It's not like they give out certificates.

Anyway. Just look at Ayesha now, hogging the table, not moving her bag, so there's nowhere for Ivana and the kids to sit down. You glower at Ayesha. She gives you the full silent treatment. And meanwhile Ivana and the kids hover by the table, making chit-chat, till at last – phew! – Ayesha stands up and chucks a note on top of the dirty plates.

'I'm off,' she says, hitching up her low-rise jeans what have slipped down to reveal a neon-pink G-string. Then, turning back with a venomous sneer snaking her lips, she hisses, 'Have fun with the rug rats.'

A trail of huffiness follows her out the door, a trail so huffy as to be almost – whatchamacallit? – visible. You turn to Ivana. Hug. And then Ivana blows a raspberry in the direction of the door and you all, kids included, get the giggles, and that's it: shoulders-down time.

'So, who's this, then?' you say after the laughter has died down and Ivana tells you their names – Ona and Tomas – cos, like, even though she's told you loads about her kids, you've never met them in the flesh before.

Minutes later, you've settled up in the café and made it to the front of the queue for the swings. But you're saddled with a growing sense of embarrassment over what happened last night, and a growing sadness and all. Being surrounded by kids, probably. Brings the missing of him back to you with an unwelcome bang. Ivana's chatty as ever, though, thank God, taking your mind off things – even if the conversation's a bit all over the shop till you get to the sandpit and the kids play with a bucket and spade by themselves for a bit.

Sitting on the grass at the side of the sandpit, Ivana hitches up her skirt, stretching out her long, tanned legs. There's a moment's peace as you both enjoy the sunshine for a minute. But it ain't uncomfortable like it would be with, Ayesha, say. It's a warming, friendly silence, what brings with it a new feeling of being relaxed.

Ivana's the first to break it. 'So, Hayleigh. Something I been means to ask you.'

Your stomach drops. What have you gone and done? 'Oh, yeah?'

'Those XXs you put on your text message.'

You blush. Like, does she not want to be your friend? Does she think you're being – whatchamacallit? – over-familiar? 'Ye-es…?' you say.

She pushes her sunglasses up on top of her head, and you can see her face properly now, her nose ruffling up in a cute way as she says, 'What do they mean?'

With a gust of wind blowing your hair over your face, there's a second to think. Like, is she taking the piss?

But as you brush the wisps of hair away you catch her expression, and it's natural and open, not making fun of you at all.

'They're kisses, babe – like, X means a kiss.'

She pulls the glasses back down over her eyes, her cheeks turning the colour of Tomas's red Peppa Pig wellies. Smacks herself on the forehead. 'Of course!' she says, 'of course.' And then she's laughing, a tinkling, tuneful laugh, what's catching and soon has you soon joining in (and crossing your legs, just in case).

'So… I was in the club last night,' she says when the laughter fizzles out and she's rescued the kids' bucket and spade from an older kid with a cob on.

You should have known the warm buzz in your tummy wouldn't last long.

'Oh, yeah?' you say, trying to sound interested. You've been avoiding the subject, didn't want to tell her about Sapphire, or Colin. Not sure why. Saving face, probably.

She looks over at the kids. Waves. 'Yeah. Queen Sapphire, she speak to me for once. Of course, she not being friendly but was feeshing, asking about something that happen with you and Colin.'

'Oh. Right,' you say.

And, as if you might be able to muster a bit of zing from its rays, you lift your face up to the sun. Try to find the right words to tell her about that shitstorm what's been at it again, pasting your life in a stinking rich coating of muck.

'Well, it was sort of like this...' you begin.

INBOX: 1 new message

FROM: MUM
SENT: Tuesday 5 June, 16.22

Don't forget your nannas birthday next week. Send a card. She's going to be 70.

Yes I remembered Mum. How's Connor? Are you having a party for Nanna?

Going for dinner at Alduomo. Don't pretend I didn't tell you about it.

Sorry forgot. How's Connor?

10

Another summer's late afternoon. A scalding white light burns your eyes as you step out the Tube station at Oxford Circus, making your pupils shrink. It was bad enough having no sunglasses or sandals in the park but here, in the centre of town, the air is tight and unforgiving, and you curse yourself for not being prepared for the weather as per usual, for not taking a change of clothes out clubbing with you.

You harrumph down the street, kicking out at the rubbish what's piled up on the pavements from the office people and tourists and all the other bastards who clog up the town this time of day.

Damn it, what's this little hissy fit all about? Usually by day four of your period the red mist has lifted, the anxiety and depression and that easing off. Not this cycle. This one's a real doozy. A gnarly old troll. A wizened old witch.

And so you have to do the walk of shame in last night's clubbing outfit, turning onto Great Titchfield Street (nearly home, thank goodness), dragging your feet along like they belonged to someone much larger than you, much heavier. If only home felt like home. Instead, a sense of dread's building. Will they be in? What day is it – Tuesday? Nah, they should both be at work, but you never know. What about the pigeon? When was the last time you fed it? And, more to the point, isn't it about time you set it free, or took it to the RSPCA?

You freeze then, finding yourself outside the Italian restaurant near the flat. It's closed on a Tuesday, nobody about, but for a split-second you imagine he's standing there – Colin – a shit-eating grin on his face, holding a teddy and flowers. A banner written in childish block capitals – 'SORRY, LAY-LAY' – waved ten foot high in the air. But no. That's your mind playing tricks. You shake your head, try and shake away the Colin and Layla Show as you walk up the marble stairs to the front door, step across the mat (no post today), avoid the big mirror, turn your key in the lock. Turn it left. Wobble it about a bit. Turn it right. Shit. The lock ain't budging. Have those cows changed the locks? You try again, left, right, left, till at last, as you wiggle it to and fro, you hear the lock unclick and with all your strength you push the door open (it gets stuck in the heat), and launch yourself into the flat. Cool, it is indoors, and silent. Much more like it.

With visions of pigeonmaggedon, you head straight for the bedroom and pull out the box from under the bed. And there he is, your little friend. Asleep in his makeshift nest of torn-up newspapers – or is he?– no, you can see his little puffed-up chest rising and falling. Good. Though, deep down, you're not sure if you want him to get well again. Like, the responsibility of it. Isn't that what you're running away from in the first place? But, then, with a shrug, you pour some water from a glass on the bedside table into the egg cup, telling yourself to remember to pop in some seeds for him before you go out.

And then you flop on the bed. Knock back two ibuprofen with the last of a carton of Ribena you bought on the way home (Vitamin C, right?). Wonder if you should have a zizz before you head for work. Common sense tells you yes, you only managed a couple of hours last night. But when did you ever follow common sense? On nights again tonight.

Hopefully you'll be on with Sapphire, so you can give her what for. That bitch. Trying to turn Ivana against you now, and all! After seeing Ivana off home to do her kids' tea, you spent the tube and bus journeys back from Victoria Park plotting ways to get Sapphire back. Telling Jez she's done more than dirty dancing, maybe. Or calling in a favour from Billy and having her beaten up. A cheap thrill runs through you at that one. But no, you think, changing your mind and checking the Hello Kitty clock for the time – there's got to be some other way, some way of getting to her where it will hurt most, without resorting to violence.

OK, so Kitty's telling you that there's time for some TV before work, but before you can even stick it on you catch sight of the wardrobe, the door slightly ajar.

That's not right.

It's usually locked. Your stomach turns over when you find, yeah, that it's open. You freeze. He's not, is he? Hiding in there? Colin? No, of course not: there's nothing in there but the usual clothes and the mothball smell. What, then? The flatmates, snooping? Yeah, you think, getting the chills, somebody's been in here; the room, well, it smells different (and not just from the pigeon), feels different – you can't quite put your finger on it. You always keep the wardrobe locked in case the flatmates poke their noses in – they'd probably be happier to see a load of meat carcasses hanging in there than your slutty work dresses. Never mind how they'd react at the drawers stuffed full with knickers. Cos the guys in the club, sometimes they want to buy your knickers, yeah? Especially the ones you've been wearing… Have to take in spares every shift, just in case. But, thank goodness, the drawer looks untouched. You delve deeper into the wardrobe, let your fingers run over nylon evening gowns, silk corsets, lace, fur. Not exactly a croupier's wardrobe. But you don't care any more if the flatmates have sussed out your real job; you've had enough of pretending. Anyhow, everything still seems to be in its place. You close the wardrobe door again. Lock it.

But, if they wasn't snooping, why was it open?

An old-fashioned kind of wardrobe, it is, three doors, roomy, made out of some sort of dark wood – the one bit of furniture you've bought since moving in. The only help Billy's ever given you, driving it over here from Portobello Road Market, helping you lug it up the front steps. *High maintenance*, he called you that day – does sometimes still. Yeah, right. A girl who can look after herself, ain't bothered if you go out together much, and has made you money from pimping her out to a lap dancing club? Really high maintenance.

In a huff, you sit back on the bed and survey the room. You really ought to buy some more furniture. Another picture, or something.

A niggle then. Not Billy... something else. What is it? You sweep your eyes over the room. Your one ornament, a statue of a naked woman standing on the edge of a shell (a souvenir from your only ever trip abroad) – well, it's still here, staring at you from the mantelpiece. Same position as before? You get up from the bed and walk across the room. Yes. Her boobs are facing away from the picture of you and Connor on the mantelpiece, her bottom sticking out towards him. Still. You can't help it, can't help a creepy sensation crawling over you, the feeling that somebody's been in here. But if they wasn't fishing about after something to wear, what – ?

No way! Is this some kind of joke? The money!

You run your tongue over your lips, but they're dry, your tongue as rough as sandpaper. You dive under the bed. Push the pigeon nest-box out of the way. Scrabble for the rucksack – still locked, thank goodness – and with shaking

130

fingers tug at the little silver key for the padlock you wear on a chain around your neck. Come on, fingers, sort it out! Finally the key comes off the chain and on one attempt, two, three, you turn it in the lock, unzip the rucksack and... *phew*! The old scarves laid on top of the money, the plastic bags with the money in, are placed just the same as when you last counted them.

You swear on your life if those bitches had had their paws on them, well... you'd... you'd... you'd claw their eyes out! Stab them up! Kill them!

Alright, alright, that might seem harsh, but steal the money – well, it'd be as if Connor was being taken away from you all over again. And it swings back to you then, that kick-you-in-the-fanny (pardon your French) despair when Mum shut the door in your face for the last time... your clothes spilling out the top of this rucksack... the rucksack chucked onto the lawn, flattening Mum's geraniums... Connor's cries, you swear on your life you could hear them from the other side of the garden window... those screams you let out till you was retching up bile... your fists battering the front door –

'It's OK, it's OK,' you mutter out loud as you choke back tears, your airways narrowing, your chest tightening. With the money, you'll get him back. You'll show Mum.

But can you be sure? Sure it's all there? What if they placed the carrier bags back just so, the scarves laid on top of one another in a copycat way, same as you'd left them, knowing you'd suss if they was put back topsy-turvy? Worry grips you then, its long, grasping fingers choking your throat. You swallow, reach your hands up to your neck, try and draw a breath, swallow the little saliva you've got left, and reach for your asthma inhaler, what you keep next to the Kitty clock on the bedside table, just in case.

You take one puff, two.

It's no use. You're choked up, a tightness in your chest what won't disappear till you've counted the money.

Every. Single. Last. Note.

Job like that calls for a beer, you think, and you nip to the kitchen, grab a can of Stella and – hating yourself – fish in your jeans pockets for the last of a wrap what you pinched from that lad's jacket last night. And, once your thirst has been quenched with half a can of lager, you lean over the little coffee table by the big sash window and rack up a line. And it's as if you was being carried off, now, on a journey. On a journey what makes you detached from all the recent crap… a journey on water with Connor, where you both glide, drift, float along till you're in the middle of nowhere on the wide open sea, cut off from the rest of the world.

But, first, you need the money.

So you make a start, taking out the wedges of fifties and twenties with care and concentration. Lay aside them pathetic tenners and fivers for now. Heat rises in your cheeks, your heart – *baba-boom, baba-boom, baba-ba-boom* – beats faster as you begin to lay out the piles of notes. *One hundred.* You can buy Connor a tricycle. *Bob the Builder*, something like that. *Five hundred.* Take him on holiday. Butlins, or a nice little cottage. Just the two of you, ice creams and donkey rides, as many as he wants, all sunny skies and toes dipped in water, ice-cold and squeals of delight. *One thousand.* Two months' rent. A flat you always dreamed off, overlooking Brighton beach, Connor racing up and down the hallway, along spacious corridors, on his trike.

Tingling all over, you pick up a fifty-pound note, calling to mind the first time you held one in your hands. One of your first days in the club, it was… a sweating, wiry, pink-cheeked bloke sticking it in the top of your black lacy knickers… you swooning over its inky biro-redness… a heart-flip as if you'd fallen in love… and you removed it from your knickers, kissed it with glee, sniffed it and all, pressing your nose against smooth, crisp paper, getting off on its dirty cash smell... the bloke so chuffed at your childish reaction that he immediately slipped you another (you've used that experience as a little trick from time to time since, pretending someone's chucked you your first fifty). Still your favourite note, the fifty. Says *money*, says *made it.* You rub the note against your cheek, see yourself earning heaps and stacks, job lots of them, next time you're in the club, and, satisfied with yourself, with your efforts, you add it to the growing pile.

Another beer, and you've reached three thousand pounds. You sniff, tasting the coke what you must have just done at the back of your throat.

Three thousand.

Cor! Think!

Think what that money could bring you! It's like a ticket. Yeah, a ticket. A ticket for Connor away from the life what Mum gave you... no shoes with holes in for him, no birthdays without parties, no life on benefits and free school meals, no hand-me-downs. Instead, new clothes, toys galore, living in your own flat... no, a mansion... And you drift off to...

... a mansion. Your mansion. You're a celebrity, famous for – you're not sure, don't matter – the mansion bursting at the seams with the latest high-tech gadgets and that; endless rooms, a swimming pool.

A photo shoot!

The mansion laid out over four pages in *Hello!* magazine. Connor kneeling by your side in front of a log fire, dressed in a shirt and a waistcoat, rosy cheeks and a gappy-toothed grin. And the mag's readers are all, like, *Ooh, he's adorable, what a gorgeous Little Man, what a lovely house*, and your heart's exploding with fireworks of pride. It's a house what says *classy*. Not a showy one like in them magazines, furnished with brass beds and chintz. You'll have a new fitted kitchen, gleaming work surfaces, a ton of floor space for his toys. A garden with a swing. A tree house!

And then... another photo shoot! *Heat* magazine this time. You've been voted Celebrity Mum of the Year. Yeah, take that, Katie Price! Connor telling the papers what a great mum you've been...

Mind boggling, you sit cross-legged on the floor, thinking yeah, that's what money gets you, your eyes gobbling up the piles of money sprouting up around you: heaven in a bundle of notes; towers of oranges, greens, blues, reds and pinky purples, and you love them all equally. Yes, you'd like to say sorry to all them other notes: that fifty ain't your favourite no more. The ripped ones stuck back together with Sellotape; the crisp ones with gleaming silver-foil lines down the middle; the soggy blue ones; the weather-beaten tenners; the ones with the bloke with that silly moustache on the back... you want to hug them all in, smother them equally with your love and affection. Yes, love and affection, you think, dreamily. Quite spaced out now, quite loved up as it goes, and it won't be long till you've finished counting, you're nearly there, totalling up the last of the piles, your entire body tingling, quivering, shaking and that's it... yes, that's it... it's all there!

Four thousand, five hundred pounds.

Anxiety loses its grip; your chest relaxes. In its place, smugness. You did this – made this money, made nearly enough to get Connor back! Nearly halfway to the magic ten grand. Worked your arse off for it, too.

And you thrill at your achievement. At knowing you've got nearly enough. Nearly enough for no more benefits! For no more accusations of being a scavving teenage mum! Enough maybe for a deposit to rent a little flat. Getting your own place at nineteen. Who'd have thought it? A flat far enough away so that Mum can't stick her nose in, but close enough so that she can babysit for you. Yeah, one of them flats on Brighton seafront, like you said. Go to the technical college there, finish your A-levels, do an NVQ.

No. Not that. Boring!

If you're gonna dream, you might as well dream big... and you're off again. The piles adding up not to four thousand, five hundred pounds – or even the original fifty grand you was stupid enough to think you could make – but to four hundred thousand.

Sod that, four million!

Four million what sees you married to a footballer. No, no, not that – you've made the money yourself: a reality TV star. You're living the dream. Forget mansion; it's a castle you live in. Acres of land. A lake. A...

... but you're now consumed by a sinking feeling. You wonder about the coke. Realise there's nothing left and it doesn't get past you, that these two things are related: this empty feeling, this sadness and this lack of coke. Besides, Mum of the Year? You flush, call up a picture in your mind of his blue face, the stillness in the cot, and you smack yourself, *slap!* across the cheek, surprising yourself. You scratch at an itch at your arm. Only the scratching doesn't satisfy the itch and soon you're tearing away at it, the acrylic nails you had done last week doing a good job of nearly ripping your skin.

The money's all there, so why do you feel Bad and Wrong? A wet blanket? Down in the dumps? And you shiver for a moment, an icicle chill going through you at the reality of it – that it might well not be worth staying up London for another year just to reach the magic ten K. You reach for your cigarettes. Then, trying to dredge your spirits up from the depths, you take the wedges of money, start lobbing them willy-nilly back into the plastic bags, stuffing the scarves down the side of the rucksack, starting to zip it back up. And, as you do so, them spirits plummet further, cos it's like you're putting away your hopes and dreams in that bag; like you're watching Connor's feet, his legs, his body, his face, disappear as you zip it up... all hopes in fact of ever seeing your Little Man again.

But look. Maybe you'll pass the audition Thursday. Then, so Kenny says, you'll soon be raking it in. You shudder, a worry about the audition growing at the back of your mind. Instead, why not go back to Plan A? Get yourself a new regular. A bigger, a better one. Even try for one of them gangsters you've avoided for months. Yeah, a gangster dripping in gold, who loves to splash the cash. One who gives you diamonds, pearls. That's what you need to reach the magic number ten.

You sneeze, rub your eyes... yawn.

Reality bites.

What you really need is a zizz. But instead you take the video remote and press *Play*, hoping that last night's recording of them nitwits on *Big Brother* will take your mind off the suckiness of your so-called life.

INBOX: 1 new message

FROM: MICHAEL
SENT: Tuesday 5 June, 17.17

*OK. Trying again. Please reply
Fox. Think it over. I miss you.*

11

Your feet *squeak squeak squeak* across the sparkling floor in the customer loos, and you blink at the gleaming tiles and bright white lav. Not much call for the women's loos in Elegance, to be fair. Not hard to see why, you think, yanking down your jeans and then your knickers, dripping blood on the seat. Christ, this period's dragging on. Suppose they did warn you about that at the clinic – about your first period after the abortion. Damn! It's soaked through to your knickers. Did you forget to change the tammie again? Probably. And now you're going to need a change of clothes for the way home, and all.

Change of clothes? Argh! That's sparked something at the back of your mind... Course: it's the first Tuesday of the month. Theme night. On the one hand theme nights are great, cos you can have a 'good night', i.e. make pots of money and let your hair down a bit. But on the other – fancy dress? There's nothing what makes you more aggy than seeing a group of men going slack-jawed and wet-lipped over you and the girls 'on parade'. Personally you can't be doing with all that fantasy stuff, so your usual theme night costume is... well, a bit lame.

Cowgirl.

Use the old lasso to reel the saddos in.

Yee freakin' har.

Yeah, you should love it. Dressing-up should make it easier to escape to Destination Imagination. And OK, that fantasy stuff might *seem* harmless, but till you've seen a grown man dribbling – and you mean really fizzing and foaming sprays of saliva down his chin at the sight of a French maid's outfit – thinking that dressing up is 'just a bit of fun' is off limits. End of.

And then you wonder, what's with the grumpiness? Are you more pissed than you thought, or, more to the point, are you coming down from the coke? Not sure, but as you bend over the loo to put in a new tammie the room starts to blur around about you and a faintness comes into your head, a faintness what makes you feel like the room and its walls are against you, bending the light, making your head spin, trying to disorientate you and that. You jiggle your arms and your legs. Try and get things back into focus, pray the blurred edges of the room will sharpen up. *Smack!* Slap yourself across the face. There, that's better.

What's that all about? Making a habit, of that, eh?

Anyway. Going back to the money from earlier today, can you just say something? All that cobblers about mansions and castles… You know that you've got your head in the clouds – somewhere high above the Heathrow flight path, probably. Like, as if you'll ever be famous! Maybe you could try out for *Big Brother*, though – get yourself on telly. Who knows where it'd lead? Modelling jobs, TV work, a book deal and that? And you spin out again, thrown off balance by this rubbish tossing and turning through your head, knowing deep down that the other girls at Elegance would have more of a chance, the ones with the big personalities and that. Cos you, you're different, yeah? Not gobby, not confident – a wallflower, didn't Dad used to call you? In fact it's slowly dawning on you that, Ivana aside, you ain't much like any of the other girls here at all.

Stomping up the stairs to the changing rooms, you chew that one over. You and the other dancers. It's like you don't have the same – whatchamacallit? – motivations as them, don't fit with the usual reasons why girls start dancing in the first place. Some of them have got what you'd call *issues*. Hate the way they look, lap up the customer attention. Yeah, even the prettiest girls like Katrina, in the game to prove something to themselves, cos they hate what they see in the mirror. What's all that about, then? And then you've got the show-offs, the girls who get a thrill from getting their kits off, like Sapphire. First night she came in the club she was giving it large in the changing room about how she'd had three orgasms that one shift. (Meantime, you'd had three fantasies about murder. Different strokes for different folks, eh?) Then there's the last reason the girls come and work here, the ones who've been for– no, not forced, but who've got blokes connected with the club who persuade them to start dancing. Sort of like you with Billy, to be fair…

Only that train of thought's put on hold when you're blown away by a blast of hot air as you walk into the changing room – in other words, Susie bawling the girls out, in one of her shitty moods.

'Late,' she snaps.

Christ's sake – why's everyone on your back at the moment?

'You're going to miss the parade.' She tugs at the zip of Katrina's schoolgirl outfit while throwing you daggers. 'Maybe even your first dance.'

And then Katrina, all zipped up, is stomping off, rubbing her back where the zip has pinched.

Oh, what now? Susie's waddling up to you (sometimes you don't believe that she was the club's top dancer back in the day), looking you up and down as you grab the tired cowgirl outfit – a frilly white blouse turned an unexciting grey and the short skirt frayed at the edges – out of the locker and start pulling it on over your undies.

140

'And isn't it about time you changed your theme night outfit?' Susie's saying – what is she, a mind-reader? 'Look,' she continues, tugging at the hem of your skirt. 'Needs a wash and all.'

You nod as though you agree, but as you stick a fake pistol in your garter you wish it was a real one.

'And don't give me the silent treatment,' she drones on, handing you a small pink tablet. 'Only looking out for you. I know Jeremy's had words about your outfits – and everything else.' And as the other girls go out the room two by two (like animals into the bloody Ark) and she closes the door behind them, she keeps up the rant. 'Look, I shouldn't take sides, but them lot – you know who I'm talking about – you're going to have to up your game, ain't you, with these new girls around?'

You wish you could stick your fingers in your ears, sing *la-la-la*! You don't need to hear this! Susie telling you what you already know deep down. You also wish you could grow a pair and tell her about what's happening with the other girls, but you know what she'd say (*playground stuff*) so you just say, 'I hear you,' setting your lips in a grimace, then popping the pink pill in your mouth and chewing.

And then you turn to your locker, rummaging in it for the high-heeled cowboy boots what you bought in Camden Market the other week. Waste of money that was, then. Meanwhile, Susie's rummaging around in the big basket of outfits she tries to sell you all. Bloody tat, the lot of it.

'Come on, try this. On the house.'

What. The. Eff? You finger the 'naughty nun' outfit she's just handed you like it was made of sick. Black rubber dress with a white trim. Fishnets. Habit. Your eyes water – hot water, salty. In the past you didn't need gimmicks to get the money rolling in; it seemed like the ten-grand target was well within your reach without resorting to sleaze. Bloody Sapphire! Bloody Jeremy and his money-grubbing! This job was actually OK till recently when he took the new girls on. But now… you make your hands into fists… now – you hate to admit it – the competition's too much.

A quiver of rage; an attempt to dampen it down. A quiver made worse by the reason for taking the pink pill and memories of the club's last threadworm epidemic…

But, even as you come over all itchy, you're telling yourself to forget it. To forget worms. Forget Sapphire. Let her get on with the dirty dancing, the back-stabbing and bad-mouthing.

Followed by a swift about-turn. Nope. No way. She's got to get what's coming. You see yourself jabbing her in the eye with the point of a manicured finger, popping her balloon tits, one *pop!* two *pop!* – watching the air *pfurt* out as she deflates. If only…

And soon you're walking out onto the main floor, cursing the thin spotty nun (yup, you gave in) you see in the mirror on your way out… and you're fuming, raging, bile swimming around your mouth to keep the acid thoughts company. And if you'd read your tea leaves this morning they would have shown that things would only get worse. Got to be your worst ever night in the club: treading carpet for ages for naff-all dances, the calluses on your feet rubbing against the six-inch stilettos, shooting pains surging up your legs. You're twitchy, anxious, the green-eyed monster blowing in on a foul-smelling wind every time you flick your eyes over to another girl doing yet another dance for yet another customer. Raking it in! And Sapphire, where's she? You saw her name on the rota; she must be coming in. In the VIP room probably, then, the cow.

Agitated and with your turn on the pole looming, you make a decision – you'll show the new girls who's boss. Pull something special out of the bag. Show them all up with a sensational new move on the pole.

But what? The banana splits? Nah, too easy. Chopsticks? Nah. Too obvious.

A flash of inspiration then. The allegra box splits! That's it! You've only managed them once in practice but you're fired-up, confident, greedy for attention. Besides, what's the worst that can happen?

So when Derek gives you the nod you peel off the too-tight nun dress and strut over to the pole with a swagger, aware of Sapphire's minions in a huddle watching you from the bar. And as you climb on stage a clatter of rock music blasts out – you're in luck: a lap dancing classic, 'Closer' by Nine Inch Nails – the ziggy guitar sounds thrusting in everyone's ears, fixing all eyes on you.

Here you go. Your moment of glory. Your rise to the top as best dancer in the club. The sure-fire way to the Queen Bee crown.

To begin, you glide around the pole with elegant ballet moves, a contrast to the edgy full-on lyrics of the song. The air gets thinner, the audience goggle-eyed.

Then, with eff-you eyes darting over to the hussies' corner, you start the climb up the pole. Only – *uh-oh* – it's greasy, slippery. The cleaners ain't been in for a while (cost-cutting). And so your hands slip and then burn with the effort of clinging on as you do a little scissor move in a build-up to the allegra box splits. Slipping further, you wonder about trying something different, but it's too late, you can't back out now: one leg's wrapped round the top of the pole for support; the bottom leg is stretched out in a split. Only, it ain't going to work, is it? The pole's way too slippy! You're attempting the climax, getting both legs parallel in the splits with the pole, the music building up its sleazy sex riff, but then... no way... your bottom leg slips and – shit.

Torture, humiliation… and you tumble to the floor in a jigsaw of limbs.

You don't look good.

You don't feel good.

No amount of conjuring up visions of celebrity, glitz and glamour will get you out of this one.

Along with pumps of smoke from the dry ice machine, laughter drifts across the front of the stage. You crawl from one end of it to the other, trying to channel porn-star sexy, to make out like the fall was deliberate. And *phew!* – you've pulled it off, cos a guy in a Lacoste shirt is looking right at you – winking, is he? But no. Second glance, course he's not. He's laughing, doubled up, slapping his thigh.

You pull yourself up, dust an imaginary legion of specks from your legs and head straight for the bar.

'Oy, Celia,' you say. 'Another vodka.'

'Yup,' she goes, not looking you in the eye, the cow.

And then you mope in the corner, pulling the black rubber dress back on, which is hard when you're sticky with sweat and embarrassment. Alcohol gushes through your body, urging you to get back on the hustle. But you daren't, cos, instead of porn-star sexy as planned, you feel about as sexy as a pig in pyjamas.

Christ, a pig in pyjamas would have better luck with this bunch of pervs.

And this latest disaster is the excuse you need to give up, to ditch all thoughts of new regulars, to slump instead on a chair at the back watching the scene, downing one drink after another, the minutes passing with brain-deadening sluggishness. It's like a battle zone out there: a battle zone of tipped-up chairs and spilled drinks and booze casualties sprawled out in each and every corner, the stamping of feet and the beat of the music thudding through your brain like the boots of a thousand soldiers on the march.

And, if it is a battle zone, Sapphire thinks she's the sergeant major or the general, or whoever the heck it is who's in charge. Too right, a battle zone – like the Blitz out there tonight, the new light show scissoring in flashes and blinks across the main floor. You scan the room for Sapphire again – got to be out of the VIP room by now, surely – your eyes blinking in time to the light show's four-four beat.

Bang! Temples throb, a slow, steady throbbing brought on by the booze or the coke or the bungled move or God knows what.

Bang! Stiletto heels grind into the floor, teeth clench, and then – you gasp – here it is. Your first glimpse of Sapphire since she bad-mouthed you to Jez. The bitch. The slut. The evil hussy who wants to destroy you.

Bang! You watch as she straddles some guy in a dinner suit, her trademark tits in his face; you smart as he puts a wodge of notes into her money pouch. She kisses his cheek, her face a picture of pleasure and delight at her booty.

And with a final *bang!* it comes to you, how you can get Sapphire back: you'll hit her where it hurts. Not with violence, not by showing her up in front of her mates, but by becoming Jez's little grafter, his little star again.

Yeah, Sapphire ain't going to win. No way, no how!

You're much prettier than her. Sexier. OK, she looks red-hot in her theme costume as Snow White, the short black wig suiting her much better than her usual dyed red hair. You flinch, bitterness and jealousy hitting you square in the jaw.

Now look, sorry, it might be the drink talking, but here comes a bit of a rant. Cos fair dos, she looks red-hot, but you need the money more than what she does. Ain't in this game for what you can get. You're doing it for Connor! Yeah, you'll show her, you think – bring it on! And you grab both arms of the chair, hoiking yourself up… not bothering to pull down the black rubber dress what has slid up revealing your flashy red thong… staggering in the black heels Susie loaned you. A new tune, one that always gets you going, blasts out and you think, that's it, it's a sign, you'll show her! Gonna make that last five and a half grand as quick as possible, then scarper from this stinking club forever, no matter what it takes.

You choke back another vodka, scanning the room for a victim. OK – him. He'll do. A suit who comes in about once a month, sitting by the stage, a right chancer you'd usually warn the other girls not to touch with a bargepole – one of them give-an-inch-take-a-mile kind of guys.

You sashay over, magic some sparkle into your eyes. 'Fancy a dance?'

'Yeah, why not,' he says, waving a fiver – a fiver! – in your face.

'That's great, babe, but you're gonna have to cross my palm with more gold than that.' You stroke his cheek with the back of your hand, bend over so that your boobs cushion his face – the way you've seen Sapphire do.

'You going to tell my future?' he says, playing along with you.

'Mmm, maybe, play your cards right.'

'Don't need to, love – I can see it already: your head, my lap.'

Eugh.

'We'll shhee,' you say. *What the fuck, are you slurring?*

'Tenner?' he goes.

Why not? you think. *Got to start somewhere.* And you dance for him. A dance geed up by all the energy and frustration of the last few hours, days, weeks. You stand up, strong, bold. Make shapes. Pose. Show off the silhouette of your arse, your tits, then turn your back, leaning over so that he gets a bird's-eye view of the shadow between your hips. He groans, grabs your arms to turn you back around, pulling you closer to him, his breath minty, his cheeks sizzling. No point telling him *look, don't touch*.

Hang on, but you can't straddle him – the rubber's too tight. Got to sit side-saddle. And you do that – go side-saddle, tapping out your movements to the four-four beat of the music, and you're swinging, swaying, putting all you've got into the dance, whipping your long hair from side to side across his chest, your eyes locked onto his, till one, two, three, four, the tune's reaching its climax and you climax with it, finishing your dance, panting and puffing, simpering and sweating, and you turn your back to him, leaning over, your arse an inch from his face.

Put that in your pipe and smoke it, Sapphire, ya bitch.

'Wow,' he goes, his three minutes up, 'how much for a private dance? Take things further?'

'Now you're talking.'

And you lead him by his Family Guy tie across the battlefield into one of the private booths. 'Oh, and fifteen, babe.'

Though you get off to a bad start, hands slipping on the filthy, greasy poles either side of the banquette, it's not long before he's paid for two more dances – nude ones, *kerching!* – and he's living up to his rep, getting way too hot and heavy: you breathe on his neck, he wants you to lick it; you strike a sexy pose, he wants your tits in his face; you swing your hips at the tip of his erection, he wants you to grind down on it; you pretend-play with your nipples, he pleads with you to tug on them till they're sore (*Come on, hurt yourself, hurt yourself* – the perv). The more he tries it on, the more you forget what to do with your hands, your feet, your mouth.

Then *it* starts. The filthy talk.

'Does nunny like to do naughty things to herself?' he pipes up as the music changes into some Eighties number. Which will be, what – the fourth track you've danced for him? But never mind. You glance at the CCTV camera, not giving two sods for the three-track rule.

Naughty nunny thinks you're a Grade A scumbag, you think, but out loud you say, 'Mmm, yeah, babe, you should see what toys she keeps in her bedside drawer.'

Dildos. Failsafe way to get them going. When you first started dancing in the club, stuff like this – the pervy, the kinky stuff – well, it made your cheeks burn (you was practically a virgin, for Christ's sake). But now bad language swims out your mouth as easy as 'cup', 'cat', 'book'. Just words, after all.

And of course, like all the others, he loves it. He pulls at your nipple. 'Go on.'

Oh, please!

'Er… she likes to put a big one in her special place. You know, her most secret hole.' Put 'dildo' with 'arsehole', and they're usually creaming themselves in seconds, and you can rake the money in, and move on to the next chump.

'*Uughreeeee*,' he goes.

Assuming this means that he's into it, you go on, filth coming out your mouth what would sound silly in the crappiest of pornos. Not that he seems to care, you must be doing something right, cos eventually, after another dance, another wodge of notes, he comes out with it. 'Dare you to finger yourself.'

Not even bothering to whisper, bold as brass.

Lucky you've got an excuse, for now. A get-out-of-jail-free card.

'Er, no, darling,' you say, hoping you won't have to explain. 'I can't do that.'

He doesn't ask why; he just scratches his beard and says, '"Can't", not "won't". Well, what *can* you do?'

And you're, like, sitting there fully nude on his lap now, the dress pulled off ages ago, your stomach lurching, cos you ain't sure how much more you can give. Then, maybe down to the alcohol or maybe down to a web of desperation being spun inside you, something makes you go for it, to go further than you've gone before, to say, 'Er... erm... how much you got?'

You feel a million miles from sexy or in control.

And the weirdo pulls out a roll of notes. He was teasing you with that fiver before. Your skin freezes, a sickly cold. Before you did your first ever lap dance, you felt just this way. Cold then hot; dizzy, sick. Only this time, you think, your knees knocking as you sit astride him, this time there won't be any going back.

And you start to dance again, zoning in on the shabby purple velvet walls as you shake about to Shakira, a new closeness of flesh and bone between you, his fingers exploring inside your mouth. But whatever you do seems wrong. It's like the usual false promises you make, of what you'll give him next time, don't work; nothing can satisfy him.

You're wondering whether to walk away, deciding enough is enough, when, with a sneer, he pulls you towards him and comes out with, 'I want more for my money than that.'

And that's it. With them words it's like you're making a leap, one giant leap for womankind – or backward step, more like – and you wish you was somewhere warm and cosy and calm and comforting, not some place cheapened by violent bright lights and raucous music and racy purple walls and by the smoke and sweat and minty breath on your cheeks and the panting – oh, the panting! – some place where your legs weren't trembling as a guy in a suit grabs your hair, making it clear what he wants.

But look, you tell yourself, it's good practice for Thursday. Soft stuff, Kenny said. This'll be sort of like a dress rehearsal, make Thursday more bearable. Can't be any worse than what this guy expects. But all the while there's another voice, urgent and shrill, a voice inside you what's shouting, *What the hell are you doing?*

Too late, too late, too late, too late to back out now, Layla replies, and the suit undoes his fly.

Next thing you know, you're lowering your head, saying 'sorry' as your head bumps his chest on the way down.

His prediction bang on the money.

Bump. Whassat? Bump. 'Shhtupid door.'

The changing room door. Four am. Your knickers stuffed with the green stuff.

Hic. You walk over to the cubicle. *Hic.* Money spilling out of your garter. *Hic. Hic. Hic.*

Shhtupid, shhtupid girl. What would Mum say? Dad? Michael? Bad enough you ain't even told them you're a stripper... but now... this? How could you tell anyone... this?

Hic, hic, hic. You rub the heartburn in your chest, then move your hands up to your throat as if by rubbing it you can wipe out the memory – biological, salty and thick – and you retch. *Hic.* Come on, body, make your mind up: hiccups or puking? Puking or hiccups? *Hic, hic, hic.* OK, hiccups. And you stumble, fumble in the locker for your handbag, somehow galumphing into a splits position to tip out its contents on the floor. *Hic.* Eyes close... room spins... you reach out for the floor, try and hold on to it for balance... eyes open. And you feel about on the floor for what you're after.... Something hard, pointy. Keys. No, not them.... Fumble, fumble... Something leathery. Not that either... Fumble, fumble... Something soft, bristly. Ah, there you go. Toothbrush.

You stand up, walk to the sinks and run the tap, letting icy-cold water flow over your wrists, splashing it onto your cheeks. And, standing over the sink with your head bowed like Mum taught you, you brush, swill, rinse, repeat, brush, swill, rinse, repeat till the door swings open and, out of habit, you look up into the mirror to see who's come in.

Katrina.

That's when you see yourself. See yourself. *See* yourself. Mascara running down your cheeks, skin a ghoulish white. Katrina catches your eye, then drops her own eyes to the toothbrush. Walks over and places her hand on your back. 'Good night? I've made a stack.'

Her voice is flat, her body rigid as she counts out piles of money on the floor.

'Oh, yes, Layla's done brilliantly,' you say, and then you're off on one: Layla this and Layla that, Layla made a pretty packet... almost believing your own hype and then with a last *hic* it hits you, a tsunami of nausea, and before you can finish bigging Layla up you're heaving... holding onto your stomach... breaking into a run towards the cubicle where you unleash a dirty waterfall of vomit into the bowl.

Later – you're not sure how much – you hear Katrina's footsteps sound out with a clanging echo on the changing room floor, an echo what gets you, right in the heart... an echo what makes you feel lonelier than you've ever felt before.

2 MISSED CALLS
INBOX: 1 new message

FROM: BILLY
SENT: Tuesday 5 June, 22.30

*Not replying to my texts.
Forgot to charge ur phone
again? Call me.*

Wednesday

12

Water running, flowing, gushing; streams, rivers, an ocean of it, spreading knee-deep over a wasteland somewhere – a place what you sort of recognise but is alien too. Now you're lying on top of the water's surface, floating on a shimmering ocean... No... not the sea, a toilet, a toilet overflowing with water and with – eugh... No way you can use it, so you have to hold it in, control the urge to –

You wake with a start. Shivering. Where are you? Ah, OK: on the steps outside the main entrance to the flats, the colours and strange coolness of dawn creeping around you like robbers, stealing the night away.

What are you doing here?

No idea.

Maybe fell asleep after getting out of the taxi?

Probably, you idiot – it's a head-say-hi-to-wall moment.

Anyway. Never mind that for now, cos you need to pee. You really need to pee. But here? On the street? *Well, why not?* the voice inside you asks. *You've done worse. A lot worse.* Another shiver and you shove all thoughts of tonight in the club to the back of your mind. All you want is to crawl into bed, into your soft, doughy, damp-smelling bed. Yeah, first a waz, then bed.

But the steps are against you. You trip up them, banging your knee on the top step. The main door is against you. You fall against it, banging your elbow. The doormat, you rage, as you trip up over it, is against you.

Everything, let's face it, is against you.

Indoors, the communal hallway is well lit, so you don't bother with the light switch. Besides, the gloom's the perfect match to your half-drunk, half-burned-out mood. You try your key in the lock, *wiggle, wiggle, wiggle*. Stiff as usual. Try again. No luck. Bang on the door. No answer. They must be in, them cows. What time is it anyway? You scrabble in your handbag for your phone but you're done in, exhausted, at the end of your rope. Tiredness is everything now. Well, that and the first sweaty thumps of a hangover. Maybe you could use your handbag as a pillow? Just lie down on the floor?

Oh, come on, this is ridiculous. They must be in. You bang on the door again. Well, a half-baked attempt. Feeble, you are, so feeble. Another try of the key in the lock. Again, no can do. You groan – it's no use, is it? – and turn your back to the painted door, sliding down it, your legs splayed out like a wino in a shop doorway. And you sit there for a minute, limp and cross-eyed with tiredness, feeling chilly and dozy, the only hint of any excitement in your brain the unwelcome thought that the pigeon probably needs feeding and might well be dead.

But then you tell yourself to forget it: you're a good mum – a good pet owner, you mean. And you wilt, wilt with the effort of staying awake, your mind too frazzled to get any further with them thoughts, too zonked to give them serious attention.

Oh, for some sleep.

And oh, to forget, to forget, to forget. Two words jeering and poking, poking and jeering all the time this other stuff, this practical stuff has been bothering you. The shame. The shame. The shame.

The shame what is sliding and slithering to stake its place in the murkiest pit of your memory, the place you keep specially for all the worst what you do: the shame of what you did just hours ago in the club, cloying its way with sticky, inky stubbornness into the chambers of your heart, replacing the fresh lightness of the blood what should flow through it. In through your arteries, out through your veins. That right? Mrs Collins, your biology teacher, would have a fit if you got that one wrong. Whatever. Not even the thought of the bundles of notes stuffed in your handbag can make up for that tacky and toxic black shame.

What the hell was you thinking?

Well, you wasn't thinking, was you?

You yawn, a gloomy grey tiredness engulfing you. Yawn again. Stretch your arms above your head. Then, with a gargantuan effort, heave yourself upright, pulling the cords on your hoodie tighter around your head, resisting a nagging impulse to think of the club shame again.

Then, like it does at times like this, the bottle of JD in your handbag springs into your mind. Yes! JD. You see yourself downing it in one, see it giving you the courage, the strength to know what to do. So you feel about in the handbag for the cool hardness of the bottle, unscrew the top, and tip the dark liquid down your neck in a one-er. It burns your throat – like you care – as you *glug glug glug* it back. Only now you're hopping about with your legs crossed; more liquid wasn't the brightest idea. Right, that's it. A decision. Give those cows a rude awakening, no matter what time of day it is.

Bangbangbangbangbang.

No answer.

Bangbangbangbang.

–

No, it's no use. You really can't hold it in… No option but to drop your knickers, let it go, worry about the mess later.

Phew. That's better.

Now to try the door again. But of course there's still no sodding reply.

Oh, sod it – there's got to be some other way in? And you cast your mind about to the back of the flats, where there's a little fenced-off courtyard for the communal bins. Yeah, and there's a window in the kitchen what looks out on the bins, slightly high up, but maybe low enough for you to climb into? Got to be worth a shot. Funny, you think, as you walk down the front steps, unsteady on your feet, holding on to the black iron railings, funny how you sometimes fantasise about being a burglar, wonder what it'd be like to wander about in the night-quiet of somebody's home, noseying over their things. Well, now's your chance...

You're a burglar, a master criminal who's eluded the cops. Britain's Most Wanted. You imagine a black catsuit, a crowbar... but then you're scolding yourself: no time for fantasies, cos you've reached the back of the flats, the ground sticky and crunchy at the same time under your new trainers where the bin men have made a mess while collecting the rubbish. Whatever. Soon you'll be lying in your nice clean... well, not clean (like, when was the last time your sheets were changed?)... in your own bed, at least.

Only, as you look up at the red brick building, you're confronted by a number of windows and you're not sure which window's which. Like, if you face the flats from the main entrance, the kitchen's on the right, so you should climb up into the window on the left, right? *Left right left right left right...* You snigger, only to yawn again and stamp your foot in irritation at how long this is all taking. Casting your eyes upwards, you see a light, a light from inside, a light what says indoors and warmth and comfort. You're drawn to it, and it gives you the courage to climb up on a dustbin and with one hand try and hoik up the window. *Oof!* No, you'll need both hands to get it open that way. For now, the other hand rests flat against the red brick wall to stop you falling from the dustbin. *Oof!* You swap hands, using the left hand to steady yourself on the wall, the right one cupped under the wooden sill and with a last *oof!* to your surprise it budges an inch. Result! And before long you've managed somehow to push open the window, get a foothold on the sill and throw yourself into the kitchen, landing with a loud crash on the floor... no, not floor, table. Bloody hell, have the silly cows been moving the furniture around? The table's usually between the two work surfaces but it's been wedged underneath the window, and what the heck's happened to the boiler?

Oh, shit. Holy bleeding crap.

It comes to you in an instant. It ain't your kitchen, is it? You walk around the table. Reach above the door to turn on a light, the whirr of some strip lighting hitting your ears. You blink at the harsh white light. A green kitchen. Yeah, definitely not yours. And you kick yourself, literally kick yourself, at how stupid you are, how stupid for having no sense of direction. For having no sense at all! How are you gonna get out of this one? You scan the room and see a photo on the fridge, a beach shot. Thailand maybe, somewhere like that. Oh, OK: her next door, the neighbour. You cast about in your mind for her name. Bianca? Blanca? Something like that.

It's a nice kitchen – clean, tidy. A kitchen what says respectable, hard-working. A kitchen what makes you feel... what is it? A feeling you haven't felt for a long while. At home – yeah, at home. The sounds of a clock ticking, the fridge humming, they're soothing, so soothing. And all at once drowsiness swirls through your body.... sparks of light explode before your eyes... sleepiness weighs down your eyelids, your mind drifting, drifting under waves, waves of tiredness what are rolling harder and faster now that you're safely indoors.

You pull out a chair from under the table. Comfy – leather padding on the seat. And it's tempting, so tempting to sit at it, your head resting on the table. Sleep is building up inside you but you're not quite there yet, a confusion of thoughts holding you off from the final plunge down.

Never going back to the club again... Connor – must remember to visit Hamleys soon, an early birthday present... cancel your plans... that meeting with Billy and his porn guy... come back to Michael on his texts...

No. That's you, jerked awake again, still not comfy enough, still not quite asleep yet, and so you drag out another of the chairs, pull the two together and settle yourself, lying sideways on them. But then...

No way! The door handle's turning!

You bolt up, flick your eyes to the window, your brain screaming *you cannot escape you cannot escape you cannot escape* as she, your neighbour (Bianca, right?) walks in, her mouth forming a perfect O.

Uh-oh, this is gonna be a bad scene.

You step towards her, a big grin on your face, to sort of like show that you've not come over all Britney, that you ain't some nutter who's broken in.

And then it comes, a weird screeching noise what charges out of her mouth long and loud. '*Aaaaah!*'

OK, so the grin and the stepping towards her was a bad idea. Perhaps soft, soothing words might do the trick? 'It's alright, it's alright, it's me...' you say.

But now she's doing all the fancy footwork of Amir Khan in the ring, her silky crimson dressing gown flapping around her like a boxing robe, and you laugh, which panics her more, and – holy shit – now things ain't quite so funny, cos she's leapt further into the kitchen, right, and is pulling out a bread knife from a knife-block on the counter. Like you said: uh-oh.

She clasps both hands around the knife. Jabs it in front of her chest. 'What do you want?' she's asking, her voice high-pitched and squeaky, her legs now spread apart in a martial arts pose, Ninja-style. *Jab.* 'What do you fucking want?'

'Nothing, I don't want nothing,' you say, backing behind the chairs, your heart hammering inside your chest.

'Well, what are you doing here?' *Jab.* 'And how did you get in?' *Jab, jab, jab.*

You can't help it – your eyes shift to the window. 'Look, I, er – I just wanted to get in the flat. Next door. I'm Hay – er – Layla. I live next door.'

You drop your bottom lip, and it quivers. Oh, good God, you ain't going to blub, are you? Damn it, you are: tears are plopping down your cheek.

The shame!

'Oh, yes,' she says, squinting at you, 'it is… you.'

And she lays the knife on the kitchen counter, frowning. Folds her arms across her chest. 'Well, sorry,' she says in a teacher kind of voice. 'I called the police when I heard the crash. They'll be here any minute.'

You sink back down onto a chair, blinking fast to stop the tears. 'What, really? It was just a mistake…' You fish about for an excuse. 'I only wanted to get in next door.'

'Why,' she asks, taking a mobile phone out from her pocket, as if to prove that she's dialled 999, 'didn't you just knock?'

You look up at her, trying to think what to say, open your mouth, and OMG, instead of another excuse you belch, an embarrassing comedy belch what's perfumed with JD.

And then she's looking you up and down like you was something what she's picked up on her shoe, and says, 'Look, I'll make you a coffee, sober you up.'

The coffee, when it's finally ready, rises back up your throat, leaving a bitter taste in your mouth. Or is it her what's leaving the nasty taste? You sip at the coffee politely, on autopilot, but you need something else, something to take the edge off this waiting. And so you ask if you can smoke. Oh, OK, should have known, cos she's giving you a look, right? – a look what says that's an even worse boo-boo than breaking into the flat. Bad to worse, she then starts lecturing that the girls next door are concerned for you, that isn't it about time you took a good look at your lifestyle? – and you remember with a slam of regret that she's all matey with Rebecca and Cathleen. Cheese and wine nights and that. Very poash.

You swear on your life it's a relief when the doorbell goes and the police arrive.

There's two of them. A man and a woman. Up themselves, the pair of them, all – whatchamacallit? – pompous and that. After the introductions, the four of you sit at the table, Bianca explaining the situation, your feet kicking at the chair beneath you, hands clasped in a sort of prayer position under your bum. But you try and style the whole thing out, make light of it. Like, why should you be embarrassed? Simple mistake. Could happen to anyone. And while they're interviewing you, and you're trying to answer their questions all, like, honestly and that, Bianca's called in Cathleen and Rebecca, cos it's like seven am and she's caught them on one of their mobiles. Now why didn't you think of that? You catch Rebecca's eye, as cold as a blooming dead fish's, and the wretchedness of it catches hold of you, a world-weariness what snags on your nerves – the misery of the past few days, of Colin, Sapphire, the club, making you skittish, defensive, on edge.

But there's hope, cos one of the coppers, the bloke, yeah, seems OK, and you think he's the more senior one. Though the woman is being a real pain in the whatnot. 'It's up to your neighbour if she wants to press charges,' she says after hearing your version of events.

'Oh, leave it out,' you say, suddenly bored of her questions. 'Like I keep saying, it was an honest mistake.'

She really lets you have it then. 'I don't think you're taking this seriously, miss. The law's the law. Breaking and entering – it is a serious business.'

Jobsworth! You roll your eyes and catch the male copper grinning at you. You toss him a coy look and he winks.

'You're good cop and you're bad cop,' you say, trying to make a joke out of things, picking up on his relaxed cue. Only that seems to get his back up.

'One more word, young lady, and you'll be arrested,' he says.

So much for good cop.

'Feel free,' you whine. 'Never been in trouble with the law before.'

'That right?' the woman's saying now, and she takes out a radio from the top pocket of her black vest. 'We'll see about that. Name?'

Then it hits you. The stupidity. Your stupidity. Like, why did you have to go and climb through that window? Now you've really dropped yourself in it.

You draw a breath, squeeze your hands tighter under your bum. 'Hayleigh,' you say, aware of the snooty shapes of Rebecca and Cathleen out the corner of your eye. 'Hayleigh Weeks.'

And alright, alright, it's a fair cop! Now you're embarrassed. All them months of pretending, of covering up your real name, and you've had to let it slip. They look at one another, told-you-so sorts of looks what make you feel stupid and small. And you sit, increasingly lonely and sick, while in the background Bianca, Rebecca and Cathleen huddle around the cooker, three witches over a cauldron, and the police woman speaks into her radio.

You don't care. So you get arrested. So what? Like, what's the worst that could happen? They have beds at the police station, right? Maybe you'll get some kip at last. Though who'd feed the pigeon then?

But then everything speeds up. The three bitches come out of their huddle formation, and Bianca's all, like, talking to the coppers and that, saying that she won't press charges but she'll be inspecting the window and expect reimbursement for damages, and the girls are all, *Yes, officer, we'll take care of her, try to keep her in line*, and you personally don't seem to have much say in the matter, but quite frankly you'd agree to buy her anything right now, so that you can just forget everything, feed Mr Pigeon then crawl into bed, let the forgiveness of sleep come to you and blank everything out. So you give it all wide eyes and big apologies, when demanded, to Bianca, to the coppers, to the flatmates.

And then they're out of there, the police, but not before the male copper's handed you a card *in case you get into trouble again* and you find yourself, by some sort of miracle, in the corridor outside the entrance to both flats, Rebecca and Cathleen walking ahead of you. You follow, your head hanging down, noticing a puddle of – what is that? – on the floor.

'Nice one,' Rebecca says, slamming the flat door shut behind her, the opposite of her usual laid-back self. 'You've really lost it now, haven't you?'

And do you know what? You understand why she's so fed up. You do. It's like, it hasn't escaped your notice what a disaster you're becoming. If only you could tell her. Tell her about the club, what happened there, about Connor, about all of that. If only you could stuff her full with your problems, make her as weighed-down and strung-out as you. She'd understand, wouldn't she?

But as you hover in the hallway, clammy, your mind beginning to fill with a grainy picture of the pigeon, dead as a dodo in his box, you can only mumble, 'Sorry,' your eyes drooping from tiredness and shame.

'And Hayleigh...?' Cathleen now – grabbing her handbag off the little shelf by the front door – off to work in a minute, you reckon.

'Yes?' you say, your hand resting on the handle to your bedroom door, eyes still fixed on the floor.

'Let's talk this evening. We've got some things we need to sort out.'

'Yeah, sure,' you say, looking her straight in the eye now, without blinking, passive, not objecting, 'whatever.'

And just when you think that's it, bed at last, sleep, Rebecca's brushing up behind you again, handing you a mop.

'Oh,' you say, getting it. 'Oh.'

SENT MESSAGES

TO: BILLY
SENT: Wednesday 6 June, 13.05

Soz for silence. Been busy.
How u?

>   *Excited!*

Oh yeah?

>   *Yeah, for tomorrow. U?*

Sure.

>   *Go out after? Have
>   one of our big nights
>   like old times?*

Mm. Maybe. See how it
goes.

>   *It'll go great. Feel it in
>   my bones.*

Kay. Catch you laters xxx

>   *That's my girl. xxx*

13

You're lying on your back, legs spread. Today's another scorcher, and you're clammy, sticky, your buttocks glued with sweat to a roll of thin white paper what's been laid out on top of a reclining bed. Above you, a skank in a white coat with a too-tight ponytail looms, humming along in a tuneless way to a jingle on the radio. One of the commercial stations. Heart FM, you guess. She seems distracted, fiddling with the lapel of the coat with one hand and a piece of equipment with the other. She's new to the job, she just told you, and you're worried that this is going to be painful.

'Whoops,' the girl says, her nose crinkling with – what, embarrassment? – and you wince.

Wince in advance, knowing that in approximately two minutes she'll be let loose on your most precious and private parts.

Usually you wouldn't give a tinker's toot about lying spreadeagled in front of another woman – it's her job, after all, and yours means you're half-naked most of the time too, to be fair. But it's just the two of you in the room, which is awkward. Plus you don't like the way she's looking at you – she can't seem to take her eyes off down there, even while she's pulling on her surgical-style gloves. You squirm. Squeeze your buttocks together. Grip the side of the bed with tensed hands. Only to tell yourself not to be so ridiculous. Not like you haven't done this countless times before. Even so, you fish about in your mind for a distraction, and soon – surprise surprise – you've settled on the flatmates.

Thank goodness they'd both left for work when you woke up, and couldn't gang up on you – though your head and your stomach are doing a bang-up job of just that. Bloody hangover. But it's not only the hangover what's troubling you. In your mind, you re-read the note what was left on the kitchen table.

Hayleigh,

We hope that you're feeling better today. If you're not working this evening, could we please have a flat meeting? Say about 7? There's something we need to discuss.

Cathleen and Rebecca

Which is a right mare cos you need to be a good girl today and get into work on time... And then you frown. Hesitate. Ask yourself if you can really face Elegance after last night. Ayesha's asked you out for a drink, though – probably do that instead. So yeah, pretty much whatever happens tonight, there's no way you'll be home around seven. Cos – do they think you're stupid? – it's pretty obvious what they're planning when they –

Ow! Your eyes water. The silly cow could have given you a warning.

Ow! A burning, a stinging, as the second wax strip is pulled off, on the same spot.

Ow! Oh, come on, everyone knows waxing the same spot over and over is no way to prevent swelling – *ow!* – and pain.

Oh, right. No, you ain't at the GP or at a whatchamacallit? – gynaecologist. Like you've said before, you're not much good at describing stuff. No, you're lying flat on your back at the beautician's, going through the motions of a Brazilian bikini wax.

'Ouch.' This time you say it aloud.

'Sorry, love – told you: it's my first time,' the girl's saying. 'I mean outside of college and mates.'

Why didn't you just wait for your regular beautician to come back from lunch? You don't hold back. 'Well, don't worry, it ain't like I need it done for work or nothing.'

Then your face burns as she leers at you. And even though she's probably got the wrong end of the stick, thinks you're a prossi or something, you clam up. *Never apologise, never explain*, Dad always said. And you lie back and think of England, wriggling back into position on the bed, even as the stinging sensation reaches its peak as she applies another strip of wax to rip off a last few stragglers.

You grit your teeth, don't say anything more about the throbbing pain. Cos it's like a test, ain't it, of whether you're a proper woman? If you can take it, then yeah, you're a Grade A stand-up female; if you can't, well, then you're probably a hairy-legged feminist or something. A freak. Like no matter how stingy and hurty this is, it's a million times better than the alternative: a muff, spiders' legs hanging out your thong. *Eugh!* So you grip the side of the bed yet tighter as – *ouch!* – the scraggy cow plucks out a ghetto of leftover hairs. You see yourself taking them tweezers and plucking out her incey-wincey brain. It's a fight between you and her now: a stand-off.

Client versus beautician.

Hair-plucker versus hair-loser.

Skank versus goddess.

No way you can let her think that you're not a real woman; you can handle it!

She comes at you again with the tweezers, a determined look on her face. You twist away, the thin paper stuck to your bum ripping beneath you. She inches nearer, the points of the tweezers within flobbing distance from down below. You can't take no more!

'Alright, alright, 'sfine, I can live with it like that,' you shout, jumping off the bed.

So. Not. Fair.

And she's rubbing her hands together in a self-satisfied way, then sort of like dusting down the lab coat. She knows she's got the better of you! You stare her out as she hands you a bottle of soothing balm. And when she leaves the room *so you can get dressed* it crosses your mind that this *is* just like a visit to the doctor, after all. Only, for some reason you can't quite put your finger on, in some ways it definitely isn't…

Never mind, needs must, you think, pulling your jeans on inch by inch over your bottom, cos if you don't –

Ouch! But oh, this burning's beyond belief, probably your worst ever waxing. And that's saying something. Maybe it's the hormones, a chemical reaction to being near the end of your period? Slowly, it dawns on you that there's no way you can go into work tonight. Not with redness and swelling. Jeremy's going to have a fit. Then again… and you breathe out slowly through your nose, your body loosening up at the thought of calling in sick. It's a good excuse not to go in after – your body tenses – after what happened last night. And, as you walk cowboy-like to the door of the treatment room, convincing yourself that you're right, your knickers rub against the sore areas. That settles it. The irritation's bad enough in ordinary knickers, but in a lacy G-string or a thong? Your eyes sting at the thought.

Anyway, as you was saying, letting some woman loose with hot wax on your nethers… Look, can you just say something? It's not like you're a feminist or nothing. Heaven forbid! The stupid cows who sometimes protest outside the club, driven by jealousy and misunderstanding of what goes on inside…

A wobble, then. Misunderstandings?

And your mind warps again, bending itself back to visions of Family Guy ties, greasy poles and toothbrushes.

No.

You don't want to think about it. Can't compute it. No way you can face up to the fact you've become close to a… to what the beautician probably thinks you are. It's doing your nut in.

So, walking out of the treatment room into the reception area, you do yourself a favour and put these thoughts firmly to one side. And the beautician, right, she's nowhere to be seen. You consider not leaving the payment, but no, that'd only bring you down to her level. Buggered if you're paying a tip, though.

Slamming down the cash on the counter, you wonder what to do for the rest of the day, wonder how to avoid the stink bomb of problems what are festering around you. You could go to the pub. *No,* your pounding head and churning stomach beg, *not that.* Call Mum? Maybe speak with Connor? You come down the stairs of the beautician's and out of the little side alley what leads onto Oxford Street, wondering if you can muster the nerve. Not likely. And all of a sudden, like it does ten million times a day, your heart bursts with the red-rawness of missing him, and you drift deeper into the busy street, brushing past the flitting shapes of the lunchtime shoppers, thinking of him as you hobble about, lifted along by a bubble of memories, the stinging in your knickers reminding you of the episiotomy after he was born. Three weeks you had to sit on a bag of frozen peas to reduce the swelling. They didn't tell you that at the birthing class, that's for sure.

And that's not all they didn't teach you, eh?

How it would really be with a little one, they didn't teach you that: that being a mum would be the very opposite of how it's sold on the adverts, the opposite of cotton and cream, snuggly and warm. Or about the exhaustion, the night feeds, the nappy-changing conveyor belt, the heartache of failing at breastfeeding. They didn't teach you how painful it would be to be apart from the baby's dad (who you really should text, you think, with a prickle of conscience). Most of all, though, they didn't teach you that cos you was a teenage single mum you'd never be allowed an off-day. That Connor would have to be cleaner, happier, more goo-goo and gurgly than all the other babies at the Children's Centre. You know, like, to prove that you could do the job just as well as everyone else, if not better.

For a moment you let your mind dwell on this, let yourself be brought to your senses by this harsh bite of reality, by the harsh fact that these difficulties might be the real reason you let him go so easy.

Deflated, you come to a stop outside the shoe shop on the corner of Regent Street, only to scuttle away past a *Big Issue* seller who tries to catch your eye. And it slams into you, the reason for this drifting, this wandering around town, this turning all the problems you'd had with Connor over in your mind.

Cos you're afraid of turning up at the flat, yeah? Afraid that in a few hours' time you might end up homeless like him. But then you have a word with yourself. Homeless like that *Big Issue* seller? Behave – there's, like, a load of places you could go! But no sooner have you thought this than the falseness of it engulfs you, chokes you up. *Really, Hayleigh? Loads of places? Like, where?* And even if you do find somewhere – sofa-surfing, living out of a suitcase – not sure you could take that again. You flare your nostrils, sniff the air as if trying to sniff out some hope in it, some sign that everything's going to be OK. But of course there's no magic answer, no magical cloud on the wind with a sign or a message that things are going to turn out alright.

Sighing, you take in your surroundings and realise that your wanderings have taken you further down Regent Street. You come to a standstill outside Baby Gap. That's it! A bit of shopping for Connor, that'll lift the mood. You walk into the shop and soon find yourself cooing over the cosy cottons and pretty pink party dresses. And you allow yourself to brood – but only for a split-second – on whether the baby might have been a girl, only to quickly head to the boys' section, rummaging through the selection of cute jumpers and adorable cotton shirts. You pull out a short-sleeved checked shirt, so darling on Connor, it'd look, you imagine. But what size? Like, you want to get that right. There's nothing else for it. Sweating, you fish your mobile out of your handbag. Dial.

She answers, all sort of bright and breezy. 'Hello.'

'Mum, it's me, Hayleigh.'

'Yes.' Voice frosty now.

'How is he?'

'He's fine.'

A noise in the background. Him? No, music. The radio, maybe. You move over to the pyjama section, away from eavesdroppers. Turn your face into the corner to speak into the phone.

'Sorry, Mum, I can't speak long, but I just want to check his size.'

'His size?'

'Yeah, size. I want to, like, buy him a little outfit.'

'He'll be two in October, Hayleigh.'

Irritation swells as if you'd been stung in your throat. 'Yeah, I know that,' you snap, 'but is he still a big boy? Big for his age?

'He don't need any clothes, Hayleigh. We're fine.'

We! What's this we?

'Fine, I'll get 18–24 months, then, yeah?'

'Do what you like; you always do,' and the line goes dead.

You press *End Call*, your cheeks stinging. Wipe a slick of sweat from the mobile. Flick your hair out of your eyes. Sense somebody next to you. A shopgirl.

'Can I help you at all?'

'No, no,' you say, 'just browsing,' and you move away from the pyjamas, walk back to the shirts, cursing the old cow as per usual, cursing her cos the other option's worse: wondering why she hates you so.

There's a choice of blue or red. Red, you think. Bright colours, they're what suit him, with his olive skin and brown hair. And, choosing a pair of long shorts to match, you take the items to the till.

'Are they a present?' the woman behind the desk asks.

'Er, yes,' you say. Then, quickly, 'No!'

Like, what can you say? Yes, it's a present. For my own son. And you blush as you snatch – with hot, sticky hands – the bag away from her, scurrying out of the shop, reminded of the shame of not being there for him, the guilt of why you left in the first place.

But as you turn a corner down onto Foubert's Place your spirits lift, cos you're there, in the moment, in the moment of dressing him in the shirt for the first time. And he looks so cute in the shirt, your precious Little Man. The cheesy grin! The chubby little arms! And it's sort of like you're in a trance now, jumping out the way of a mountain bike what's hurtling down the pedestrian street, cos you're looking but not seeing, your mind fixed on his cheeky face as he plays with his toys in the new gear. You're giddy, happy, riding a wave of elation! Your steps become feathery and light, a weight lifted from your shoulders now that you've bought him something new. Cos that purchase, that whatchamacallit? – transaction brings him closer to you, don't it? Means that he's still all yours? And you crack out a smile, flash your white teeth, at the next person who walks past. An old girl, Asian, wearing a crazy purple suit and a floppy sunhat.

'Nice hat,' you say, and she stops for a minute, only to shuffle off again in a hurry. Like you was some kind of weirdo or something!

Like you care! Not your problem if she don't share your sunny mood. Cos how gorgeous everyone looks, how dreamy the world is today! You look around, a thrill running through you, not at all bothered if anyone notices the grin what's spreading out on your face, a sort of like ridiculous display of happiness for all to see.

Further down the street, a young guy shuffles past, a druggy type, scabby clothes and a manky old rucksack on his back, walking with the help of a stick.

'Nice day, mate,' you say, and he flinches, growls something what you can't make out. Waves his stick at you.

What's his beef? Never mind. How could he be unhappy on a day like this? On a day when your boy has a new shirt, a new shirt what will make him the cutest Little Man alive! And again, you imagine dressing him in it. Brushing his teeth. Combing his hair. Imagine the sheer joy what you'll take in doing them everyday things for him, as soon as you see him again.

Only as you turn onto Carnaby Street a couple deep in an argument piss on your parade. 'Nah, you've got it all wrong,' this young lad in a suit's saying, tugging on his girlfriend's sleeve. 'I never text her, it was her.'

You want to tell him, *Don't be daft! Today's a beautiful day, a wonderful day, not a day for arguing, for fights!* And a daring and a boldness floods through you, these thoughts of

Connor toughening you up, making you uncharacteristically courageous and brave.

You step closer to the girl, get in her eyeline, say, 'Are you OK?'

She looks you up and down. Scowls. Then screeches, 'Mind your own fucking business.'

And now they both turn to you, turn on you, and the bloke starts up a rant. Tells you to stop poking your beak in. Christ, is he going to – ? But no, he backs off as she starts screaming at him again and a police community support officer walks up to them.

And that's it. That uniform. It makes you come crashing back down, the giddiness leadened by the overwhelming black weight of reality. Cos the uniform's a reminder of last night, yeah? – of the supposed break-in, what led up to it and what happened after. You glance up at a clock outside a jewellery shop. Three-thirty. A few hours till D-Day, till homelessness. You scratch nervously at your leg. Stand watching courier bikes whizz past. You can't go back to the flat. Not yet. A strong sensation of numbness is getting to your limbs, to your hands, to your brain, holding you back, and it's not just anxiety over yesterday's screw-ups. Maybe you should walk down the street to Liberty's? While away some time in the concessions there, cheer yourself up with a taste of luxury just by smelling things, touching them: the cashmere, the exotic perfumes, the expensive oriental rugs. Why not? You could afford them, anyway, if you wanted. But you're not in the mood for the piercing shopworkers' eyes, and so you continue down Carnaby Street instead. Maybe check out the Miss Sixty shop?

The thought of it, of having something new, of a crisp store bag tied with ribbon, of taking a new garment out of its tissue at home, it's frustrating: it should make you feel better, but somehow you're sluggish, in the doldrums, slinking zombie-like from store to store, window-shopping outside some shops, lingering a while inside others, each with its own banging music or classical soundtrack, each with at least two sets of eyes boring into you as you walk in, shop girls with looks what say, *Don't touch what you can't afford.*

If you're not going to shop, what else is there, though? What else is there to pass the time? Your tummy growls, but you ignore it. Haven't managed to eat anything but toast since those fancy eggs you had with Ayesha yesterday. You catch sight of yourself dithering in a bookshop window and realise, with a start, the unvarnished truth, the truth of what this shopping trip and the visit to the beautician's are about. Delaying tactics. Obviously. Putting off what you've got to do. And so, head down, you allow yourself to give in to it, give in to what's got to be done, i.e. pack your bags; move on… jump before you're pushed. And now that your mood has changed to acceptance you walk briskly through the quieter early afternoon streets, giving yourself a talking-to, running through a mental to-do list:

Work – speak to Jez, call in sick, tell him you're going to have to take a few days off cos of the dodgy waxing.

Billy – no way you can audition tomorrow with your down-below in this state. Phew, a get-out clause.

Connor – well, you've reached the flat, so you can lay that biggie aside for now, all thoughts turning to packing up your things, getting out of here before the two cows come home to give you a dressing-down.

Fifteen minutes later and you're hauling the big rucksack out from the under the bed, cramming it with clothes and toiletries, the money safely stashed at the bottom. Only then, as you check under the bed for anything what's got kicked underneath it, among the used tissues and God knows what else, you see it. The cardboard box. The pigeon. How could you have forgotten? You flick up the flap and peer in. Mmm. Not dead yet.

What to do?

Picking at your fingernails, you lay this decision to one side for now and scan the room in case you've forgotten anything else. There. The photo on the mantelpiece. Your Little Man, your darling boy. And you smother him with kisses before popping the well-thumbed print in your handbag. And what about this? You clasp your fingers around your statue of the naked woman. OK, it's naff, this souvenir, but it's a sort of like reminder of happier days, you'll take it for – whatchamacallit? – sentimental reasons. But, hold on – her hand is broken. You scan the mantelpiece and can't see the fingers, the hand anywhere.

You knew it! You knew they'd been in here! Those snooping cows. And there was them, letting you think you was going mad, letting you think you was paranoid and that.

You look in the mirror above the mantelpiece and catch yourself looking smug. You was right all along. You're not mad! Not losing the plot! And they come across as so right-on, but they're no better than you – a pair of snoopers... scum, lowlife. You take another look at yourself in the manky glass, almost seeing the turning wheels and cogs of your brain as you dream up ways of taking your revenge: flipping up your skirt and rubbing your crotch on the kitchen surfaces, wiping a slick off what's left of your period on their toothbrushes, pissing in their beds, smashing the windows.

Then you think of the bills what will be left unpaid – next month's rent, that electricity bill, your share of the phone – and you smirk, cos leaving owing them money is sweet revenge enough, right?

No – no, it isn't. Not for the months of ganging-up and harsh questions and cold shoulders and that.

And then it comes to you. Of course. The pigeon. You'll leave him behind, a parting gift. Let them deal with him. No way they'll do him any harm. You see them in your mind's eye, flapping over what to do, over his injury, the shit and the terrible smells.

Sorted!

Only riding roughshod over that little problem is another one, a major one, that's been letting your brain know it's around since you began packing, with a thrumming and throbbing in your temples. Where will you go? Is your only option to crawl back to Billy, begging to kip on his sofa or, worse yet, to share his bed?

But no, you swore on your life you'd never go back there.

Where, then? Your heart plummets. Peacehaven? Home? Give Connor the clothes in person?

No, no, no, not yet! Fear takes a hold and you scrabble in your handbag for your inhaler, with your chest squeezed, your airways tight. One puff. *Soon, soon, you'll go back, but not yet.* Two.

Then, at last, something sparks in your mind. Ayesha. You can say yes to that drink for tonight, ask if you can stay over. Confident about this new plan, you drift into the kitchen, sit for a last time at the table – feeling pretty much diddly-squat at the fact that you're leaving, to tell the truth – reach for the home phone (use up a bit of their bill, why not?) and dial.

And Ayesha's like, 'Sure, come over now, stay with me for a while,' and you light up a fag, exhale, wonder if there's anything of yours in here what needs packing. A Brighton and Hove Albion mug. A steak knife Billy bought you at Christmas, being as you're such a big carnivore. You shove them in the front pouch of the rucksack – never know when they might come in handy – catching sight as you do of a photo on the fridge of you and the two cows, taken at a Hallowe'en party last year. The one and only time they pretended to like you cos they wanted to dress up as three witches.

A little flutter of your heart, a choked-back tear. You sniff. Hard. No, you won't allow it, won't allow that diddly-squat to be replaced with the truth; won't let yourself get upset.

Anything else?

Never mind – a *beep beep* from outside tells you that your minicab's arrived.

And so you:

rush back into the bedroom, pick up the box with the pigeon and place it on the kitchen table...

rip up Rebecca and Cathleen's note and leave it, alongside your keys, beside the box...

walk across the creaky floorboards with solemn, quiet steps, and through the front door.

You won't look back, you promise – not once.

INBOX: 2 new messages

FROM: DAD
SENT: Wednesday 6 June, 14.30

*Come on princess. Let's not
fall out. Knock knock?*

FROM: MICHAEL
SENT: Wednesday 6 June, 15.57

Fox????

14

'Happy Christmas,' you breathe, pleased with yourself, with your joke, looking down at the fairy lights garlanded across your tummy, winding up up up towards your chest. You rub where a star, a red one, has dug into your shoulderblade, scratched the skin. Broken it, even. *Twinkle twinkle, little star...* You exhale. Try and focus. If only your eyelids would stop swooping down on your pupils... 'How I wonder what you are.'

'What?'

'What what? I didn't say nothing,' you say, your eyelids fluttering again, up down, up down. Up. Now you see it: a bathroom cubicle. Smell it: a piss stench. Feel it: a heat so clammy that you can taste it on your tongue. And them, you see them: the two lads.

Oh, yeah, the two lads. In the background, laughter. At you? You let your eyelids swoop down again, escape back into the comfort zone of your thoughts. *Up above the stars so high... No, world.*

'World,' you say, a wobble in your voice.

Connor, little Connor, singing this to him. Warm and cosy, you feel, remembering his face light up when you shared the rhyme together, and you do the actions with your fingers, twinkling them left to right, right to left across your middle, beyond the land of the fairy lights, and you giggle. Only to worry you've missed something.

'Say that again.'

Or are you hearing things now? Hard to tell cos you've got cotton wool ears, everything fuzzy and muffled and that.

You cast your mind back to earlier. To: hitting some bars with Ayesha... vodka, gallons of it... a dab of MDMA, maybe more... then... an angry brushstroke painted across the evening, an argument, Ayesha doing her Cinderella act, heading back to Hackney to see whatshisname, her new fella. Followed by a gap: a black hole in your memory till being in here with the two lads.

'What you are,' you repeat.

The lads, who are sandwiched either side of the toilet, share a look. The lads. Oh, yeah, you think, screwing up your face with the effort of trying to get everything clear. *Yes, sir,* you think! *Crystal clear, sir!* The lads are cute, both blond, both wearing light green T-shirts. Confusing. Then you notice *it*, a little envelope laid out on top of the cistern, a tenner rolled up and three lines in a row. *All in a row, row, row, pretty lines all in a row.*

'Come on, then, hurry up,' Lad One says, the tall one, hopping about on an Adidas trainer. 'And close the bloody door.'

But you can't manage it; you're teetering, tottering, leaning on the doorframe for balance, a human Christmas tree – always did dream of two Christmases a year, why not one in June? Besides, the lights are so pretty – *like a diamond in the sky*, you want to sing out loud – but now Lad Two has you by the elbow, steering you towards the cistern.

'Nooo,' you sort of moan, suddenly shy, and he goes, 'Alright, then, I'll go first,' and you try to bring things back into focus...

... the dare to wear the fairy lights... an urge to have them sparkling, twinkling on you... your idea to strip down to your bra, wanting to see the lights tremble and glow against your naked skin. Only the lights went out when you unplugged them, of course. *No go on the glow*, you giggle. But, even so, you draped them over yourself and then the two lads invited you in here for a line – or did you ask them? – you can't remember, and it doesn't matter really, cos you're being led by the elbow again and you stretch over the toilet bowl, the string of fairy lights swinging towards the cistern and Lad One – or is it Lad Two? – rescues them before they take out the coke and then you're steadying yourself, ignoring the warnings flashing into your mind, and after you've snorted the line you lift your head and notice a sign what reads 'THIS BAR HAS A ZERO TOLERANCE POLICY TOWARDS DRUGS'.

You laugh out loud.

'What's so funny?' Lad One says as you pass him the note.

Thomp thomp thomp. The sound of heavy boots on the floor.

Thomp thomp thomp. Now the pummelling of fists on the cubicle door.

You wedge yourself between it and the lads, the cubicle a squish-squash of legs and arms, flapping your hands as a warning to stash the gear. Too late: the cubicle door's being pushed open as best the bouncer can – yeah, must be a bouncer – with the three of you squished against it.

You poke your head out.

'Out in a sec,' you say.

He's a big guy, meaty, handsome – the bouncer, right? – a cartoon villain scowl drawn on his face.

'Out – now,' he says, backing off to give you room.

You fold your arms across your chest – how silly you feel to be in your jeans and bra! – and step out of the cubicle, into the bathroom, zeroing in on the sparkly vinyl on the floor. *Twinkle twinkle, little floor.*

Lad One trails behind you, his voice squeaking, a frightened mouse, as he says, 'Come on, chief, we weren't doing anything.'

'Pockets,' the bouncer's saying.

You hover behind him, nearer the main bathroom door, holding your breath against the chemical whiff of the urinals, thinking you can make a run for it, to escape, and as they turn out their pockets it hits you, the line, and you straighten up a bit, which only brings on a familiar slam of desperation. Like, how did you even get here... if you leave, where will you go... and where's your top... your bag?

But of course the real answer to the question *how did you get here?* – in a piss-smelling bog, half-naked with two strangers – is, where else would you be?

'So, uh, laters,' one of the lads is saying, as the bouncer shoves them both out of the door, and you turn your back to them; they're part of your back catalogue already.

'You too, love.'

'Huh, what?'

'You too,' the bouncer's saying. 'Pockets.'

And you smirk, cos he's aiming his eyes way above your chest. First time that's ever happened.

'And I think those are our lights?'

'Well, I, um, I don't have nothing,' you say, and you dig your fingers into your pockets, although truth be told you ain't got a clue what you'll find in there.

But it turns out you're – what do they say on American telly programmes? – clean, and the bouncer's all, like, sorry that he had to chuck your mates out, and you're, like, *Oh, no, they weren't my mates, my mate left hours ago, in fact what time is it anyway, how long since my mate blew me out?* then he's telling you that he recognises you, he's seen you in the bar with Ayesha before, and you tell him how Ayesha's bolted on you even though you're meant to be staying at hers, and you realise after a while that you've been rambling at him, and that you was wrong before when you said the line had hit, cos it's only really just hitting you now, that's what's making you ramble, and you say this out loud and then go 'whoops' but he doesn't seem to care that you're caned and he's like, *Easy, tiger*, as you stagger into him, and then he's shifting his eyes towards the door, asking, *Where's your clothes?* and you're telling him, *Not sure, in the ladies' maybe?* and then he's, like, leading you in there, covering you up with his jacket as you cross the bar – what a gent – and yeah, they're there – the bag, the shiny red top, on the floor of one of the cubicles, bunched up next to a puddle of loo water, or is it wee? – and he's saying, *Five minutes to sort yourself out, then I'm coming to get you.*

Ooh, just like Davina, you think. Only this isn't reality TV, worse luck, it's just your shite reality, so you bolt the cubicle door – good to have some space at last, not to be sardined in with them lads – and sit with your head in your hands, thinking you might have been too hasty not to leave with Ant and Dec or whatever their names were, what with being all out of drugs now.

Wallowing in self-pity, you sit like this for a few minutes, till, with maximum effort, you lift your head, your teeth gritted, only to spy a piece of graffiti on the wall saying, 'FUCK YOU'. And you think, *Well, that's nice, ain't it?* and, disgusted, you wipe it off with the side of your hand cos you guess it might be written in eyeliner and then you realise why you're guessing that it might be written in eyeliner, cos in fact you *know* that it's been written in eyeliner, being as you now remember that you were the one who scrawled the words on the wall in disgust, after Ayesha bolted.

What's got into you?

You swear on your life you've not always been such a loser. Mum would have an eppy if she found out you'd been writing graffiti. *Sorry, Mum*, you think, and, shame-faced, you take a piece of bog roll, wiping off the remaining 'K YOU' what hasn't been smeared by the side of your fist.

Right, cos writing graffiti's your biggest worry. There's the club, the audition, nowhere to live, Michael's texts… Connor. It always comes back to Connor. And, as if the mum who lurks inside was telling you to, you tug down on the loo roll holder again, take another square of paper, and rip from it a smaller piece, what you stick on the end of your nose with spit. You and Connor, yeah? – you'd play this game where you'd wet some loo paper like that, and stick it to your nose, singing *My mummy flies pigeons, whee!* as you blew the paper across the room and you'd both laugh as it flew through the air. And then Connor would look up at you with them big brown eyes, wanting you to do the pigeon thing over and over, and that one time you was doing it when Mum came in the room and scooped him up while you was still laughing, with an *Ain't you got some homework to do*? and he flew into her arms and said, 'Mu-ma,' and you was left to feel like the lowest of the low, like something what had been left by the side of the road, and it comes back to you so clearly, so clearly –

Rat a tat tat. A knock at the door.

You rub your eyes and jump up. Undo the bolt. Sit back down. Then the bouncer, your bouncer, he pushes the door open and kneels down. Doesn't shout at you or what have you, like you expect – doesn't give you a telling-off, or chuck you out – just bunches up his face in a question as he crouches opposite you. Then he's leaning towards you – oh, shit… he's not going to, is he? – and you flinch, only to realise he's trying to pick off the loo paper from your nose.

'Oh.' You manage a light little laugh, watching the tiny bit of loo roll flutter to the floor. 'Long story.'

'Tell me about it?' he says.

'What. In here?' You let him follow your eyes around the cubicle. 'Now?'

No, he means go for a coffee, he's saying, if you can wait half an hour for him to finish; he knows some place where you can get food, cos he bets you're hungry (which goes to show how clueless he is about drugs). And that's where you find yourself an hour later, in a café with wooden benches and tables what's buzzing with people. Chatting. Kissing. Just munching away on their chips and cheese or what have you. No licence; not the kind of place you usually hang about in. And the thing is, this bouncer, he might be alright, you think, watching him as he whistles while the waitress plonks the food on the table (his food – you still ain't hungry), and rubs his hands across his thighs. But is it an act? Who knows? And anyway, you need to concentrate, cos he's going on about his job.

'Yeah, I know all about bouncers,' you say when he finishes his spiel, the sentence coming out like four-letter words.

'Oh, yeah?'

'From my job.' But, as soon as the words are out, you wish you could suck them back in.

He picks up a fork and shovels a huge chunk of, you think, chicken pie in his gob. 'Oh, yeah?' he says again, crumbs sticking to the corner of his mouth. 'What's that, then?' he says, wiping away the crumbs.

'Dancer,' you mutter.

'Sorry, didn't quite catch that...'

'Dancer,' you say.

He meets your eyes, still munching on that sodding pie. God, you wish he'd hurry up and finish it – the sight and smell of it is making you nauseous. Anyway. You know he knows what kind of dancer. You used to say *exotic dancer*, it sounded well, so... exotic, but that you can't even bring yourself to say *that*, can't let them words slither out your mouth. Just goes to show, doesn't it? How far you've come.

Or how low you've sunk. The way you couldn't say it, it makes you stop and think, and all at once you feel submerged in the shame of it. As if you was being buried alive in it. You're lying down under the filth of it, the dirt of it, barely able to breathe. And all this time, he's been sat watching you as you twist a napkin in your hands. Twisted up inside too, hating yourself for hating, for not trusting nobody for such a long time.

Then he says something what surprises you.

'Look, I know all about doing a job that disgusts you... like I've been saying.'

Your ears prick up.

He lays his fork to one side and leans back on the chair.

'Yeah, mate,' he says. (Mate? That how he sees you? Bummer!) 'I've had enough of it. Enough of little tykes like those lads thinking it was their God-given right to shove Ajax up their nostrils. Enough of the hours. Enough of working nights, standing outside in the cold or the heat, bored out of my brains, trying to look butch. But mostly I'm fed up how people look at me, fed up how they see me. Like when you flinched back at the bar when I reached out to you.' You blush. 'So, I'm off,' he says. 'Off to teach English somewhere. Go somewhere hot. Did a TEFL certificate recently.'

You look blank.

'Means I can teach English anywhere in the world. Thailand. South America. Anywhere.'

You do a little whistle through your lips at the possibility of it. All them countries out there. And, even if you don't know where they are on a map, you see in them a chance of escape. And you feel… what's that? Jealous? Yeah, jealous that you can't seem to leave London, never mind the country. And you feel another twinge and all. A twinge of disappointment that this bloke is going off somewhere.

He goes on about these plans for a bit, and then finally he asks about yours and you tell him, tell him that you'd like to go back to your A-levels, finish the history one, start an English one, retake your maths GCSE. You don't mention Connor, though, which is weird. Cos usually when you meet new people you want to tell them right away, but with him it's like you want to keep something back, just in case…

'Anyway. What's wrong with the bouncers where you work?' he says, after a bit.

Pulling your knees together tight under the chair, you make a decision. You don't know if it's the coke or all the booze or The Problems ganging up on you again, or the glint in his eye, or the need to get something off your chest, or the tiredness, the nagging and niggling tiredness what's stinging your eyes, making your muscles ache, but your decision is this: you will open your heart to this man, you will put your trust in him, take a punt. So you launch into it.

'What's wrong with them? Well, we pay this house fee, right, and they're meant to protect us, that's what the money's for supposedly, but still the customers paw you, try and touch your – er – bits through your knickers…' his turn to blush '…shit like that, and they turn a blind eye. The bouncers, I mean. They only get involved when somebody's really out of line, or you're in danger and that. And then, right, when they're not looking down on you, like most of them, there's the ones who want to rescue you, try to tell you a girl like you shouldn't be working in a place like this – '

'Can't blame them for trying,' he interrupts.

You let that go for now, continue as you were ' – as if it wasn't your decision to work there in the first place.' And you look at him, like, meaningfully, before you carry on. 'But it ain't the bouncers who are the worst of it. It's the managers. The customers. Being paid for the number of eyeballs you attract. So weird when you think about it. And then there's the other gir– ' But then you change tack. 'Oh, I don't know. It's confusing; it's, like, been OK, my job, quite liked it till – '

'So, it's not all bad, then?' he interrupts. And with them words you clam up again, zip your lips tight shut.

'Look, way I see it,' he says after a bit, 'we've got similar jobs.'

You pull a face.

'No, really. A job where people don't see past what you do. Like, if you're a policeman or nurse or what have you, people only see the uniform, but that's OK cos the uniform says "good person, a helper" – it's socially acceptable. But us: the opposite. People look at us like we're scum, don't even think there might be a heart beating inside there, a brain ticking away.'

You lay the napkin you've been twisting to one side, cos there's something about what he's saying, about his plans, his job... they've given you a flash, a hope sparked something deep down.

'Yeah, maaay-beee,' you say.

'No *maybe* about it,' he says. 'I think about it a lot.'

Oh, come on, like you don't think about it and all. Only it's like, you can't put it into words as easily as what he's done. You pick up the napkin again, begin to shred it into pieces in a distracted way. You've have had enough of this conversation, of this man you can't quite figure out. Like, what's his angle? There's always an angle. A catch. A black curtain of tiredness drops behind your eyes. You try and

191

remember how much sleep you've had in the last couple of days – four, eight, maybe ten hours? – and, scraping the chair across the floor as you half rise out your seat, you say, 'Sorry. Thanks for the coffee and that, but I'm off.'

He looks like you've just let the air out of his tyres. 'Oh, right, OK.'

You see him grabbing your wrists, wedging the café door closed with a boot to stop your exit, using his strength to get the better of you, and you cower back a little, saying, as offhand as possible, 'I'm just really tired – been a very long day.'

'OK, that's cool.' Then, he says in hushed voice, not meeting your eyes. 'Can I have your number, though? I'd like to see you again.'

You get a 'yes' out quick before you can change your mind, sinking back into your seat. And after he's reached into his pocket for his phone and you've given him the digits he says, 'What's your name, anyway?'

It comes out like the truth. 'Layla.'

'Oh, like the song,' he says.

And you regret it right away. 'Sorry, no. Hayleigh,' you say. 'Force of habit.'

'Well, Hayleigh, I'll get you a cab home and we'll speak soon, yeah? And you can tell me the long story.'

'Eh?'

'Why you had that piece of bog roll on the end of your nose.'

Your eyes meet and a melty, fuzzy feeling hits you, the words *love at first sight* filling your head. *Don't be silly, Hayleigh*, you tell yourself. *Calm down, love!* But as he walks you to the nearest minicab place, by your side, not too close but closer than mates, you can't help it: an unfamiliar warmth is spreading over your body, head to toe. Only it's mixed with a weepiness too, right, cos you're close to bawling your eyes out, your mind on one track: dreaming of Ayesha's sofa-bed.

And, as you skip to the front of the queue (he's mates with the minicab people) and throw yourself into the cab, he makes a hand gesture for you to wind down the window, mouthing, 'I'll call you.'

You nod, thinking you might like this gentle giant giving you a ring. And, giving the driver Ayesha's address, you let yourself be swallowed up in the comfort of the back seat... close your eyes... drift in and out of sleep while the cab stops and starts as it weaves its way across East London, endless questions stampeding across your mind.

Could he be nice? Could he be OK?

Could you not be gay, after all?

Could he be the –

You wake up with a start, thrown forward on your seat, the seatbelt digging into your boobs, into your neck, and all.

'Sorry, love,' the driver says, and as you give him evils through his rear-view mirror he drives off again, leaving you with no idea why he stopped so suddenly.

You rub your eyes, so dry, so itchy. God, why did you have to go and wake up? You could have done with a few more minutes' kip... hours... days, in fact! You huff and puff to yourself for a minute, then remember your bouncer – never did ask his name – and it's like a switch has been flicked while you slept.

Who cares if he calls? With your luck he'll be just the same as the others, fit into a box like the rest of the blokes you've met since coming up to London: the knight in shining armour; the too-cool-for-school trendy; the bit of rough. The driver pulls up at a set of traffic lights, another cab revs up alongside yours – a black London one – and you peer in its back window, goggling at two lovebirds necking in the back. The sight makes you want to bang on the window, to scream, to shout! Yeah, and just why did he take you for a coffee anyway? You was in a right mess. All that Prince Charming stuff – load of baloney, weren't it? And as the cab sits in traffic, petrol fumes and the smell of a pine car-freshener start making you feel sick. You wind down the window a tad. Yeah, and if he hadn't liked the way you looked, if he hadn't had a good lech at your body earlier in the bar, would he have helped you?

A wave of disappointment tears through you. It was Layla he liked the look of, not Hayleigh. No wonder that was the name you gave him when asked, the name what first sprang to mind.

And then, you think, only too well aware of the letter, as if it was a barrel of rocks in your handbag, there's Michael to consider. Like, you can't exactly shag around if he's going to be back in the picture.

For a minute your mind freezes – *what to do? what to do?* – and you glance out the window to see how far you've come. OK, Hackney Central – not far to Ayesha's now. Then, you think about it, how far you've come, but with a different meaning in mind. Not far, eh? Letting a bloke have your number! Like he'd be any use to you, if he even calls, that is. You check your phone…

What the – ? Eight missed calls.

From him?

No, of course not.

And that convinces you. Time to go it alone. No Billy, no Jeremy. No guilt trip texts from Michael. No men with no name. Time to take control. You wind the window down more, the quiet of the early morning city streets humming through the gap, and with a flick of your wrist eject the mobile from the car, listening with satisfaction as it clatters and shatters on the pavement outside.

'Easy!' the taxi driver says, looking back at you. 'Those things are expensive.' Shaking his head.

You nod. You smile.

8 MISSED CALLS
2 VOICEMAILS
INBOX: 1 new message

FROM: BILLY
SENT: Wednesday 6 June, 23.54

Not funny Hayleigh.
Answer why don't you?!

Thursday

15

Victoria Park. You're sitting on a bench, your face tilted up towards the sun, a slave to the thought of sleep now. You picture yourself lying across it, the bench, feet dangling from its metal edge, listening to the leaves in the hedge behind you rustle in the wind, letting the kids' squeals and shouts from the play park opposite soothe you to sleep. But you daren't. Daren't fall asleep in case somebody nicks the rucksack, steals the money, taking with it what little hope you've got left. You feel like all eyes are on it – the tramp who shuffles past, his shoes flap-flapping on the stone path, the sole of one shoe always one step behind him; the dog walker who's being pulled along by a pack of yapping dogs; the group of well fit black lads, jostling and dissing each other... all of them eyeing up the rucksack. You start fretting that any minute now any one of them, even the tramp, could get the better of you, grab the rucksack and run off with it. They wouldn't even need to hit you or nothing. You've got nothing left... no energy. No fight.

Cos of Ayesha.

So you turned up at her flat this morning, right, after a dressing-down from the minicab driver for vomiting out the window, about six-thirty am. And Ayesha, yeah, she's cold, barely speaking to you, so you lay on the sofa, had a short zizz, then woke up and switched on the TV, cringing over an episode of Jeremy Kyle. Didn't stop you wondering what the results of the DNA test would be after the ad break, though. Anyway, at the same time as having one eye on the screen, you was also trying to figure out Ayesha's beef when this lah-di-dah bloke comes in her front room, floppy hair, joint in hand, a Hugh Grant soundalike, and she's all, like, in a whiny voice, telling you that she's changed her mind about you staying – that, like, she's really sorry, but you can have a shower and a sleep and then, if you don't mind terribly (*terribly?* – that was for his benefit, surely), could you find somewhere else to stay this evening?

And you were like, *Yeah, sure, of course.*

Too tired to argue.

But when they went out for some breakfast you tossed and turned on the sofa, the discomfort from the waxing keeping you awake, sleep being a sort of like faraway place you'd once visited but you couldn't remember how to get there, its landscape or its climate. And you were angry, and all. An anger what blinded you to everything else, keeping your heart rate up, making your brain pulse with negative thoughts. Like, Ayesha, how could she? Telling you in a soft voice when Andrew left the room that he's *the one* (giving new meaning to the word *one*), that she's really sorry (like fun she is) but that he's a keeper. Like, she knows your situation, your whatchamacallit? – predicament. And so, yeah, you didn't sleep any more, and left before they got back. Couldn't stand the thought of having to look her in the eye. Did manage to stick two fingers up at her, though, by swiping the last of her coke what you found on a coffee table in the lounge.

Never did find out if Bradie was the father of Karen's twins.

If you're honest, though, you're not all out of juice, out of energy, just because of Ayesha. It's cos of everything. The job, the baby, Michael, the drugs, the termination. Worrying about missing that stupid meeting with Billy and The Bloke. All them reasons are why you're sitting here alone.

You pull your knees up to your chest, your trainers resting on the bench, and turn your head away from a group of old codgers passing by. All your thoughts, your actions, your worries, they're dragging you down now, down down down into a deep trough of loneliness. Till you're stuck there, caked in it, encrusted in it, and it's shut down all of your senses: you're glassy-eyed, not seeing; cloth-eared, not hearing. Everything is silent, grey, even if all around you is hubbub and colour and light – if that makes sense?

It's the same in the club. You see that now. When you first started you felt like one of the girls, like you fitted in. But soon something wasn't right, something you couldn't put your finger on. Now you recognise what it was. It was loneliness trampling over you, crushing you, making you small. Yeah, it was like, in spite of all the colour, the energy, in spite of all them people scampering around you, and the constant hum of conversation, of bickering, of laughter in the changing room, with each splash of colour, with each buzz of gossip you was getting lonelier, feeling yourself fade, drift away. Till Tuesday night, yeah, when you, like, overstepped the mark, and now you're sat here, invisible, not loved by anyone, a ghost.

You mull all this over on your bench, trying to feel part of the wide open space of the park in front of you, trying to stop being so tiny and insignificant, and while the sun still shines and puts a warm glow on your cheeks you reckon there might still be some hope. Only not long after, the sun disappears behind a cloud, and any promise of a brighter future is stolen away. Cloudier today, not as humid as the past week. In fact, you're shivering: it's come over a bit cold. Or maybe it's Ayesha's unfriendliness, the chilliness of her sending you away with a flea in your ear, with an 'I'll call you later', what's cooling your blood. Just goes to show how little she listens, being as you told her you'd lost your phone.

A rumble in your tummy then, a diversion from Ayesha's treachery. Maybe go to the caff in the park, have some brekkie? But you hate to eat in public. Can't face speaking with the waitress, the other customers. It's like, the lonelier you feel, the less you can face other people. Strangers. It's like, odd, right, cos being around other people should make you feel better, shouldn't it? Only it's the opposite: thinking of even one single encounter, well, it's the pits, the end.

Instead you try and gee yourself up by sitting up straighter on the bench, dropping your feet to the ground, crushing your trainers into the stone path for support. But somehow, looking down at that stone, a glass bottle smashed a foot away, a cluster of cigarette butts by your feet, doesn't provide the inspiration you're after.

Make a decision. Go somewhere! Anywhere!

But where? Where is there for you? You think of the bouncer and his plans. Maybe you should head for the airport. Can you get a passport in one day? You think of ancient ruins, of tropical beaches, of coconuts and bananas, tree-climbing monkeys and caw-cawing parrots – of worlds you've never seen. But no, of course you can't go abroad. How could you? Being a mum, well, it's like wearing handcuffs, ain't it, even if you can't be there for him? In person, you mean.

Look, can you just say something? Just cos you ain't with Connor doesn't mean you don't feel it – that tug, that bond with him. All it takes is to think of him, or to look at his photo, and you can smell his porridgey baby smell, feel the touch of his sometimes soft, sometimes rough pudgy skin. Yeah, it's an invisible thread what ties you to him, without even being in the same room. Or even the same city. Jesus Christ! How did your life go so wrong? How did you end up – you start sobbing – so alone, when you have so much love for someone, for your Little Man?

You stumble forward as you try to lug the rucksack on to your back. Damn, it's heavy. Sod it. All them work clothes what you packed, spares what don't fit in the locker at the club – do you even need them any more? God knows. Elegance seems a million miles away now, Tuesday night's disaster making the club shift from being a part of your everyday life to a memory what trails behind you, leaving an imprint in your mind like the horrors of a bad dream. You stagger, what with the back-breaking bulk of the rucksack, and walk a little further into the park, past the war memorial, and it hits you in waves.

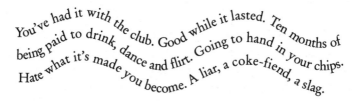

You've had it with the club. Good while it lasted. Ten months of being paid to drink, dance and flirt. Going to hand in your chips. Hate what it's made you become. A liar, a coke-fiend, a slag.

And then your thoughts become clearer, more straight-lined again.

Cos… to think!

To think that, when Jez auditioned you, you felt lucky – lucky to be picked out from the six girls dancing full-frontal naked for him that day. And you think back to:

pacing up and down beforehand in the changing room

lips bleeding from sunken teeth

fingers trembling, stomach churning… shame-faced in your nakedness

crippled by nerves.

But even so, yes, you felt lucky, cos being picked meant that you was the prettiest, right? – the sexiest, even though you hardly knew what sexy meant back then. Soon had to learn, though, didn't you? How to be sexy… what men like…

Like letting them get one over on you, letting them think that they're smarter, more in control. Nothing they find sexier than that. Except maybe using foul words against you, telling you the twisted, sick fantasies they wouldn't dream of telling their girlfriends or wives. The simple act of opening their wallets making them think they own you, can possess you, humiliate you.

Call that lucky? you think, heat rising in your cheeks.

Lucky? you think, spying a rubbish bin out of the corner of your eye.

Lucky? you think, tears rolling in giant drops down your cheeks as you head towards the bin.

As if!

And carefully, undoing the padlock and zipping open a small gap at the top of the rucksack, you fish out some of the clothes what are poking out of the gap: camisoles, expensive silk and cheap polyester – now surplus to requirements. Red lacy thongs, silky orange French knickers, a blue peephole bra, flimsy see-through panties; a rainbow of lingerie appearing from the bag like a never-ending stream of hankies out of a magician's sleeve. And you laugh, wiping tears and snot from your face as you pull them out, your movements becoming more frantic, your eyes wild and excited and all. And then, with a final magician's flourish, you stuff the revolting clothes in the bin through a small space on top of a fish and chip wrapper. *Abracadabra!* The velvet evening gown what you wore for your audition misses the slot and slips to ground. *Alakazam!* A leopard-print bra – rubbish! Pants, a suspender belt, stockings! All rubbish! You don't care if anybody walks past, sees what's wagging in your hands and now spilling out of the top of the bin. You'd tell them. It's rubbish, all rubbish!

And it's like you're on a high! Buzzing! Reeling! Chucking this stuff away, it's setting you free; it's a whatchamacallit? – a revelation, a release, the loneliness of earlier being wiped out by a kind of ecstasy, a rush. And, filled with a new kind of freedom, a giddiness, a spinning in your head, you put the rucksack on your back again, your mouth breaking out in a toothy grin as you fasten the waistbelt around your middle.

Making light little taps on the ground now, you scamper away from the bin, your mind reeling, and you set out for... you don't know quite where yet, but you don't care. You're lost in nature, in the sounds of the bees buzzing near the plant life, in the soft summer wind fluttering past your ears. You reach out and touch a tree, hum a tune as your fingers brush its gnarly old bark. You're happy, free. And your load – well, that's lightened now, in both ways, now that you've made your decision.

But somehow decision-making also makes your eyelids droop, your eyes sting. The rush, for what it was worth, is on a low ebb now, quietening down... Good while it lasted.

But now, a zizz.

You must sleep.

Your strides become weary and long and you drag yourself further into the park, eventually finding a grassy area filled with people. You settle for a patch near a group of mums and their buggies. Safety in numbers, right? And then you lie down together with the rucksack, rolling over onto your side, hugging your legs into the bag and then shifting about to stop the chafing down below. Then the worries return. Like, nobody's going to steal the rucksack, are they? They'd have to steal you with it. And slowly, thinking of Connor, of his chuckle, his babbling, his chubby legs, you drift off...

A little later you wake up. Your arms are aching from gripping the rucksack, so you must have been asleep a while. Your tongue is dry. Your eyes are dry. But everything else is wet. Your back's covered in sweat. And it hits you, sledgehammer-hard, now you've had a zizz. What a mess you're in. Like, a week ago you had a home, even if it was sharing with those cows. You had a job, even if it was – you gulp, hard – sex work, dressed as something else in a veil of glamour and glitter. You had hope. Now. Nothing.

No home.

No mobile.

No Connor.

No clue.

No clue what to do. Like, should you go and meet Billy after all, lie about when you thought you was meeting? A storm of leaves is whipped up in a gust of wind and you watch them dancing across the grass. A black labrador runs around its owner, its red leather lead bouncing off the dusty park ground, what's cracking from the dry heat of the last few days. A ball rolls towards you from the group of mums and toddlers, who are sitting in a circle a few metres away, and you pick it up, roll it back. Time stands still.

Two pigeons peck the ground next to you, making a dust cloud, and you think of Connor and your pigeon game, and of your pet pigeon and all. You feel sorry for pigeons. People think they're dirty. But it's like the bouncer said, about your job: people don't see what's inside with some things, with some people – animals too. You reach out to stroke one of the pigeons, the big browny-grey one, only to jerk your hand away as it pecks nearer. Just as afraid of the disease and of the different, of appearances, after all, aren't you? Hypocrite!

You close your eyes and not much else happens for a bit, till, opening them, you notice that the park seems busier, noisier, kids everywhere. You spot a loved-up young couple walking past, giggling, and you stop them with a wave.

'Excuse me, got the time, please?'

'Quarter to four,' the woman says, smiling at you, and they walk off, linking arms, carrying on the laughter from before. Quarter to four. Just after school finishing time.

Then somehow, as if planted in your brain by a friendly spirit, it comes to you. How could you have been so dumb? Ivana. You can stay with Ivana. She said it only took her half an hour to get here on Tuesday, door to door. And before this thought has even reached its conclusion you've leapt up, dusted the specks of grass and dirt off your jeans, scanning the park with eager eyes for the nearest way out.

11 MISSED CALLS
4 VOICEMAILS
INBOX: 4 new messages

FROM: BILLY
SENT: Thursday 7 June, 11.21

*So, where are u???? We're
waiting 4 u here.*

FROM: BILLY
SENT: Thursday 7 June, 12.34

*U blew it, I'm coming 4 u.
Better watch out.*

FROM: ELEGANCE
SENT: Thursday 7 June, 15.35

*Left you 2 messages. Call me.
Jeremy.*

16

You take a breather outside a fruit and veg shop, shifting your weight from one trainer to the other cos of the pain from the corns and the blisters. In fact, name a foot problem, you've got it – a nice little leaving present from the club. For a couple of minutes you stand squinting at a number of vegetables you couldn't name if your life depended on it. Fruits, and all. Spiky purple ones. Ones with red bumps what look like they've been infected with something. Tasty-looking ones too, to be fair. Shiny red apples, juicy ripe peaches and your favourite, huge plump watermelons. You imagine taking a bite, the juices running down your chin... If only you could stomach food these days. Haven't eaten for – what is it? Twenty-four hours?

You look left, right, down the street. Green Lanes. Didn't take long to get here on the train. Standing room only, though, the journey spent in a stressed-out flap, each part of your body giving your nerves away: fingers gripping the straps of the rucksack, ponytail sticking to the back of your neck, eyes shifting to the floor every time someone dodgy-looking got on, head banging with worries – oh, the non-stop worries, of being homeless, of Connor, of Michael, of work, of Billy, pulsing through you. And then you was pitched forward by the crowds leaving the train, up the tunnel and out of the station, propelled onto Green Lanes into a swarm of traffic noises, the first of the rush-hour workers on their way home, the shoppers in a hurry, and afterwards into a street full of foreign-looking shops: African beauty shops, kebab takeaways, halal butchers; all sorts of food for sale, delicious-smelling breads knotted into strange shapes, foul-looking red, pink and brown meats. You study them, the shops, cos you know that Ivana lives above one. Pity you can't remember which sort.

Thirty minutes of traipsing up and down the street and finally you come to it. Of course. How could you forget? A nail bar. Striped, polka dot, Union Jacks – all kinds of acrylic nails in the window, a flashing neon sign promising 'NAILS AND TANNING'. Ivana's mentioned how useful it is having the nail bar there; she can get her nails done while the kids watch telly upstairs.

You yawn. How tired, how done in you are. But, if Ivana's home, everything'll be OK. Cos it's your last chance, yeah, before turning up at Billy's? And that – you shudder – is a last resort.

Open curtains and the sound of a TV blaring from a window above the shop give you hope, give you the oomph to cautiously step into a corridor at the side of the nail salon through a small metal-framed door. You take the steps leading up to the flat two at a time, *please be home, please be home* a little poem running through your head.

You reach the door of the flat – *please be home, please be home* – read the name MIELKUS by the bell – *in the right place, thank goodness* – and ring the doorbell, hear it buzz distantly.

Ivana's down to work nights this week, so she should still be home.

But there are no footsteps. Nothing.

Please! Please be home.

Another minute's wait with your heart groaning in disappointment, and then you lean on the bell again, a worry monster gnashing its teeth, ripping up all hope with its claws, coming for you. *Please be home, please be home.* You think of the money in the rucksack and of a hotel, but you've never stayed in a hotel, let alone on your own. Do they take cash? Which one to choose?

But that thought's put on hold cos – hooray! – Ivana's opened the door, just a crack, and you catch the surprise and – pleasure? – yes, pleasure! – in her face when she sees that it's you. She swings the door wide open, gives you a hug.

'Hayleigh, so lovely to see you.'

You dither in the doorway, feeling small in its frame.

'I came to say goodbye, and ask if… if…' But you hold it in, uncertainty getting the better of you. 'If I could stay here a day or two. Sorry, I'd've called first but I, er, lost my mobile.'

And she's ushering you in, 'Of course, darling, of course,' helping you over the threshold of the flat, walking in front of you, kicking an explosion of toys and shoes out of the way, pushing her hair off her face, saying, 'Sorry, sorry for the messes.'

She looks pretty without her warpaint on. Lovely, she is. A face what lights up as she says, 'Come in, come in.'

In the living room, CBeebies is on the TV, Tomas with his lively face and brown kiss-curls toddling about in front of it, one finger pointed in the air as he dances an unrhythmic dance along to the theme tune of *Tweenies*. When he spots you he races over and jumps in your arms for a hug. And then Ivana, right, she's speaking in her own language to him and Ona, who you didn't see at first, who's sitting on a sofa, cuddling an ugly plastic doll. When she stops speaking, the children squeal with delight.

You cock your head towards Ivana.

'I told them they could keep watching television while we speak.' She rubs her temples. 'Lovely you here actually, they did my head up today.'

You follow her down a corridor decorated with children's drawings, family snaps, your heart sinking at each step. Should you have come here? Being around kids again after Tuesday in the park – well, it's just another kick in the teeth, another reminder that you're apart from him, ain't it?

'Marko in?' you say, anxious to know if her husband's home, taking off the rucksack from your sweat-soaked back, resting it on the kitchen floor, your stomach growling at cooking smells in the air. You've never met Marko, and, though Ivana has told you nice things, is dead keen on him in fact, you're not in the mood to now.

'Work, darling. Late. And I was meaning to work in club tonight. I think he work longer on purpose so I can't go in; I had to call in sick.'

'But I thought Marko didn't mind you working at Elegance.'

Ivana picks at a silver acrylic nail. 'He don't mind? Well. Sure. He's – you know, political, Marko. He says a woman can do what she wish with her body. I tell him to leave it off. I don't care whether he agrees; I know I can do as I wish. Anyway, I like my work. I know things have got bad in club, but I know where to stop, how far to – '

You return her gaze, sheepishly.

'Oh,' she says, 'sorry.'

So rumours are going round the club already, are they? Not them made-up rumours from before – ones about that guy on Tuesday night, you mean…

'Look, it don't matter. I don't care what the girls are saying about me,' you say. 'I've decided to quit, anyway.'

'Quit?'

Oh, right, you forgot her English ain't perfect. 'Leave. I've had enough.'

Her face scrunches up, not so pretty now. 'But…' And she fidgets, shifts about on her chair.

'What?' you ask.

'You say *quit*, but I thought you...'

Your forehead crinkles in a frown.

'What? You thought what?'

'Well, I was in work last night and Jez call a meeting, say he sacking you because of... you know.' She looks away. 'I thought that was why you here.'

You lean back on your chair. Flick at a bit of lint on your hooded top. Think of the mobile phone what you chucked out of the taxi, the calls you must have missed. Sacked, eh?

The kitchen suddenly feels stuffy, airless. You grip the chair, fight for breath, wonder if you remembered to pack your inhaler. Was it, like, in the bathroom cupboard at the flat? Did you remember to clear that out? But who cares? It's not asthma what's making your chest tight, your head spin, is it? To think! To think you'd decided to tell Jeremy where to stick his rotten job anyway. But him, sack you first? The bloody cheek of it! The – and you flush, head to toe now – the bloody nerve of it! Tears well up in your eyes. Before you had a chance to say your piece, to tell him what you think of his stinking club, of his playing favourites; what you think of his sodding *bottom line*. Him and his double standards. One rule for you, one for the Essex girl slags! Unbelievable!

You try and compose yourself, meet Ivana's eyes.

'Sorry,' she says, for like the millionth time since you arrived, coming around the big wooden table to kneel down in front of you, placing one hand on your knee. 'Sorry. I thought you go to the club today, this why you come.'

'No, no,' you say, a distance in your voice. 'I – well... I got chucked out my flat. Lost my phone... Got a dodgy wax...' Your eyes flit over the kitchen counter, what's scattered with piles of colourful chopped and unchopped vegetables, and you can't help feeling a spare part... in the way. 'Look,' you say, 'I'll go.'

213

She follows your eyes and says, 'No, no. I make dinner. You join us.'

'Well, I, uh…'

'Not a question. You have bath, then you join us. Then we talk more when the childrens sleep.'

A tiresome dragging in your heart and the pounding of a thousand drums in your head stop you from putting up any kind of a fight. So you just say, 'Lovely, thanks, babe. Can I borrow a towel, please?'

Within minutes you're in the bathroom, hunting for a tammie in the cupboards. Your period's nearly over, the flow light, but you need something all the same. Then you remember that Ivana has a coil, she don't get periods, so you decide that you can make do with a bit of bog roll stuffed in your knickers after the bath. And then you're easing yourself into the bath, relishing the heat, the bubbles and the softness on your skin. But it's weird. No matter how much you scrub with Ivana's loofah, you still feel filthy, stinking, not right. Like, when did you last have a proper wash? You think back to Friday, to your last bath, when you read Mum's letter, and Michael's. And you turn both letters over again in your mind, turn over thoughts of Mum, of Connor, of Michael, of the last few days in the club. But somehow this makes you feel dirtier, filthier, and so you scrub harder, a soapy scum forming on top of the bath, till at last your skin is pink-sore and gleaming, and you put the loofah to one side.

You close your eyes. You relax.

You don't know how much time has passed when you walk back into the kitchen in Ivana's bathrobe, with a towel wrapped around your head. And there's Ivana at the kitchen table, reading the children a story.

'*Oh, help! Oh, no!*' she says, her accent thick.

'*It's a Gruffalo,*' the children reply, in perfect English.

A stab of jealousy shocks you. If only it was you... you and Connor, you're thinking, guiltily, and Ivana catches you staring, pats a chair next to the little girl.

'Come, sit down,' she says, and you do, Tomas smiling, Ona hunched over a piece of paper, not even looking at you, and you think maybe she's got no manners, till moments later when she hands you a drawing.

'Look!' she says, beaming. 'Cat!'

'Oh,' you laugh, 'that's lovely, Ona. Show Mummy.'

And Ivana's all, like, busy then, getting them to clear away crayons and books and placing a salad drenched in mayo before you on the table, vegetable rissoles on the side, encouraging the kids to eat, zooming aeroplanes into her son's mouth, her voice rising sometimes in her language, and even you manage some dinner, then offer to do the washing-up while Ivana bathes her kids, squeals of delight floating out of the bathroom, followed by crying and shouting. You've just had a chance to start on the drying-up when she walks back in the room. It's like she's aged ten years.

You wipe up a final cup then wipe your hands on a tea towel, saying, 'No wonder you don't want to leave the club for the kids' bedtimes sometimes.'

'Yes,' she says, laughing. 'Yes. When Marko can do it, do the kids' baths, I'm happy. Anyway,' she says, 'they should sleep now. Let's drink.'

You put down the tea towel, gladly – you hate doing chores – and follow Ivana into the living room. It's a small room, but homely. Posters on the walls. The TV still on in the background. Loads of books on the shelves. And, oh! – you spy the little toy chihuahua. She must have brought it home when she found out you'd been given the boot.

'Sit down,' Ivana says, and she waves a hand at the sofa, placing a tray with wine and two glasses on a little coffee table. You watch in silence as she pours out two large glasses, your body screaming for a drink. 'So, you think you'll speak to Jeremy, try and get back in?' she asks, taking a big sip.

'Oh, I dunno, I doubt it,' you reply. 'I wanted to leave anyway, like I said. And how about you? Can you stand it any more? Like, it's hard to say while we're in the club with all the earwigging, but ain't you had enough too?'

'Ah, it's OK. I enjoy the people.' She flicks the remote, stops at one of the soaps, asks if you want to watch that, and you nod. 'Well, the old girls, not the new. But I do like it, even if it make things difficult for me and Marko. He get over it when I've saved enough to buy us new home in Kaunas, start our business too. Then I stop.'

'Oh, right. So he isn't OK with it?'

'Well, sometimes. But husbands, they are like cars. You work on them, put stuff in to make them run smooth. You know,' she says, her eyes sparkling, 'like good food, like sex. The marriage it break down all the time, but you don't have to sell it, buy a new car. You see?'

'Er, yes, I think so.' You'll miss Ivana and her random bollocks.

'So you leave the club, then, so what now?' A pause, then, 'You go back?'

How many more times? 'Definitely not. Maybe just the once, to talk to Jeremy, see what's what.'

She puts her hand on your knee.

'Darling,' she says softly, 'I mean go back home.'

You bristle. 'No… no… I can't…' And you stand up, thinking you might have to make your escape. Like, she's getting too near… too close to what you can't face up to.

And she shoves you back down onto the sofa, stronger than what she looks.

'Why you so scared?'

You turn away, eyes drawn to the TV's white-blue light. A lorry goes past and the whole room shakes.

216

She looks at you and shrugs. 'Cheap rent.'

You smile, but the way you're twisting the stem of your glass in both hands shows the real truth: the edginess, the nervousness what's churning up your insides. Still fake-smiling, you take a big glug of wine and she does the same, refilling both your glasses as soon as you're dry. Then for a while you both focus on the TV. And after another ad break, another glass of wine, you finally feel like going there, opening that can of worms. Like ripping open the can, in fact, digging them worms out with your bare fingers. Telling her why you feel you can't return home... about Mum, about all the arguments.

'But darling, it's still not clear,' she says, 'why you can't go back.'

It's no good – you can't sit still. You get up, walk over to the window. It's not dark yet but the street below is bright with neon signs, the smell of kebab meat drifting up to the flat from the rotating spits, what are spinning around and around. You lean your bum on the window ledge.

'I don't have enough money.' *Still fighting it, Hayleigh, still fighting the truth.* 'Haven't saved enough to get Connor back.'

'Nesamone,' she says, or something.

'Eh?' you say. You can't hear her over the TV and the street noise.

'You do have the money – you do. Why do you lie? Why you not say why she chuck you out?'

You turn your face away from her gaze. Don't dare fess up to her that she's right. Cos, what difference does it make? Five grand? Ten grand? Fifty grand? Even a million would be no guarantee you'd get him back. Even a million wouldn't balance out the emotional price you'd have to pay to earn it. You wish you could tell her this, wish you could also say, *I'm scared, I ain't got the bottle to face up to Mum, cos I know she was right in a way.* You want to tell her, *I'm a coward, that's why I won't tell you what happened, don't want you to think badly of me.*

But, phew, you're saved, cos Ivana's getting up, brushing down her skirt, giving you a look.

'I go get more wine from shop,' she says, 'You listen out for childrens?'

You nod.

'Back soon.'

With a grunt you acknowledge this, walk away from the window and flop back onto the sofa. You haven't come here for a talking-to. What's she doing, poking her nose in? You put the wine glass on the coffee table with a clunk, wring your hands together. And you can't help it. No matter how much you want to bury it, the real reason you fear going home, images of that terrible afternoon when Connor got sick creep into your mind...

... his little body, pale and bluish in his cot... choking out hot, stilted breaths... his skin cold and clammy, his hair damp when you placed a hand to his head... green paramedic uniforms, raised voices; Mum screaming... you calm, alert, eyes wide open... And then... being pushed out the way of the cot by the paramedics... fighting with Mum over who should travel with him in the ambulance... the alien world of intensive care, Connor lying there, octopus-like, all them tubes coming out his body. And then, the diagnosis from the consultant: septic shock, septicemia aggravated by the heat in your bedroom.

And, when he finally got out of hospital, how the blame game cut in. Jabbed. Stabbed. Cut into your and Mum's relationship. Only weeks later, Mum chucked you out, blaming you for his illness. But it wasn't your fault. It was Mum's!

'Hayleigh?'

218

You lift up your head to see Ivana looming over you, another wine bottle in her hand. And you realise you've been crying, tears pouring down your cheeks, snot dribbling out of your nose. You wipe it all away with the sleeve of the bathrobe, catch Ivana looking, say, 'Sorry,' as she hands you a tissue and you blow your nose with an embarrassing honk.

She opens the new bottle, not saying nothing. Hands you your glass. Sits down. Looks at you.

'Come on, Hayleigh, you must tell.'

But where to begin? You look at a poster for an exhibition on the wall. 'Outsider Art' in Berlin, whatever that is. You take a breath. And you begin, trying to tell it from an outsider's point of view, to describe it in simple terms. No feeling, no emotion. No talk of blue skin and rapid breathing and sweat pouring from his head and favourite teddies left behind in the ambulance (another one Mum blamed you for). No talk of wet knickers from the shock, of puking in the ambulance from the comedown, or of the guilt, or of the mind-blowing, heartbreaking shame that he got sick in the first place.

'But then she is wrong, she should not have Connor,' Ivana says when you've said your piece. 'You must go back for him.'

You can't look her in the eye.

'Look,' you say, 'that's not all.' You suck up another huge glug of wine. Dig your knees into the sofa edge. 'If I hadn't been out clubbing the night before he got sick, Mum would have forgiven me.'

'Well, OK. Clubbing. Not so bad?'

You shake your head. She's wrong. It was so bad. And you dredge it back up, the sodden, filthy shame of it... The night out. You'd felt like you were owed one, see? You hadn't been out in the ten months since the baby was born and you were gagging for a dance. But you'd been so tired that evening, what with college and looking after Connor, that you'd dipped into some whizz, a gramme, maybe two… dancing on the podium, you and Michael, letting your hair down for once.

You tell Ivana this. 'And the next day, well, I was on a comedown, right, from the speed? Didn't get back till seven am, and that's when I found Mum on the sofa with him. He hadn't eaten all evening, had been up all night with a fever, his breath was all funny and fast. And she was going mental at me for that, saying I should have been there. Only soon – ' you drop your eyes to the floor, hoping the shame you're feeling won't be too obvious ' – she got off that subject cos there was no hiding that my pupils were popping out my head; she sussed what I'd been up to. And Oh My God the row what followed. In front of him! In front of the baby! Mum went through my bag, found a little plastic wallet with two more wraps in.' You cringe at the memory, look up at Ivana who's nodding, and you're like, 'Then she threatened to call Social Services! And so – ' you blush at the memory ' – I slapped her in the face. I was, like, so angry and worried…'

'But I still don't understand why she blamed you?'

'Well, like, after a while I had to beg her to let me have a zizz. And I slept through Connor's lunchtime. So it was Mum who put him down for his afternoon nap. Put him down overdressed in that bloody hot room, when he had a fever, that's what made him so poorly in the end. And she had to go out and I was meant to check on him, yeah, two hours later? But I went back to sleep, so he was in there for hours, getting hotter and hotter and hotter, and it was only when Mum got back from the shops and yelled at me to check on him…'

You trail off. Cos how could anyone, anyone, describe *this*?

And you see now, that this blaming – blaming Mum for what happened – it's not getting you anywhere. Like blaming Mum for bathing Connor each night, blaming Mum for being the one to whizz up his apples and pears in the blender, blaming her for bonding with him more than what you did.

Blaming her for letting him – your mind freezes; you can barely even think of the words – nearly die.

You recognise now that this blame game is pointless. And that it was you. Who could have been stronger. Who could have put your foot down. Could have begged Mum not to chuck you out, begged her to let you stay.

Still, even if you no longer blame Mum, can you be sure that she'll no longer blame you – that you can no longer blame yourself?

'Look, Ivana,' you say, cos she's just sitting there expressionless – you wish you could read her mind – 'can I just say something? I know it sounds like I'm the wicked witch. But it was my eighteenth that week. And there'd been no cake, no nothing from Mum.' You draw in your breath, pick at your fingernails. 'So, like, that night we went out, it was the first time I'd been out since Connor was born.'

But *damn it damn it damn it,* you think, stuck some place between acceptance and agitation now. If only you hadn't gone out! If only Michael hadn't persuaded you to go to the after-party. If only Mum had called the doctor as soon as he got sick! But no. Again, don't blame Michael, don't blame Mum. You should have told him to let you make your own decisions; *you* should have called the doctor! If you hadn't been on such a slit-your-wrists comedown from the drugs, you would have done and all.

Sobbing, you rock back and forth on the edge of the sofa, not bothering to stop when you sense Ivana right next to you.

'Alright, you don't need to say it,' you tell her, 'I'm a crap mum, the worst,' and then, between sobs, 'I don't deserve him.'

She puts her arms around you, gives you a squeeze. 'No, you're wrong,' she says, rubbing your arm. 'How old is he now, your little boy?'

You wipe your nose again with the sleeve of the bath robe, and say, 'Sorry, sorry. He's nearly two. Two in October.'

And you know what she's thinking. Guilt flickers across her face. A bit younger than her Tomas. She edges closer to you, puts her hands together on her lap.

'Hayleigh…' she begins – and she talks to you in a soothing voice, and you drink them in, the comforting, calming, kind words what she's saying, words you've wanted to hear for months.

An hour later you lie on the sofa, half covered by a duvet, bathed in an alcohol sweat, looking up at the ceiling. It has a pattern, waves and lines what you follow back and forth with your eyes. You know Ivana's right. Home. It's been on your mind for weeks now. The lap dancing. That porn stuff, the audition. My God, what were you thinking? It was a diversion from the right track.

And all this blaming has been a diversion and all. A diversion from the fact – and you brace yourself at the honesty of it – that you were relieved to get away from the responsibility of looking after Connor. From the shame of being a teenage mum, of being on benefits. My God, the relief you'd felt getting on that first train up to London! Like you was breathing out for the first time since he'd been born. Not holding your breath at the heaviness of every moment of caring for him, of making sure he was happy, well-fed and warm, of proving that you was a good mum, not just some teenage slut.

But you're ready now.

Ready to look after him again.

Ready to hold your breath, even if you don't exhale one single little puff till he's all grown up, leaving home at eighteen.

And you roll over, turning your face in towards the sofa, trying not to breathe in the unfamiliar smell, a homesick-making kind of smell, and though you toss and turn, your head spinning from the wine, you can feel it coming, you're looking forward to it – a full night of guilt- and anger-free sleep, the first proper sleep you'll have had in three days.

12 MISSED CALLS
4 VOICEMAILS
INBOX: 6 new messages

FROM: CATHLEEN
SENT: Thursday 7 June, 17.33

*Not going to dignify your
pathetic moonlight flit with
a response.*

FROM: REBECCCA
SENT: Friday 8 June, 10.52

R U OK?

Friday

.

17

It's the seahorses what make you think of him. You goggle at a couple of yellow ones, their tails wound around one another, bobbing along two-as-one as if they was on a date or something. You read the caption next to their display tank, the words on it making you come over a bit – whatchamacallit? – sentimental and that, the bridge of your nose stinging, your eyes filling. The male seahorse gives birth, right, which seems like one of Mother Nature's better ideas, and – wow, how cute! – when they find a mate, they mate for life. Alright, they might not live for long, but it's still kind of romantic.

'Adorable, ain't they?' you say, cos Ivana's sidled up to you, pulling you out of them thoughts.

She nods and the children run up behind her, their noses pressed to the glass at the bottom edge of the tank. Ivana lifts Ona up so that she can see the baby seahorses better, and Tomas lifts his arms towards you, with an expectant look on his face. You lift him, surprised at how heavy he is for someone so little. And then of course *he* muscles into your thoughts. Connor. How much does he weigh now? Huge, he was, when he was born. Nearly nine pounds, strapping. No idea if he still is, what with Mum giving nothing away on the phone – for all you know, he's a tiddler these days.

The little boy tugs on your sleeve then, wants to get down. Grateful, you turn away again from them thoughts, and after he's *oohed* and *aahed* over the seahorses a bit longer he grabs your hand while you continue the tour. But, even as he holds your attention with his chirps of excitement and endless questions, your mind's floating closer towards Connor.

To tell the truth, you're bored of it now, though. Of thinking about Connor. Bored of the waiting, the worrying, the being kept in the dark. Lucky he'll be yours again soon, then, you think – yours again soon if you follow Ivana's advice and go home. Tomas's little hand, cupped in yours, squeezes you, and again your heart ripples with a wave of longing, looking forward to the moment when you'll do this with your own baby boy. And then he's off again, Tomas, rushing along the little ledge at the bottom of each tank with Ivana chasing after him, Ona running alongside.

Yeah, so seahorses. The father giving birth. Funny, that, cos you went to the Sea Life Centre in Brighton on your first date. Michael met you outside with a box of chocolates, and you were both, like, trying to be so grown-up. You snort.

Michael.

Grown-up?

As if!

And you bring to mind the birthing DVDs his mum gave you to watch, what you had to switch off after Michael's, like, fiftieth *Oh mate, that's disgusting* as a baby made its way out of its mum's vagina. You hated Michael's mum for those DVDs. Shame, that, cos you can see now that she meant well. Your own mum, though she wanted to be at the birth, didn't give you any advice. Well, other than *Should have kept your legs shut*. Michael's mum is a nice lady, though. Doesn't fuss. Doesn't blame. Even when Mum doesn't let her get close to Connor. Mum thinks Michael's scum, yeah, cos he wasn't interested, wasn't there to hold Connor as soon as he was born.

Look, can you just say something? You know you haven't said much about Michael yet, but it ain't like you've forgotten him...

You lean your head against another tank, grateful for the soothing coolness of the glass, deep-breathing for a minute as a giant fish swims heavily past. You feel safe in here, in this dingy, dank space. Secure. And it's sort of like being here breathes life into thoughts you've kept hidden, allows them to grow, to push out the negative thoughts what have been taking up so much space in your mind. Like the letter. The letter from Michael you've been carrying around with you, a few extracts of it set like cement in your brain now that you've re-read it so many times: *Want to make up with you, be a family... You and your Mum didn't give me a chance... Got an apprenticeship at a joinery... I can look after you and the boy... Miss you, Fox.* Fox. His pet name for you.

You're not sure. Like, you're dead proud of the time what you've spent looking after yourself, thanks very much. But even so... even so, he's got you bang to rights over the not-giving-a-chance thing, and, even more so, you're wondering if you've been a bit harsh about him. Cos, look, when you said before that he wasn't interested after the birth, it's not that he done a runner. Came round after school some days, sometimes helped with the bath and that – when Mum let the pair of you crack on with it, that is. But she made it hard for him. Told him he was useless, a waster, that kind of thing. So, could you blame him for not putting up a fight when you dumped him? He was just a boy then, really, still doing his GCSEs when Connor was born. And for all that he's let you down, let Connor down, there's a softness in your heart for him, a caramel centre, like one of them chocolates he was always giving you.

The next display case along, you feel sorry for the fish: *sand gobies*, it says. They're kind of plain and miserable-looking, a boring beigey colour compared to the blues and neons of the fish in the tropical tanks. You read the caption above the display case: 'Female sand gobies prefer good fathers over dominant males'. And you think, maybe Michael does want to be a dad. Besides, why shouldn't you depend on him for a bit? Why not use the four and a half grand as a starting point for you and your little family, and then let Michael look after you both?

A mewling impatience comes at you then, everything what's happened in the last few days – Colin and Sapphire, Jez, Rebecca and Cathleen, the neighbour, the pigeon – all of that fading, lost in a grey cloud of memory, suddenly meaningless, your mind stuck on what you discussed with Ivana last night. About leaving: leaving Billy, the dancing, the porn stuff... leaving all that behind. And your head swims with the possibility of it. You're possessed by the natural beauty of it. Laughing out loud at the common sense and simplicity of it. Of making a home. With Michael and Connor.

Only no sooner have you thought this than – palms sweat, jaw clenches – anxieties surge. Like, have you left it too late? And it's as though, if you don't do it soon, then it's going to be too late. Too late for kisses and cuddles and whatchamacallit? – recon-silly-ations and laughter and family fun. All them months spent dithering, putting it off, being yellow, being weak, and it comes down to this: it has to be now, it has to be – gulp – well, why not this week?

You scan down the long, dingy corridor for Ivana, picking her out by the seahorses' tank again, Tomas on her shoulders with his legs kicking at her chest, Ona looking tiny at her side. Your heart thuds and you race along the smooth concrete floor to catch her up; you just have to share your decision.

Only the kids want your attention; you can't get a word in. So you suggest a sit-down in the café, buy a juice and a biscuit for the kids, a coffee for you and Ivana, to give you two minutes' peace.

And when the kids are finally tucking into their snacks you're able to say, 'So, what you was saying last night.' Ivana puts down her coffee cup, peers at you. 'You're right. If I could just stay at yours again tonight to pack up my things, I'll see Billy tomorrow, then head...' pause '... home.'

'That's great, really great,' she says, and she squeezes your hand for a second, only to quickly reach out to grab Tomas's juice before it tips up over the already dirty table. 'I think you do the right thing.'

And she's right! You know she is! And suddenly another of them highs what's swooped down on you recently pounces again, a high what you cling on to with all of your might, what you won't let go of, in case it shifts back into the opposite, into yet another low. And so you take hold of Ivana, grasping her shoulders, excitement swelling through your arms, your hands, your fingers, and kiss her full on the lips – not in a pervy way, there'll be no room for *them* kinds of thoughts now – trembling at the thought of the world what's waiting out there for you, for you, for Michael and for Connor.

And for once you're in luck, cos for the rest of the day that high is a little bird what flits and flies around about you, keeping you happy and calm. And, even as you get caught up in the Friday night rush hour while you make your way back to Ivana's, you'd swear on your life you could hear it, that high, chirping and cheeping the sweet sound of success all the way home in your ear.

As soon as you're back at the flat, the packing begins. You start by sifting through the mess in the rucksack, where you find a packet of sanitary towels hidden away at the bottom. Great. Just when you don't need them no more. Can't think when you bought them; they're the bulky night-time ones. After the abortion, maybe? It takes a while to sort things out, and you get lost in a dream for a bit as you repack the money, asking Ivana for some rubber bands to hold it together, making sure it's tightly wedged in between your now few clothes. You make hard work of an easy job, and by the time you've joined Ivana and Marko in the kitchen the kids are already in bed.

Ivana's sorting out her work bag as you walk in, Marko, dressed in filthy overalls with rolled-up sleeves, washing his hands at the sink.

'So, OK, I leave you with Marko tonight?' she says, going back to an earlier conversation. 'I want to work in club,' she told you before, 'not made much money this week.'

'Sure, that's fine.' But you grin sheepishly at Marko, who's walking back across the kitchen, slight butterflies flitting through your tummy at the thought, being as you barely know him.

'And you sure – you go? Tomorrow? You can stay longer, of course,' she says, pulling a face at Marko, 'but…'

You ain't so stupid that you don't see Marko stiffen. 'No, I'm going. Definitely,' you say, with another put-on grin.

But at that your heart rate increases. Sweat drips down your back, a series of doubts suddenly cramping your style, crowding out the plans what have been wheeling merrily – roundabout-style – though your mind. You turn to Ivana, your mouth dry. 'I'm a bit worried about the trains, though. Like, sometimes there's rail works on a weekend.'

Right away she sees through the excuse. 'So get coach. Or check trains. You'll get there – if you want to.'

The butterflies become full-on stomach flips now. And then a genuine reason to stay pops into your head. 'But what if Mum ain't there? Sometimes they use my nanna's caravan and go away for the weekend.'

She smiles, as if she'd expected you to come up with yet another half-baked excuse.

'So call first. Make sure they there.'

You mumble something evasive and Ivana leaves the room with a little flounce. Comes back. Hands you the phone. 'Call,' she says. Kind but firm.

'OK, OK,' you say, leaving them to it in the kitchen, Marko now hanging a row of colourful knickers on a clothes horse alongside *Dora the Explorer* and *Bob the Builder* PJs.

The phone a dead weight in your hands, you walk into the living room and settle your bum on the big window ledge, looking out onto Green Lanes. You're already used to the traffic noises from last night, so much so that the flat feels quiet, too quiet, with the kids tucked up in bed. It's a quiet that's – whatchamacallit? – unnerving, unsettling as you run through the number in your head. 923 on the end? 932? Yeah, 932. You press the small phone symbol for a dialling tone, then listen to your breath – rapid and shallow – back down the line. *Brrr brr brr* as the number kicks in. You're on the point of hanging up, but then:

'Hello?'

'Mum, it's me again.'

'Me?'

'God, Mum, don't you even recognise my voice?'

'Oh, you.'

'Yes, Mum, Hayleigh.'

Silence.

'How…' You twirl your ponytail around your fingers, eyes shifting to a bloke arguing with a couple of coppers on the street outside a pub. Another deep breath. 'How is he?'

'Same as the other day. Fine.'

Suddenly a drunk-looking bloke starts putting up a fight, flailing his arms at the coppers. You try and concentrate, straining your ears to hear something of your Little Man in the background. 'And you? How are you?'

'Fine.'

Ask me, ask me, ask ME! Go on, dare you. Ask me how I am! 'And Connor, what's he doing?' you say, ice in your voice.

'What do you care?'

You look away from the bad scene outside, focusing on a pane of glass higher up the window what's covered in a thin layer of muck. Writing a 'C' in it with your finger, you say, 'Of course I care.' Like, how many times can you have the same conversation? 'That's why I'm calling.'

Nothing but bitterness and blame hum back at you down the line. Then, a shout. Him? Your heart leaps.

'Mum?'

'Yeah?'

'I don't blame you no more. I know – ' you choke back the guilt of the last few months ' – some of it was my fault.'

Silence.

'Mum?'

'Got to go, Hayleigh. Try me again later.' Pause. 'If you're not drunk.'

'Yeah, Mum, OK, but before you go can I ask a quick question?'

More silence.

You've barely any spit left now, have to roll your tongue around your mouth to wet it before you say, 'So, like, are you going to be home the rest of the weekend?'

It comes out quick this time. 'Think so. Why? Listen, Hayleigh, I'm letting you go now.'

'Mum – ' you say, and you think you catch her before the phone line goes dead. 'I'm coming for him.'

And you slam down the phone on the window ledge. It falls BANG! to the floor. You pick it up, slam it again.

BANG! Against the wall. BANG! It bounces back, taking a piece of chipped white paint with it.

It's not fair, it's not fair!

You want to hit out, scream, punch the wall, rattled by a sudden rage what sets your mouth in a hard straight line, turns your knuckles white. It's been in storage, this rage. A rage what has been revving up inside you all week and now thrums in your ears. This rage what has, to be fair, been keeping you going; an engine of anger, a powerful motor of it, what's been keeping you alive. And this rage you thought was directed at Sapphire, at Jez, is really, you think, dusting down the wall where the paint has chipped, directed at Mum. Cutting you off, even when you're trying to make up!

You stalk away from the window ledge. Fall onto the sofa with an animal grunt. And there you lie, sobbing, groaning, moaning, bashing a cushion, till later on – you're not sure how much – somebody (Marko?) puts a blanket over you and them sobs take you at last into a deep and damp-eyed sleep.

18 MISSED CALLS
6 VOICEMAILS
INBOX: 8 new messages

FROM: UNKNOWN NUMBER
SENT: Friday 7 June, 16.30

Great to meet you. Fancy a date some time? ☺ *PS told you I'd be in touch*

FROM: BILLY
SENT: Saturday 8 June, 02.30

Tick tock tick tock

Saturday

18

Stepping out of the Tube station onto Tottenham Court Road, you try to avoid a couple of chuggers in jolly green Greenpeace tabards who are hanging about by the exit. Not being funny, but their loopy grins seem a bit forced, a bit sad really. Don't stop them inflicting them on innocent passers-by, though. Oh, no… he ain't. Yes. Yes, he is. One of them, the dreadlocked white lad, is criss-crossing the hordes of people on the pavement to slink up alongside you.

'Hello, madam, would you like to save the planet today?'

'No, thank you,' you say, then, under your breath, 'got to save myself first.' And you scamper away, as best you can with the bulky rucksack on your back, towards Oxford Street, and then Soho.

Soho. Where your first stop will be to pop into the club. Mad, eh? But Ivana convinced you this morning to go and see Jez, before you try and find Billy, right? Said that Jez was asking for you last night, that he told her he might have been too hasty in letting you go. Said that he hinted there might be something in it for you, if you turn up to see him and all. Nice to be wanted, you think, and – hard as it was to say goodbye to Ivana – nice to have spent time with her the last couple of days and all. After another big heart-to-heart this morning you exchanged addresses and numbers and she promised she'd write, promised she'd come with the kids for a seaside visit as soon as the dust settles at home.

Occupied by this happy plan, you turn onto Dean Street, your pace picking up all the time. It's a sort of like gut impulse now to see Jez and Billy then head for Victoria and get back to the little baby. And so your footsteps are quick-smart and speedy as you walk past Pizza Express and you're sort of like panting, in a rush now, as you sidestep some gasworks what are jutting out into the road. You don't even mind that it's started to rain, that wet kind of rain what sticks to your face. Like you care. It's wonderful, that rain: it's zippy and zingy and zesty, it's exciting and go-getting; it's just what you need right now. *Yeah, bring it on!* Bring on the wind and the rain, bring on the storm of Billy and Jez, of Mum and Michael and Dad, and all. You can handle it. Handle them.

Easy.

Easy-peasy.

Japanesey.

You laugh, only for a reality check as you walk with long strides past the Crown and Two Chairmen, and a pulse of anxiety throbs through you. Like, will Jez truly have a nice word to say? In fact, is there anything left to say? Will Billy give you a hard time for leaving? Will he even care? But soon you're ignoring these thoughts, psyching yourself up again, all steamed up with the possibilities, not sure this is all really happening – a quick chat with Jez to square things away, a goodbye to Billy if he's there in the pub, and then…

And then you stop. Dilly-dally on the pavement, getting lost among the grimy hustle and bustle of Soho in the raw, the streets, pubs and clubs bursting with life, spinning you out. And it's all too much for a second… life has sped up beyond all control, and you're not sure if you're ready. Not sure if you're ready for these final steps home.

Sheltering from the rain, you huddle into a doorway to light a fag, an old man in a mac ruining the moment as he bumbles noisily down the stairs. Leaning against the wall, you scan the badly written sign what's Blu-Tacked to the stairwell. Great, just great. It's the crappy titty bar Jez is always moaning is too close to the club. The old git's pure old-school Soho, all comb-over, spirits breath and nervous twitch. Insult to injury, he looks like he's got – what's that? egg? – mulched into his beard. Drawing heavily on the fag, you think you couldn't make it up, this kind of guy coming out of a place like that. Yeah, you think, as he turns back to ogle you, he looks just the type. So, when he opens his mouth, you cut him off sharpish with a 'Don't even think about it; me standing here ain't what you think.'

It's no surprise when he ignores you and starts to mouth off the usual filth (same shit, different day) and so you move off again, in a hurry again, determined again, to sort out your last bits and pieces, before the final stretch home.

And suddenly there it is, leering at you from across the road. The windows painted black. The illuminated sign with the second 'E' missing; the word ELEGANC hanging vertically in meant-to-be-alluring bright red lights. The cheesy silhouettes of women in sexy poses decorating the greyed-out windows upstairs. You hesitate. Like, do you really have anything left to say to Jez? What can he offer you now?

A blurriness hazes your vision. You lose focus, thoughts scattering like confetti away from nice goodbye chats, drifting instead to the dirty realities of the club, to the customers...

to the oddballs asking you to hurt them, to dominate them, hit them with the back of your hand, with your palm, with your fist, with whatever you could lay your hands on...

to the brain-ache from hours of endless thumb-twiddling, waiting for a dance...

to the bum-ache from hours of sitting at the bar during quiet nights...

to the jaw-ache from hour after hour of sweet-talking, of chatting up guys, sleazy Z-List kinds of guys, guys who you'd give the two fingers if they sidled up to you in a nightclub.

You dither, up on tippy-toe inside your trainers like a runner on the starting blocks, the rucksack weighting you backwards. Looking up at the ceiling of smoky-grey clouds, you wonder what's holding you back, cos, like, one toe, the big one on your right foot, is nearly there now, nearly tipping you over the edge of the pavement. Tipping you over the edge. Tipping you towards what'll probably be an embarrassing showdown.

Nah, there's no point going in, is there?

Cos you don't owe Jez nothing. No apology. No goodbye. In fact, he owes you! Owes you for the hours of unpaid emotional labour, for the long hours sitting there trying to read the guys who come into the club. Is that one a spender? A perv? A loner? An oddball? A good guy? Does he want this? That? The other? Unpaid for the emotional exhaustion of being nice to every guy who walks in the room. Too right. Nothing, that's what you owe. Yeah, that's it – he ain't worth it, Jez. He ain't worth using up one iota of energy, one ounce of the little strength you've got left.

That's the decision made, then. You won't go in. Relieved, you feel your body become limp as you dart a last backward glance at the club. Only then... a catastrophe, a calamity... cos there she is, there SHE is. THERE SHE IS!

Sapphire. Air-kissing the bouncers, Derek and Iain, on her way down the stairs. You duck two doors down into the doorway of a small sandwich bar, the smell of fried bacon wafting out. She's the last person you want to bump into. Still wearing her stilettos – typical of the silly cow; you're straight into your trainers when your shifts end – strutting down the street all tits and arse, with a *click, click, click* of her metal heels, so tinny and loud that you can hear them from across the busy road. Then another person comes down the steps and – oh, my God, this you can barely believe. Cos it's Colin, yeah? Stealing down the stairs out of Elegance, baseball cap pulled over his stupid bald head. Skulking past the bouncers. Walking in the same direction as the porn-version Oompa Loompa. Following her? This is all it takes for your heart to pulse and throb, throb and pulse with anxiety again.

Briefly you're torn between right and wrong: the bitch on your shoulder goading you to let them get on with it, let him do his worst, let him follow her, molest her, get whatever he wants; the angel on your shoulder begging you to tell her *Sapphire, be careful* (never did find out her real name). Yeah, pleading with you to help her out, despite the catcalls, despite the bitchiness, despite what she done to your dress.

But your stomach has dropped to the floor (*What are you, chicken shit? Afraid of him?*) and too late you cry out 'Sapphire!' – a half-cry, cos she's already out of there, turning into Old Compton Street, Colin trailing a few steps behind.

God, look, can you just say something? You know you're going back on everything, on all them bad things you've said about her. But, end of the day, you don't blame her. It was Jez. Jez who set you up against each other. Besides, this pain of being stabbed in the back by him, it's like a real blade has been punched into you, this realisation where his loyalties lie. Jeremy, yeah, what is he like? Turfing you out on your ear so that Colin could come back as a customer. Putting Colin's custom above all your hard work. Letting a man – you grit your teeth, make your hands into fists – who followed you, who, like, mauled you, come back into his club.

You swear on your life if Jez was here...

A random vision of the steak knife in the rucksack's front pocket comes into your mind; at the same time bile coils its way around your gut, only to sneak its way upwards. Good

God, you're going to be sick. Properly sick. You reconsider going into the club, just to use the loos, but no, thinking of the club just speeds up the process and instead out spews the bile, the poison – *bleurgh* – and, as another wave hits, you let it surge up your chest, burning your heart on its way past, spraying out in a splatter over the pavement, and all the while you're ignoring the sandwich man who's peering out his window from behind a tall tower of baps. It takes a minute or two to stop heaving – wet retching, then dry retching – and only when there's nothing left to give do you wipe your mouth, repulsed by the acid taste what's filling it up.

You think of the damage what you could and should do to Jeremy.

Yes, damage.

Damage.

Damage.

That word. You relish it, relish the d, the a, the m, the second a, the g, the e – let it surf over the other worries and thoughts in your mind. What damage could you cause, could you inflict? On Jeremy? On the club? Stung by a sort of self-loathing and misery, you stand still, weighing it up. Weighing up the option of stepping further over the line, of doing worse than in the past few months, doing worse than near-prostitution, worse than breaking and entering, worse than leaving your son. All of this seething and foaming inside like a kind of seasickness, a sickness what gets worse every time you think of that word: *damage*.

But when the sandwich man comes out his shop to yell, 'Clear off!' you lurch into the road at a slow, steady pace and it comes to you. No. You will not do anything. Won't do any dam– and now, unlike two minutes ago, you can't bring yourself to think the word. Cos it ain't like you to do wrong. To yourself, yes, you've done wrong: going too far with that customer, taking yourself away from the baby. But it's like your London life has made your boundaries skew-whiff, made you wide-eyed and weak. Not any more. You'll be strong now, for Connor, yeah, for the baby?

Cos you are not a bad person.

You are not a bad person.

You are not a bad person.

'I'm not a bad person,' you say out loud as an old dear in a posh get-up walks past, and she speeds up, shoulders hunched.

And it's weird: now that this new sense of right and wrong has lit up inside you, it's like it was a cosmic signal, guiding you, back to where you was first thing today, steering you as if you was following a bright star in the sky back to goodbyes with Billy then to Peacehaven, to Michael, and to your Connor.

With a jump of joy, of excitement, you move faster, faster away from Elegance, from Jez, that place, that man who both changed you, made you rotten – if not quite to your core, thank goodness. And you leap, the rucksack light on your back now, over the cracks in the pavement, an old childhood superstition coming back to you out of left field: if you step on a crack, you will die.

But, as you listen to your footsteps bounce down the street and the bright star in your mind burns brighter still, the opposite idea takes hold, together with a spasm of pleasure.

You will not die. You will live.

VOICEMAIL: FULL
INBOX: FULL

19

By the time you're outside the pub where you hope to meet Billy, you're no longer fizzing with energy. It's not that you're afraid of telling him you're leaving. You've been mulling it over on the short walk from Dean Street. Like, Billy, he once said he loved you (to be fair, he was high), calls you his girlfriend, even, so there's a chance he might be a bit bothered. Not that you can remember the last time you did anything normal together (movies, the pub, a meal), never mind – and you shudder at the thought – have sex.

A strong sense of shame warms your cheeks then, so you reach over and pull off your hoodie now the rain's stopped for a bit. This earns you a wolf-whistle from across the street. On autopilot you turn around, thinking it might have come from Billy, but it's just some random showing his appreciation for what's under the hoodie, you guess.

Still got it, you think, with a smug wink and a smile, and you realise that you're almost looking forward to this goodbye with Billy.

Look, you don't mean to sound heartless, but, Connor, yeah, he's way more important than any man, any boyfriend could be. And you swear on your life you don't mean much to Billy. Be glad to see the back of you, probably.

Even though rainclouds are simmering again, there's a crowd of afternoon drinkers outside the pub, smoking and knocking back pints; must be rammed inside. Whatever, you hope there's a seat in case you have to wait. Cos, even though you managed another unbroken night's sleep at Ivana's, tiredness is still thumping away at you, the action-packed last few days a burden, beating you down. Never mind the hangover from the shock of seeing Sapphire and Colin.

Of course it *is* busy inside the pub, worse luck, as if being there alone wasn't hassle enough. You strain your eyes but can't make out Billy at his usual table, or anywhere else for that matter. Oh, well, it was a long shot. Might have to pop around to his flat in a bit, to see if he's hanging at home. Meantime, you push your way to the queue at the bar what's two people deep. Shit, it's going to take you an age to get served. You hover behind a throng of tall blokes, and even small blokes, who you know will get served before you. Yup, there you are at the front, and a scrawny bloke behind you waving a fiver over your head is asked by the barman, 'What you 'aving?'

You spin around and scowl at the customer and he grins, says, 'She's next,' to the barman. He looks at you expectantly, and you turn back again in a huff. What does he want, a medal?

It's not one of the regular barmen and you don't feel like asking for Billy, so instead you just say, 'Two double vodka-lemonades.'

Oh, come on, you ain't being greedy. *To fail to prepare is to prepare to fail*, ain't that what they say? Besides, Billy might turn up in a mo, yeah – take one of the drinks off your hands? And if he doesn't show, well, no need to queue again.

With the drinks paid for, you push your way towards a free seat at a table. And then, in a sort of like trance, you're taking the rucksack off your back and wrapping the cords from the waistbelt around your chair, sitting down, checking the clock on the wall. Quarter past four. A twinge of impatience. You wanted to catch a Brighton train before all the weekend daytrippers head home. Still, not going in to see that backstabber Jez at Elegance has given you a bit more time. Give it an hour here, then, followed by a quick trip to his flat if he doesn't show up? Pretty much all he's worth, ain't it, an hour or two of your time?

And then you're scolding yourself, while taking a first swallow of drink, telling yourself not to be harsh. Like, he was the one who introduced you to Jez and the club, helped you get on your feet when you first moved up London, wasn't he?

See, Billy's a friend of one of your cousins. This cousin, right, she put you up for a bit when you first moved up London, till she got all shirty with her bloke, thought he was trying it on with you (which he did, to be fair, not that you told her) and so Billy, yeah, you was introduced to him one night when you was all out on the razz, and he was all, like, charming, shelling out for drinks and that, dishing out compliments and fags. Then, after a few meetings, you moved in with him. Just like that. Sofa at first, then bed, and, well… the rest is history.

Yeah, history, thank goodness, you think, raising a glass to yourself, getting a bit squiffy now, what with drinking on an empty stomach after the recent vom. A history with Billy what began by taking coke for the first time, hitting the bottle more than ever before, then losing your whatchamacallit? – inhibitions, him encouraging you to do stuff you'd never have dreamed of six months earlier: watching porn, talking dirty, auditioning for the club. Naked! (Like, not even Michael has seen you naked.) Taking risks, especially after the abortion… And your and Billy's shared history ending… well, you'll soon see how it ends, if he shows up.

The pub seems suddenly small, the air close. And that red-hot loneliness what's been burning through you makes you realise you've spent too much time thinking about this kind of stuff, and not enough time doing or living. Yeah, you've been wrapped up inside your head for too long, acting the ditz, spending too much time relying on blokes who let you down: on Billy, on Colin, on Jez. Letting yourself get sucked into their squalid greedy world, forgetting about the other stuff, the real stuff, about light and air and food and family, about all them things what keep you healthy – healthy up here (you tap your head), you mean.

A light-headedness comes over you, a little fluttering in your heart, and you place your palms on your lap for support. The hour you've given Billy's already up, the table in front of you telling its own story of the last ninety minutes or so – three empty glasses, one half-full, an uneaten packet of crisps. In a moment of madness, you consider another snort of Ayesha's coke what's taken you to the loos once or twice since you arrived. But you shrug off the idea, cos them lines have given you the jitters, the small worries you had when you arrived in the pub growing into monster fears the more what you've done. Like, since Billy mentioned the porn thing, wanted you to meet – what was The Bloke's name? Kenny, that's it – something's been bugging you. Yeah, yeah, you know you should be grateful to Billy for thinking that you're pretty enough, sexy enough to be in one of them films, but… But, no, the thought is a feathery one, the kind you can't quite catch a hold of… And there it goes, floating off – gone.

You swill back the last of the vodka, plunging you into new depths of wooziness. That's it, time to leave, you think, and you stagger up, tripping over the rucksack – God, the rucksack, you almost forgot it for a minute – your arse brushing past jam-packed men and ladies out for a good time. Only standing up makes you spinny, dizzy, guzzling down air – like, are you a bit drunk? – and you make a beeline for the door, not bothering with the usual apologies, not bothering with sorries and excuse-mes and holding open doors.

Yeah, too right, you think, no more tongue-biting, holding back, no more chickening out. Like, not having it out with Jez, that's got to be the last time you wimp out, got to be your last act as a cowardy-cowardy custard. All of this rushing through your mind, adding to your irritation as you near the pub door. And then you spot him – Billy – and them words *you cannot escape* hit you, just like they did in Bianca's flat. You break out in goosebumps. Shrink back. Maybe you can sneak out the side door? No, too late. He's spotted you… and what the – ? His face, it's draining of colour, turning the white-grey shade of pissy-weak tea.

'Hiya, babe,' you say, over the head of a small lady walking past who's doing a balancing act with a tray of drinks, and you try to ease the tension in your forehead, to appear relaxed. 'I was just…'

'You,' he says. His voice is flat. Toneless. Like, isn't he happy to see you? Again he says, 'You.' And his face flushes red and purple now, the veins on his neck throbbing to an erratic, off-key beat. 'Didn't you get my messages?'

'Messages?'

His right eye twitches and he jabs a thumb towards a free table. You follow, sinking onto a chair, trying to squash a growing sense of dread.

'Yeah, messages. You know. Voice messages. Text messages.'

'Oh, I, er, lost my phone. Look, I'm sorry about – '

He cuts in, with a 'Don't worry about it. Not like they was important or nothing.'

The voice… the throwing a whitey when he saw you… the saying none of it matters – what is all this? You chew a fingernail, a line crinkling up the usual smoothness of your forehead.

251

'But I am, Billy. I know you was waiting for me the other day, but my phone, er, broke, and then, you ain't going to believe this…' cos, right, he hated those bitch flatmates, he's bound to be on your side '…them two cows chucked me out and I – '

'So why didn't you come to me?'

'Er…' you say, and your eyes dart around the room, as if it will provide the answer. Why on earth did you think coming here was a good idea? 'Well, I didn't want to put you out, you know, like last time. I kind of…' But you trail off, cos he looks mean now. Mean and angry.

'Right. I'll get us a drink.' And he's sort of like stroking, sort of like lightly tapping your cheek, as he rises out his chair. 'Don't move, will you, baby?'

At that your stomach drops as if you was racing down the slope of a rollercoaster.

'No, no, I can't stay, Billy, that's what I come to tell you. I'm leaving.'

'What?' He drops back down onto his chair.

'I'm leaving, going back to Pea– ' but something stops you from saying Peacehaven, and you continue, 'home.'

'No, you're not.'

You swallow a lump in your throat, swallowing back with it all hope of seeing Connor today.

'Not what?'

'Not going home.'

A bloke in a stupid hat comes up then, asking if he can take a free chair from your table, and it gives you the chance to sort of like gather your thoughts. You manage a hoarse little laugh from your lips and wait for stupid hat man to leave till you say, 'Er, yes, I am.'

'No,' Billy's hissing, and he's, like, leaning towards you across the table. 'You're not.'

'I don't… understand.'

'Nobody shows me up like you done. You're doing that bloody audition, right?'

'No, Billy,' you say, gently. 'No, I'm not.'

It comes out of nowhere. A slap – *whomp!* – in the face.

A stab of pain on your cheek. The room spins. 'Crazy in Love' on the jukebox. Colours swirling, smoke belching, voices grating. Leaning back into the chair, head swimming. A red mark on your face? Backs. A sea of backs, people turned away, not looking. Not looking or pretending not to look? Pretending they didn't see? Billy's lips full, top lip curled, triumphant.

'Well,' he says, 'well.'

Which doesn't even mean anything, right, and this confusion, this being fazed at them words brings you out of your trance, and you're waiting for it then. The apology. The *Sorry, Hayleigh, I love you, I shouldn't have hit you, don't leave me*. But it doesn't come. Instead people carry on as before: drinks sloshing over glasses, loud chatter, football songs, smoke stinging your eyes. And Billy, yeah, he's sitting back down again, no tension in his face, in his body, his legs spread, silver suit stretched over his stupid teeny-tiny bollocks. Sitting there, the Big I Am, like it was his right, his right to smack you in the face. Like... like he sort of owned you or something.

From a distant, unused part of your brain it comes to you: a realisation. Like, he's a user, on a power trip, ain't he? All this making out like he was helping you, it was just an act. Like the finder's fee he got from Jez when the club took you on (one hundred quid – is that what you're worth to him?), the money he'd make as your so-called manager if you went ahead with the porn. You see now that you're nothing but a trophy to him, your body an object what he can buy and sell to his mates.

What happens next is a sort of like blur.

You get up. You tell him, 'No, Billy, you can't do this to me, I'm leaving,' and you stand up ballet-exam straight, bursting with the confidence of a thousand Hayleighs, a thousand Laylas as you pick your way past the deaf and dumb bastards in the pub. But then somehow he winds up in front of you, and as you step over the pub's threshold onto the pavement you're face-to-face and he's leaning towards you, his beer breath a hoppy mist under your nose.

Nostrils flare, teeth chatter, legs tremble at the violent look in his eye. Like, is he dangerous? Why ain't you seen that before?

If he hits you again, you'll scream for definite, you think, bending backwards towards a table of outdoor drinkers, knocking into one of their legs what gets you a *Hey! Mind out* and not a *Can we help, you OK?* and you realise that nobody gives a shit, you're nobody's problem, a piss-stain on the fun of their Saturday afternoon, and then, right, you can't quite believe it, cos he's sort of half cuddling, half wrestling you, and you're nearly keeling over what with the weight of the rucksack, and you're twisting around so the bag don't make people's drinks go flying and you notice the front pocket is flapping open – shit, have you been pickpocketed? – but you can't close it now, cos he's got a hold of you – *ow!* – by your ponytail and he's sort of like dragging you along by it, pulling you away, away from the table, away from the not-helping people, and you trip over your feet in the effort of keeping up with him, of being carried along by him, all the while trying not to lose your grip on the rucksack. And the next thing you know you're:

running

sweating

gasping for air

visions of a better time, a better place filling your mind… and then you find yourself in a little piss-smelling alley and

254

he's shoved you against the wall, blocking your way and no, nobody's followed, the pair of you are alone.

You are alone.

You are alone.

You are alone!

A snapshot what's never been taken pops into your head: of Connor, you and Michael, a family snap, the two of them so dark and handsome, two peas in a pod... and then it fades away, this image, the colour washing out till you can't even picture Connor's face any more.

To your surprise he shoves you away then, takes a breather, wiping mud or dog-shit or God knows what off the leg of his shiny grey suit. You eye both entrances of the alley, but it's narrow, too narrow to make it past him easily, not with the rucksack.

Billy flobs on the floor. Leans back against the wall. Lights up another fag. And all the while his eyes, frozen and blue, are on you; there's no chance of making a run for it.

You cannot escape you cannot escape you cannot escape. Again, those words chase through your mind and with them a sudden terror: never mind today – will he ever let you see Connor again? Will he let you out of here unharmed?

Now you do try and make a run for it but he's on you in a flash, his hands gripping at your throat. You stretch your hand around to your back. Scrabble at the rucksack's front pocket. The steak knife – you packed it, right? Yes, yes, you did, you think, your fingers touching its handle. Lucky for you, it's whipped out the rucksack before Billy understands what's happening.

'You.

Don't.

Own.

Me.'

you say, and when it happens you feel your fingers punch

the knife into his leg… a terrible screeching, and you pull the knife out. He drops his hands from your throat and goes for the knife. You push his hand away with all your strength. Punch the knife in again. Think of Ayesha and her betrayal. *Punch*. Think of Colin, of Kenny, of Jez. *Punch punch punch*. Sweet and sharp. And you think that maybe the screeching's getting louder, or is it your ears what are whistling, a buzzing in your head what's drowning out everything else? In a daze, you crouch down by the wall, the knife lodged deep in his leg now.

A loud moan. Sirens in the distance. A splash of rain.

You watch him rolling around, and you are afraid. Afraid to watch his eyes bulging, the tendons in his neck straining; and you're weeping, yeah, weeping as you wonder if the shock is worse for you or for him.

'Nooo! he yells as he pulls out the knife, his face bleached of colour, blood slopping from the gash.

The rain comes down harder. Billy tries to get up. His hands smother the wound, stemming the blood. Then, from his crouch position, he lunges.

You pick up the knife. You run.

20

And you keep on running. Running in a mad rush like you was whizzed-up on amphetamine but not in a good way, your senses and sense racing away from you, so that you're nothing but five foot six of pure sweat and pulse in a ponytail, stripped of all feeling and thought... and then the rain starts chucking down harder... dappling your cheeks with ice-cold splashes... stirring up something inside of you... stirring up them senses again... and now your throat goes against you and all, closing up with the fear of it, the fear of him chasing, the fear that you've damaged him, or, worse, that you haven't. (*Is he after you, is he OK, should you dial 999?*) Then out of nowhere come the distant drums of a memory, of feet pounding a dance floor just as they're pounding the pavement right now...

dancing stuffed into a nightclub with Michael, so hot, too hot, hair swept off your face with a scrunchie as you bounce up down up down on the dance floor, disco lights in primary colours whirligigging across the DJ deck, blinding you, spinning you out...

hoodie pulled down over your face, running all the while, you reach out your hand, as if you was in that nightclub, to hold hands with him, with Michael... But he's not here, is he? On paper, in the letter, by text, yes, he's here, but not in the flesh, not holding your hand, helping you along...

and your heart is four empty chambers, aching for him, aching for his not being here, which makes matters worse and you trip, your feet not keeping up with the pace of your heart, with the blood rushing inside your head, with the frenzied in-and-out action of your lungs.

You come to a stop. Heave. Heaving up them vodka-lemonades from the pub, heaving up a puddle of green-yellow bile. You spit it out onto the ground. (*Is he after you, is he OK, should you dial 999?*) Damn it, you're unfit. All them hours sculpting shapes on the pole, perfecting the art of looking weightless, and a minute's running knocks you right out.

Only when you reach the corner of Oxford Street do you realise the knife's still in your hand.

Panic sets in. You stash it back in the rucksack. Picture Billy grassing you up to the police, or lying in a hospital bed. (*Is he after you, is he OK, should you dial 999?*) And then you wonder whether you should get to a doctor yourself. Maybe ask for a prescription of beta blockers, Valium – anything to stop your pulse galloping, your heart racing like this. Or perhaps call that copper who gave you his card at Bianca's? Like, this was self-defence, right? Only you push that question away, cos it's a dumb one, and you're wheezing, panting, fighting for breath, zigzagging across the pavement till a woman with a pram has to swerve out your way, nearly knocking the rucksack off your back.

'Sorry,' you say, in a rasping voice, scared that you might have an asthma attack, scared that you might burst even, and so you tell yourself to slow down, to go back to them breathing exercises from the midwife what have worked before.

RE-LAX. RE-LAX. RE-LAX.

Till, breath by breath, little by little, your heart rate begins to come down...

... like it did on that night out with Michael. He took you to the chillout room, worried you might have caned too much speed, huddled you into a corner, stroking your hair as the clock struck midnight – it was New Year's Eve – and you thanked him by spewing up all over his Reeboks. The first night you spent together, that was, coming up on your first pill under the covers of his mum and dad's bed later on, while they spent New Year at their timeshare in Portugal. Your first time together. Your first time ever, in fact. His too. Like, sexually, yeah? The night that Connor was made... the night the condom split...

A man in a suit brushes past you and you jump (*is he after you, is he OK, should you dial 999?*) back on the pavement again. It's the reality jolt what you need to pick up your heels and start running again – ignoring the fact that your laces have come undone, that one lace is wet from the rain and is whipping up dirty great grey-brown splashes onto your legs – running with your chest heaving up and down, with your lungs pushing in and out, running with all of your strength and your power, with no sense of direction, with no sense at all, till you reach as if by magic – legs trembling, sweat sticking your hair to your forehead – a bus stop, the bus stop what can take you to Victoria Station and to him, your Little Man.

Cos no taxis for you today, right? you think, your brain working for once. No chance of being remembered by some beady-eyed taxi driver. And it's not long before a bus pulls up to the stop... and you jump on board... swipe your Oyster card... collapse onto the back seat. And soon the bus is moving off, taking you past Marble Arch, past Buckingham Palace, turning the corner into Victoria bus station and the minute the engine's switched off you're out of there, running again, running till you're all out of puff, all out of worry and fear.

You slump to the floor of the station concourse, leaning your back on a concrete post, wrapping your arms around the rucksack in a bear hug, the tears what have been gathering for the last sixty minutes streaming down your face, streaking your make-up. You're not just crying cos of what happened, though – you're crying cos of relief, cos of a comedown. Not a comedown from the drugs and booze – to be honest, you're still slightly off your head from the coke, from the booze, from the madness of today – but a comedown from the hopes and plans of the past twelve months, the fear that reality might burn a hole into the fantasy of you, you and Connor, spending your lives together. Fragile and flimsy as a piece of paper, you're done in, knackered, weak. Can barely summon the energy to worry about what happened just now, outside the pub...

A man, Billy's height and build, shuffles past, munching on an enormous baguette. (*Is he after you, is he OK, should you dial 999?*) Your stomach somersaults, an icy coldness cooling your blood. But no, he's Asian, Billy's white. You're seeing things.

In an attempt to relieve them worries again, you look up at the departure boards. Shit, you've just missed a train. Oh, well, time to buy a ticket, you think, dragging yourself up – time to get yourself together, to sort your head out. And as you head for the ticket machines your stomach does cartwheels at the thought of just *why* you're getting yourself together: the thought of getting home. Getting home in time to put him to bed, maybe... to kiss him goodnight, to drench yourself in that sweet baby smell...

Only with these thoughts alarm bells ring, and you dash out of the queue into M&S to buy one of them mini cans of V&T, for your nerves. Cos you know it's going to be tough – that you've built up Connor in your head to be a little prince, that you've been doing the head/sand thing over the stresses and strains of being a mum. But you're ready for it. Ready for the challenge. The things what bored you so much before – the nappy-changing and the bottle-sterilising, the laundry and the trips to the doctor – you're looking forward to these as much as to kisses and cuddles right now. And so, even as you pull the ring on the can, you're telling yourself to be strong, to be a mum.

Yeah, you're thinking as you reach the front of the queue at the ticket machines, and then walk towards Platform 15 with slow, cautious steps, your head all agog with high expectations, forget fragile, forget flimsy... and you imagine yourself as that piece of paper you mentioned before, the story of your life so far written on it; imagine crumpling it into a ball, crumpling away them worries, them stresses, them problems what have built up around you, what have made you weak. And, as you crouch down on the floor outside Smith's to wait for the train, you see yourself taking the ball of paper, throwing it upwards, and as it sails in an arc through the air you watch yourself kicking it, kicking away all the headaches of the past, kicking away all them mistakes you've made – *slam! dunk!* – into a wastepaper bin.

And with that slam-dunk you're forcing yourself to put today's events behind you. Who cares if Billy's after you? Who cares if he's OK? Who cares if he's – you sniff – alive? It's time to focus on the good of the past few months now: on making friends with Ivana; on coming to terms with all the issues with Mum. And, not being funny, it isn't every girl who could have saved nearly five grand in ten months. OK, so it was meant to be fifty at first, but, well, you ain't that – whatchamacallit? – gullible little girl who'd believe that's possible any more. Who'd believe you could do it without getting damaged.

There's that word again. *Damage.* You shiver. From the worry? From the fear? Or from the fact that the high of that last line has finally worn off? You grunt, disgusted at yourself.

And something else is gnawing at you now, in your gut. What is it? Not Billy, surely? you think, trying to shunt any more thoughts of him from your mind. Not period pains; you've waved goodbye to them for another month. Then you realise: it's hunger. A hunger you haven't felt for months, since the termination, since all the trouble at the club. It's a hunger what seems to flood through your intestines and your stomach all at once. You could eat three quarter-pounders, the meat red-raw, ketchup and mayo dripping from your mouth. A kebab. An entire tub of ice cream. Only that appetite isn't just for food; you're a different kind of hungry and all. You're hungry for their touch, their love, Connor's and Michael's. Not for the kind of love and affection them blokes at Elegance showed – not plastic love, not tits-and-arse love. Not trophy-girlfriend love either; not Billy's kind of love. But true from-a-boy-to-his-mummy love, true boyfriend-to-girlfriend love... and you hear in your head, not for the first time, Connor saying those words: *Love you, Mummy.*

The day he was born, your baby, your Connor. Panic tugging you at them first labour twinges... Mum trying to stick a Tens machine on you... the panic rising in short, sharp shocks, the vomiting, the diarrhoea... The calming deep breaths you'd tried so hard to practise fleeing out your mouth in scary, fast puffs in the hectic taxi ride to the hospital... the farmyard smells, the animal groans... and then, the pain... the ripping, searing, never-thought-it-could-be-this-bad pain... leaning over the bed, on your knees, the weight bearing down on you, the burning – Christ's sake, the burning as he squeezed and squelched his way out of you... and then the doctors and midwives all over him, taking him away from you, checking him over... Mum trying to cuddle him first but that midwife, the skinny black one – you'll never forget how grateful you was – placing him on your chest wrapped in a blanket, and then he was there, in your arms.

He was yours.

Yours!

Yes, Mum, yours. It's your... your... you scrabble around for the word... it's your *right* to have him. You're the one who squeezed him out; you're the one who made him with Michael. You're the one who loves him to bits.

The robot voice on the tannoy announces *Brighton train, Platform 15* and you leap – yes, leap – up, run-walking to the ticket gates, putting your ticket through the barrier, your hand rock-steady, and you're happy! alive! born again!

So what if you look like an idiot as you break from your walk-run into a real run, an ear-to-ear grin plastered on your face, your trainers sticking then sliding on the concourse, all the while your hands clinging on to the straps of the rucksack what are fastened across the front of your chest, your future inside it, yours and Connor's – Michael's too if he comes through on his promises? You speed along the length of the platform to the front of the train, to get to him all the more quickly at the other end. And you're almost laughing out loud as you sit in a double seat, the grin stretching all the way around your face now, Joker-wide.

Although when you first sit down it feels like you'll be waiting forever, or at least till the moon and stars begin to shine, it's not long till the train pulls out of the station, pitch-black in the tunnel at first, then a piercing blue light, a blue light filled with the brilliant hope of a summer's evening, with the hope you have for the rest of your life. And this light, together with the train's ice-cold air-conditioning, it's soothing, relaxing, chilling you out.

Only then, you notice the streak of blood on the right cuff of your hoodie.

Your breaths become freakish and fast. Sweat pours down your face, the last of the make-up what you applied at Ivana's this morning smearing off.

RE-LAX, RE-LAX, RE-LAX.

It takes two stations – till East Croydon, that is – before you're breathing easy again, before your skin is more sticky than wet. You must look a right old state, but you don't care – no more worrying about that. No more worrying about looks, about waxing and plucking and self-tanning and hair extensions, about hair-dyeing. Hell, you might even grow your leg hairs long just for fun. (No, you'd never go that far.) No more worrying about how Connor's doing, if you'll save enough money to leave London. No more worrying about whether Mum will call or write. No more worrying about Billy and his sodding 'Great Blokes'.

No. More. Worrying!

But hang on. And suddenly your mind is swamped with *what ifs*. What if Billy gets in touch with your cousin and finds you? What if he's badly injured? Like, a knife wound – that can kill you, right? What if the flatmates track you down, come after you for the unpaid bills? Worse yet, what if Connor doesn't love you? What if Mum goes nuclear when you try and take him back? What if you can't talk her around? What if – and this is a biggie – you can't explain away your earnings; what if they suss out where the money's come from?

Already gloomy and glum, your mood takes a turn for the worse, and the nearly done gramme of coke from last night starts burning a hole in your pocket. Just one little line. A last one. A goodbye if you like, to your London life. *A little livener*, as Billy would say. And the thought of him only makes you long for the charlie all the more.

The problem is where to do it. Can't leave the rucksack; can't be arsed to take it with you to the loos. The train pulls into a tunnel then, and you see yourself in the window. See yourself. SEE YOURSELF. *Like, a line, really, Hayleigh?* You steal a look around the carriage; it's fairly packed.

Sneakily zip open the rucksack. Feel about for – *ow!* – a scratch on your finger and you remember you still have the knife. *Christ!* This is the spark what gets you searching more urgently for the coke and, with your hoodie covering your hands and the bag, you take out the little envelope, looking left-right down the carriage, gritting your teeth at the waste of it, then stuffing the half-full wrap of coke, together with the knife, in the little bin at the side of your seat.

Phew.

And it's as if, where five minutes earlier them problems were still clenched tight in your fist, now you can imagine them passing like water through your fingers.

Cos you will not be a coke-head mum. That's it with you and the drugs now; that's it with you and the dodgy characters and the dodgy lifestyle. You will not break the law, not with Connor to care for. And then you're having a word with yourself. Cos, like, wasn't hurting Billy breaking the law?

No way. Self-defence, wasn't it?

And as the train rattles along past all them familiar stations you do the three monkeys, letting the worries and temptations fizzle away...

Out of the window to the left, the silhouette of the countryside competes with the darkening blue of the sky as if to see which could stand out more, which could be more in-your-face. No sooner is the view in front of you, though, than it's gone and the train's at another stop. Haywards Heath. So close now – the journey's flying by! What will you do first? Look at his face? Hug him tight? Drink in his baby-fresh skin? Wivelsfield. The light outside the window is softening from the bright blue of before into a balmy, comforting pink. Burgess Hill. Nearly there!

And you wonder if that wet on your face is tears again, cos a woman sitting next to you (when did she creep on?) is saying, 'Tell me to butt out, I don't mean to pry, but are you OK…?'

and you're surprised at her being there, and at them tears and all – you're happy, after all, ain't you? – and so you wipe snot from under your nose, sniff hard and reply, 'Yes I'm fine, Layla's – no, Hayleigh's fine,' and she nods, but not in a shitty or patronising way or nothing, you don't think, and goes back to her book as the train pulls into another station.

Hassocks.

Hassocks!

So close, so close now to kisses and cuddles and snuggles over his bedtime bottle of milk. *Chuggedy chug* – you imagine changing his nappy, or will he be potty-trained now? – *chuggedy chug* – singing him a lullaby, playing his favourite game *My Mummy Flies Pigeons, whee!* Then another burst of worry: bet that ain't his favourite game no more – *chuggedy chug* – Preston Park. One more stop! Who cares? You can learn new games, new songs together and –

no way: the train's slowing. In your belly, somersaults; on your forehead a lake of sweat. You're all cooked up, your heart beating so hard that you fear it might pop out your chest.

Ding… *We will shortly be arriving in Brighton, your final station stop.*

Brighton!

You look out the window over the rooftops, the train groaning and crawling its way into the station, and you get a kick out of the familiar, pretty, coloured houses of arty-farty Hanover to the left, a sense of safeness from the never-changing scraggy grey rock-face to the right. Your legs are jelly, your hands shaking as you secure the rucksack to your chest once again, stepping off the train in a hurry, only to get caught up in the gentle flow of people making their way to the exit.

Only: shit. No way.

A group of police and dogs are on the other side of the barriers. Waiting for you? Can't be. But what about the coke? Then you exhale, remembering you chucked it in the bin, thank God. Eyes down, you walk towards the exit gate, your heart racing ten times as fast as it's done at any point today. And with baby steps you're almost tiptoeing past the coppers... a strange look from one of them... a wink... and then... freedom! Of course they wasn't there for you.

Outside, on the station concourse, everything's familiar and strange all at once. In fact everything is opposite, is topsy-turvy, right now. You're heavy in the legs what will take you to him, light on the shoulders what are now rid of London's weight. London's ugly black smog has gone and all, you think, sucking up the fresh light air of the seaside, enjoying the first seagull squawk you've heard in over a year. Like, Connor's only a bus ride away now, a short journey along the cliff tops to Peacehaven, so you should be on top of the world – but somehow it seems unbelievable, almost too good to be true.

Look, can you just say something? You know it sounds mad, but, now you're nearly there at the bus stop what will take you to him, there's a sudden flatness in your mind, a cool-headedness; you're not in any kind of rush. You strain your eyes and catch sight of your bus, the number 14, waiting, not moving, turning over its engine. Have you got time to catch it? People are flooding down the street from the station and you can't face barging past. For some reason your legs won't play ball either, and anyway... too late. You crane your neck to watch the bus pulling away from the stop. Is this an omen? A warning? No, you ain't having that! You ain't going to buy the nonsense of the little voice inside, not today: no silly thoughts about your plans driving off with the bus. Only as you check the timetable your heart sinks – the next bus isn't for another half-hour. Maybe take a cab? Then a talking-to: no, got to be sensible, save every penny for Connor now. Just have to catch the next bus, walk through town to the next stop and get things straight in your head: what you'll say to Mum; maybe call round to Dad's first, get him on side; how you'll deal with Michael and his mum. You want it to be perfect, like the pictures you've made in your mind.

And with them thoughts you're running again, enthusiastic again, longing to see Connor again, still gripping hold of the rucksack of course, chasing down Queen's Road with its skanky pubs and kebab shops, the pavements splattered with seagull shit, and down, down, down the hill you keep running, pausing to catch your breath at the Clock Tower.

And there's the sea!

Your first proper glimpse! So calm it looks this evening, so inviting.

Picking up the pace, you start sprinting, sprinting down grotty West Street, sprinting till you can almost swallow up the sea what is there on the horizon, your mouth open, your heart open, your mind open to what life is offering you now. Then you come to another stop at the bottom of the street, Brighton Pier to your left, the creamy-coloured Regency buildings beyond it, the sky above you painted in beautiful watercolour tones. You fill your lungs with air before moving again, pushing on quickly along the promenade till you're taking in the squeals and shouts from the pier what cut across the traffic noises on the roundabout. Jaywalking across it, you have to catch your breath, so close now to the bus stop and the last leg of your journey – gulp – home.

Minutes later, you sit on the bright red bench at the bus stop, the bus stop outside the bars and clubs you was so desperate to get into when you was sixteen. But something tells you that it's time to say goodbye to that lifestyle, time to say ta-ta to that kind of fun. Ouch! A burning in your stomach then, a reality check deep down in your gut. Like, will it be all that easy, to kick the drugs into touch, to give up the partying? No, you can't bear it, can't compute it, so it's back to thoughts of the number 14 again.

Come on, bus, this is torture!

You turn your back on the clubs. Look out at the busy promenade and the comings and goings on the seafront. And you're clutching the rucksack to you, thinking of estate agents, of college, of what the money inside it will bring. In other words, thinking of grown-up stuff what makes your knees knock, your hands tremble. But also something new. A sort of like feeling that, despite them knee-knocking fears, you'll be strong for Connor, yeah? That together you'll be able to fight anything. A dynamic duo. A team.

The sky, tinted with the baby pinks and blues of a nursery, stretches above you, and in it you see a cloud in the shape of a ladder stretching up up up across the pinky-blue. A sky what's so far away, but you feel like you could reach out and touch it, like you can with the future now within your grasp. You do that now. Reach out, try and stroke the sky with your fingers. Tickle it. And then you're painting a picture into it, a picture of you and Connor, side by side, happy and laughing, climbing that cloudy ladder. A flock of seagulls dances across the sky, bringing visions of the chorus on stage in *Swan Lake*, and you see you and Connor, soaring up with them, floating off, the earth spinning at your feet.

Together, we'll dance, we'll fly.

Acknowledgements

For encouragement, support, advice, friendship, editorial insight and more, a huge thank you to Corinne Pearlman, Adrian Weston, Holly Ainley, Vicky Blunden, Candida Lacey and all at Myriad Editions. To copy-editor supreme Linda McQueen and eagle-eyed proofreader Dawn Sackett, a thousand thanks.

Many thanks to Arts Council England for the Grant for the Arts which helped me complete this novel.

Heartfelt thanks to Anna Morrison who designed the eye-catching cover.

Thank you to everyone at my writing group – Amy Zamarripa Solis, Robert Smith, Mathilda Gregory, Mark Sheerin and Ed Siegle – for their feedback on the first chapter of this novel. Likewise, a ginger-beer cheers to Liam Bell for his helpful comments on the entire first draft.

I am enormously grateful to Dr Billie Lister for meeting me to talk through her professional understanding and personal experience of lap dancing culture. Her testimony, together with those from ex-dancers on the website of the campaign group Object, was crucial to the authenticity of this novel. Several books were also useful, particularly *Dirty Dancing: an ethnography of lap-dancing* by Rachela Colosi; *Stripped: The Bare Reality of Lap Dancing* by Jennifer Danns; and *Stripped: A Life in Clubland* by Samantha Bailey – this is reflected in some of the content in this book.

A shout out to Louise Fuller… for listening.

Roly and Lily-Belle, you never fail to be supportive, even during the most challenging times. Much love and thanks to both of you, as ever.

AFTERWORD :

BOOK GROUP GUIDE :

1. Has the action of the novel, particularly the scenes that take place in Elegance, changed your views about lap dancing culture?

2. Discuss Hayleigh's relationship with her body, and whether you think women today feel a similar pressure to be toned, tanned and hair-free.

3. In what way is *Layla* a 'feminist' novel?

4. When Colin follows Hayleigh home from Elegance, she says: 'You know what people think: *Asking for it, isn't she, working in a place like that?*' Discuss public perceptions of lap dancing as a job and the sex worker's role in society.

5. Why do you think *Layla* is written in the second person? How did this affect your reading experience and your relationship with the main character?

6. How is motherhood, and the notion of being a 'good mother', portrayed in the novel? Is Hayleigh a 'good mother'?

7. Is Hayleigh really confused about her sexuality?

8. What is Hayleigh's relationship with Billy Rousseau?

9. Where do Hayleigh's moral boundaries lie?

10. The novel contains some sexually explicit moments, particularly in the lap dancing club; how does the author depict these without being overly graphic?

11. How are female relationships portrayed in the novel? Do you think this reflects reality?

12. Why do you think the male characters are kept in the background of the novel?

13. How does the mobile phone give us another insight into Hayleigh's hectic lifestyle?

14. Is Hayleigh a good or bad person? Is there such a thing?

15. Hayleigh fantasises about earning huge sums of money. How is money characterised throughout the novel, and what is her relationship to it?

16. What is the significance of birds in the story?

17. How does the author use Hayleigh's voice to reflect her background?

18. With whom would Connor be better off? Hayleigh or her mother?

19. With the exception of place names, could this be any city, or is the atmosphere very identifiable as London?

20. What future do you envisage for Hayleigh and Connor?

If you have enjoyed *Layla*, you might
like Nina de la Mer's critically acclaimed
debut novel *4 a.m.*

'Mesmerizing. And kind of frightening
that a female writer can crawl so far
into the male psyche.' John Niven

4 a.m.

NINA DE LA MER

For an exclusive extract, read on...

Chapter One

Fallingbostel British Army Base, Germany

Cal

I nick tae the block and check on Manny. Are my eyes playing tricks or what? Forty-eight hours later and he's still buzzing – sprawled on his pit, throwing out shapes wi his hands in the air, music blasting fae his stereo. Still, the vital signs are there, so I fling him a 'Back in a bit' and march across the parade square tae the cookhouse.

Ye've got tae be kidding me.

The kitchen thermometer's only went up a degree in the few minutes I've been gone. Insult tae injury, it's an Indian summer and the fans are on the blink. One degree higher and that'll be me, melted away tae a greasy spot. But there's bugger-all use complaining, so I get tae work, my hands shaking as I dice the onions and mince the beef, my eyes watering as I add the sweating bulk tae a vat of oil. *Hisssss.* The air clags thick wi bogging, fatty smoke. Oh, Christ, I think, my mouth swimming wi liquid, I'm never?

I am.

I'm gonnae boak. I'm defin-ately gonnae boak.

Deep breath in… deep breath out… and the danger's over, just in time tae add the garlic before the mince mixture burns. From the other side of the kitchens Corporal Clarke throws me daggers. I wince.

'Wilson!'

That's him, Clarkey, his temples swelling in irritation as he shouts over, 'Look lively! That food's going out on the hot plates in half an hour… and counting!' he adds wi a fake smile.

'Yes, boss,' I reply wi mair enthusiasm than I feel, a shower of sweat pouring fae underneath my chef's hat. I wipe it away, my hand wilting in the heat. Whoops! A few beady drops splash intae the spag bol. I grin.

'Slop jockeys', the other squaddies call us. A slagging I wouldnae contest, the night.

Today's going fae bad tae shagging worse.

Nine hours I've been here working like a daftie, huvin as much fun as an ice cube in a sauna. Manny's only got himself a sick chit, and guess who he buttered up tae cover fur him? Aye, right. Muggins here.

But hang on, before yous take me fur some kind of misery bucket, chill out – it's no my usual style tae pish and moan. In fact the other lads call me Happy, after wan a they seven dwarves. They'd say that's 'cause I'm 'happy-go-lucky'; I'd say they're taking the urine, 'cause I'm only five foot five in my bare feet.

Anyway. Truth be told, the reason I'm on a downer is on account of all the dirties Manny and me done this weekend. Dirties? Dirty rugs. Drugs, yeah? Which reminds me. He's needing something tae bring him back down. I know! Orange juice. Manny's always on at me: 'Vitamin C's a bender-mender; it sorts you right out.' I huvnae a clue if he's right. But who knows? Mibbe it'll huv wan a they – what d'ye call it? Placebo effects.

C'moan, Cal, concentrate! 'Scuse me a minute while I deal wi the spag bol – a bit of seasoning here, a stir there. Nope. Still looks and smells like shite. Whoah! Here comes the boakiness again. If Clarkey doesnae let me vamoose soon, my liquid brekkie's gonnae end up in the lads' dinner. I do a recce tae see how the land lies fur a quick exit. Nae chance.

The others on duty the night are just the type of cunt tae land you in it, if ye let on ye've been out on the randan.

'I'm watching you, Wilson,' Clarkey bellows over the din of ten lads and lassies scuttling like ants across the cookhouse.

My face becomes a mask of pure hard graft.

That Clarkey, he's an arse-wipe, so he is; loves a whinge mair than he loves himself. Just. I'll gie yous a fur instance. Say he parked on double yellas and the man gied him a ticket, he'd make a fuss, get violent even mibbe, even if he was in the wrong. Or say I made a mistake in the cookhouse, that'd be me in the *merde*, even if I apologised my cock off and all that malarkey. That's just the kind of cunt he is.

Och, c'moan! I'm gonnae fuckin burst if I don't get out of here, right now, this minute! There's nothing fur it but tae raid the fridge and shove an OJ carton under my whites, telling the other lads, 'I'm away fur a pish.'

Clarkey watches me, eagle-eyed, but what can he do? If ye've gotta go, ye've gotta go, eh?

Still, I cannae be too long, so once again I bolt back tae the lines and find Manny Bert-alert, eyes hanging out his heid, continuing his manual re-enactment of the raver's favourite dance move – big box, little box, big box, little box.

No change there, then.

I decide it's time fur action. 'C'moan, pal,' I say, 'yer no gonnae come down if ye carry on like that!' and, offering him the juice, 'Here, get this down yer neck.'

He doesnae move a muscle, but. I fling the OJ carton at him in frustration. Tae my shock and surprise, he catches it. No flies on him, even if he is in fuckin la-la land. Not that he drinks it, mind, just tosses it fae hand tae hand like it was a ball or something.

Is he acting it, or what?

'C'moan. I huvnae got all day. Gonnae just make an effort…?'

Silence.

'For me?' Fuck me, he's almost got me begging now. 'Please?'

Then, out of nowhere, he gives up, opens his gub, and knocks back the OJ carton in a wanner. Watching him gulp it down, my own comedown smacks me in the face, as if tae say, *I'm here, ye stupit bastard, did you really think ye'd got away wi it?*

Away tae fuck – I'm no huvin that!

I check the coast is clear and rack up a quick line of speed, putting two fingers up tae the comedown, as well as the regiment. Aw, c'moan! Yous can hardly blame me. Only a wee wan tae get me through the arse end of my shift. The minute the bitter white stuff hits the back of my nose and throat, my heid clears and I waken up. Right. I can do it – a wee while mair and I'll be in my pit and in the land of the big zeds. Besides, going back tae the cookhouse doesnae seem so bad wi a wee bit of billy up my nostrils.

Och, no. What now? Manny's only back at the happy-clapping, grinning at me, making zero effort tae come back tae the land of the living.

I am beelin now, so I am.

'Nae bother!' I spit out sarcily as I turn on my heel tae leave. I mean! He husnae thanked me fur risking my backside tae bring him the juice *or* fur covering his arse again. Double whammy! I storm out, imagining masel like wan a they comic book characters, smoke blowing out my ears, clouds of dust following behind.

Back in the kitchens I take a pure maddy, banging the pots and pans and accidentally on purpose smashing a few plates. My anger doesnae last long, but. I mean, Manny's my best pal here. We've pallied about thegither since haufway through the basic training, even though he's a soft southerner. Aye, he tried tae pull the Big Man act when we first met, was up himself 'cause he'd started his Army career training fur the infantry. Still, the rest of us chefs soon twigged how hard he is – about as hard as a bag of marshmallows, if yous want tae know the truth. It was mibbe when he put his Take That calendar up in the kitchens that we finally hud him sussed. The numpty.

If ye forget the boy bands, we've a lot in common, me and Manny, so we huv. Both scored the same on wur Army entry tests. That is, no very highly. Not that I came up the Clyde in a banana boat, as my granda used tae say. I mean tae say, I'm no stupit. Manny neither. The main thing we huv in common, though, is wur love of the rave. Kept us sane back at the training down Aldershot. Okay, yous've got me. Insane's probably mair like it – going tae the dancing Saturday nights, getting zebedeed fur days on end.

Anyway. Ye know how an Eccy buzz makes you pally up wi folk, even if yer just after meeting them? That's how it was wi Manny and me. Pure bezzie pals after wan all-nighter at the Rhythm Station. There we was, hammering the dance flair tae the sounds of DJ Slipmatt when we clocked wan another across the smoky room. Buzzed off each other all night, then broke back intae camp, tunnelling through a piece of broken fence. And that was that – bezzie pals fur life.

Talking of the rave, it's often misunderstood, if yous want my opinion. Folk that aren't on the scene, they think raving's all about drugs, forgetting that it's the music that sends most ravers mental. Och, okay, scratch that, it's the combination of the two that's magic: like bacon and eggs, beer and fags, Kylie and Jason… Alright, alright, I'm kidding yous wi that last wan. But tae get back tae my point. If yous huvnae a Scooby what I'm on about, yous'll huv tae take my word fur it: there's nothing beats hardcore rave music on this Earth. The banging bass lines, the breakbeats, the speedy-up vocals. Sorted!

Oh, and while I'm on the subject, I was forgetting another reason the lads call me Happy. I'm intae 'happy hardcore': it's got mair BPMs than your common-or-garden hardcore, it's mair euphoric and uplifting, working harder tae get yer heart racing and yer blood pumping. Problem is, Manny and me huv seen mair of the above than a fitba fan at an Auld Firm game, so we thought we'd knock it on the heid fur a bit. Ye know? Go straight; sort the heids?

Aye, right. The other day wur pal Taff turned up wi some Eccies we'd asked fur a while back, and Manny had the bright idea tae arse the whole lot in the wan go. Nice wan, pal! You see, I'm no intae double dropping so it was a mathematical certainty he'd end up in a worse two-and-eight than me.

So, he starts off on Thursday wi two tablets – snowballs they were, the wans that fuck you right up. Aye, I know I said he was soft, but when it comes tae the dirties he's harder than a fuckin brick wall. I took just the wan tae start. I'm no being funny but I like the dancing too much, so if I'm on Eccy and we're no at a rave I hold back, otherwise my mind can go off on a ramble. Sometimes I even think of the bad stuff, like my da dying, my ma's love of the cheeky water, and how the Army's no lived up tae expectations. Aw, c'moan, yous can put yer hankies away. Plenty of time tae use them by the time wur stories are finished.

Anyway. Where was I? It's Thursday, Manny's double-dropped, I'm on the wan, we're both trying tae act casual, waiting fur the Eccy tae work its magic, when he says tae me, 'I'm thinking of jacking it all in, mate, going back to Southend. Fuck the consequences.'

Kick in the baws, or what? I mean, I know he isnae huvin the best crack ever, but leaving? So I goes, 'C'moan. Who'll I pally about wi if you go AWOL on us?'

His answer? 'You'll always be alright, you will.'

And I was thinking, *What's he mean by that?* but I didnae huv time tae mull it over 'cause my fingers were tingling and my heid was birlin, which could only mean wan thing – coming up – so I made my way tae the lavvies fur a dump.

Job done, I took a look at masel in the mirror. I get obsessed by my reflection when I'm coming up 'cause the size of my pupils tell me whether the gear's working and how far gone I am.

That night they wernae saucers, they were fuckin flying saucers. I was defin-ately buzzing.

Thing is, the rushes were coming on so thick and fast that my eyes went skelly. Took me a pure hauf-hour tae feel my way along the corridor tae wur pit, me and the wall being best of pals by the time I'd finished. And obviously I avoided the eyes of any square pegs walking past me in the block – nothing worse than huvin a serious blether when the dirties are kicking in. But would yous believe, by the time I got back, Manny hud only gone and dropped his third E?

Houston, I thought, *we huv a problem.*

Little did I know he'd wind up doing four by 4 a.m.

Which reminds me. Best check on him again. I glance at the clock, willing it tae be heading towards six. Wicked! Five to!

'Come on, you mongs!' Clarkey bellows, and the whole kitchen becomes a hive of activity: tomato soup, kedgeree, spag bol, raspberry bombe and baked Alaska all on the menu, the night.

My part of the menu's ready, so I lug this culinary delight tae the hot plates in the mess hall, and wi a, 'Night, Clarkey,' I lug my ugly self back tae the accommodation; my eyes going thegither now, I'm that shaggin tired.

Ah, here I am at wur block, my pit and my pillow just beyond the door, which judders as I open it, my body screaming fur some –

C'moan tae fuck! Yous willnae believe what Manny's up tae now, the crazy bastard?

'Manny! Oy, Manny, get down fae yer pit!'

He's standing on his bed, wearing nothing but his boxers, by the way.

'Aooooouuuuuuh!'

Who's he think he is? Tarzan, King of the Jungle?

'Hoy, Manny.' I go. 'Keep the heid.'

Aye, yous are right, it's a losing battle – he's away wi the fairies this time, mibbe all the way tae Neverland, and without a return ticket. My throat closes up and my palms start sweating – somebody's sure tae come in and clock what's going down.

'Come on, ye tube, pull yersel thegither!' I say. I've lost all patience with his antics now.

'I am invincible.'

What's that? He's mumbling something at me, through a spittle mouth.

'Manny, pal, gonnae speak – "

'I AM INVINCIBLE!'

Alright, alright! Nae chance of missing that yin: he's pure hollering now.

But no sooner has he opened his gub than he buttons it and falls back ontae his pit, launching intae some major zeds. There's nothing else fur it. I lay him in the recovery position and bunch down next tae him, in case he takes a baddie.

Aye, I could leave him there tae choke on his own boak, but – as yous huv mibbe already guessed – that just wouldnae be me.

Pte C. Wilson
231042189
BFPO 179
4 Sept 1993

Dear auntie Edie

Its bean a while so I thought id drop you a line and let you know how im getting along. Lifes treeting me not so bad but I do still spend too much time board out my brains.

Sometimes youd think we serve up shite with sugar on top seeing the looks on the other lads faces! As you would say, so I don't feel bad for swaring. I cant wait for my next leave when Ill cook a rare feast for you and uncle Bob.

Im looking forward to a wee hug as well as I do get lonely sometimes. Ive got my pals around me. Remember Manny and Iain? There good pals and make life bareable and we all go to the dancing when we can which just about gets us through the boardom. Though Ive been trying to take it easy and consintrate on my work the last couple of weeks. I hope uncle Bob is okay and helping with the messages and that while your legs bad. Sometimes I think hes so lazy he wouldn't get out of bed if he won the Pools. I hope your getting on and not missing me too much.

Please write soon and tell my cousins to stop being so lazy and write to me. There letters put a smile on my face.

Love from Cal

Fallingbostel British Army Base

Manny

I'm sweating worse than a paedo in a playground, so I shake the gorgeous girl lying next to me awake. *Babe, open the window, will ya?* Phwoar! While she does as she's told – good girl – the towel wrapped round her slim, tanned body slips to the floor to expose her massive... (Manny!) She pouts, her fuck-me eyes pleading, like some grot-mag slapper. *She really wants it, she does*, I think, as her hand slips towards my... (Manny!)

What the fuck? It's Amy! My ex! Nause! How did I...?

'Manny! Wake up, ye lazy cunt. It's seven o'clock.'

Seven o'clock? Fuck about. Must be a PT morning. Physical training. No chance of me making that – ten hours' kip and I still feel like a bag of shite. Then I remember, nah, it's Sunday, on duty but no PT, and I slouch back into the comforting filth of my bedclothes and the filthy comfort of my woody... Cal's bang out of order cutting my dream short just when things were getting interesting, even if I was fooling around with my ex. Can't be arsed to go into that messy little story right now. 'Aw, mate, give us five,' I say. 'I'm well sketchy.'

'Now there's a surprise after what you pulled this weekend. C'moan. I'm no kidding. Up. Shower. On duty.'

'Oy, oy!'

The fucker's only dragged off my sheet, exposing my naked body – crown jewels and all! Alright, alright, I know sleeping naked in a shared room's weird, but if you had to sleep in a feckin' sauna, you'd have yer kit off and all. Anyway. There's no effing way I'm getting up: my head's pounding, my mouth tastes like a badger's arse and my comedown's probably gonna cling to me all day like a bad fart. I screw my eyes shut, trying to drift back into the sexy mood of my dream.

Not if Cal has anything to do with it. 'Your fuckin funeral, pal, if you want tae end up on ROPs again, and no weekend passes.'

Shut the fuck up, you big girl's blouse! That, I'm screaming on the inside. Out loud, I just go, 'Yeah, yeah, whatever.'

'Laters,' our other roommate, Jonesy, says, flobbing out the window on the way out.

'Oy, oy!' I shout – meaning at the spitting. Christ, that lad gets on my tits with his filthy habits. Been following us about like a lapdog recently and all, trying to get in with us and that. Trust our luck to land only three in a six-man room, but end up with Jonesy as the spare prick.

Anyway. Cal really lets rip now he's out of the picture. 'Cheers, pal – what happens then about wur trip tae Hamburg this weekend? I'm no being funny but yer no just fucking things up fur yersel, are ye?'

Fair dos. Stay in bed now and there's no way I – or anyone else – is getting battered at the Tunnel Club in Hamburg, Saturday night. The thing is, no other fucker's prepared to drive, so if I land up in the punt they've had it.

'Alright, alright, keep yer knickers on,' I say. 'Give us a minute.'

Fuck all this 'going straight' malarkey. Couldn't take another weekend without a healthy dose of my medicine, if you catch my drift. I mean, I ain't being funny, but the only thing's gonna get rid of this comedown is coming up again. Specially when OJ's done nothing for me this time, apart from leave a ton weight on my pelvis.

I am fucking aching for a slash!

Pissing in my pit's not an option – I get enough shit from this lot as it is – so with maximo effort I kick off my sheets, scowling at Cal as I make my way to the bogs.

'Good doggy, off you trot,' Cal goes, flicking me on the arse with a towel – the wind-up merchant.

A toxic stench swamps the late summer air, overpowering me as I get nearer to the bogs. Yup, that's it – the unmistakable reek of *eau de crap*. I cough up a glob of sick and wipe it away with the back of my hand. I guess one of the lads has only gone and staged another dirty protest. Would you believe some joker finds it funny as fuck to smear his own shit over the cubicle walls and graffiti in it with his finger?

Here we go: *You are fuckin dead meat.*

Whoah! That's well suspect. My eyes dart about; that ain't aimed at me, is it? Wouldn't fucking surprise me. I'm not exactly Mr Popular round here.

Not surprised the graffiti shit artist has lost it either, mind you, living in this fucking dump. Still, don't give him the right to fuck up the bogs for the rest of us, does it?

Lucky I only need a slash for now, so I head for the urinals... pull out my dick as I go... steady myself against the wall with both hands as I empty... try to control my breathing. It's difficult, 'cause when I think of the amount of gear I done over the last forty-eight hours, my chest squeezes in and out like one of them accordions. I close my eyes for a second, try and blot the anxiety out. Wish I hadn't bothered.

Behind my eyelids my own guilt and dread gang up to chew me out:

Only got yourself to blame, intya, ya gob shite?

Better to open my eyes and deal with looking and feeling like shit in the cold light of day. Fuck, no, that ain't much better! There's still a load of negative thoughts twittering through my brain.

I feel like kicking something, like blubbing, disappearing into a black hole. It's as if everyone hates me, and I hate them; or something bad has happened or is about to happen; as if something's not right with the world but I'm fucked if I know what.

In short, my chums, I'm consumed by The Fear, that nagging post-drugs-binge worry that you did something majorly not big or clever the night before.

Right now, I have got The Fear big time.

I mean, did I say summit to Cal last night that I shouldn't have? Did I fess up to what's doing my nut in? Nah, couldn't have done, wouldn't have done. He's been a blinding mate to me. Still, there are some things – some things you don't even tell yer mates.

Got to watch each other's backs in this game though, innit? Especially 'cause Corp Clarke's been breathing down my neck more than usual recently. He's always had me down as a loser, a fucking nobody, 'cause he knows the truth about me leaving the infantry training. Now though, he seems to really have it in for me. Went and reported me to the troop sergeant for having an 'incomplete kit' the other week, and I copped a beasting – had me marching around the football pitch carrying a sack of spuds on each shoulder. Yeah, yeah. Doesn't sound that bad, does it? But it was twenty-five degrees in the shade that day; he's lucky I didn't get heatstroke.

Still, could have been worse. Corp Clarke's got form for dicking me about.

Yeah, and we all know why that is, don't we?

Fuck about! Things have gone pretty tits-up when even yer own thoughts have turned against ya, eh?

I try and block them out by humming a favourite tune as I slope over to the block.

I'll take you up to the highest heights,
Let's spread our wings and fly away...

By the time I get back the dorm's empty. Cal must have fucked off to the cookhouse without me. Oy, oy! I know what you lot are thinking, but get back in your prams. Yeah, he's been good to me. Being late for once in his life wouldn't fucking kill him, though, would it? Fuck's sake, where's my fucking gear – my whites? Could have sworn I had my kit out ready before we started our session the other night. What a top buzz, though. A shiver of pleasure runs through me. Worth the agony I'm going through now. That's what it's all about, people: the agony and ecstasy. What I'm all about.

Course Clarkey's waiting for me when I finally rock up to the kitchens. Two minutes late. It might as well be two years.

'Oy. You. Manning!'

He's striding towards me as if I've told him I fucked his mother. In the arse. Here it comes. The Payback.

'SNCO kitchens – and you're lucky that's all I'm dishing out to you, you woeful little cretin.'

He's got to be kidding me. I don't mind rustling up the scran for the lads – quite enjoy the banter as it happens. Cooking for the officers, that's a different story. Fucking complaining wankers, they are. Everything has to be 'just so'.

And this, he's having a laugh, ain't he?

Got to make two hundred marzipan rosebuds to go on some Rupert's wedding cake! A cunt of a job at the best of times, never mind when my arse is hanging out my elbow.

I glance sideways at the other lads. Yeah, course. They've only gone and jiffed me up, 'cause I'm late again. Nothing like sticking up for your mates. I throw out evils to anyone who catches my eye. Cal don't have the guts to look at me, of course, making himself busy chucking potatoes in the chipping machine. Still, at least I'll be flying solo, can get lost in my own thoughts, not have to speak to any fucker.

Like they want to talk to you – loser!

Fuck about! There's them negative thoughts again. I try and shake them off as I walk over to the counter.

'Right, mate,' Clarkey goes, a token gesture of friendliness 'cause he knows he's landed me in the *merde*. 'Made these before?'

'Um, yeah. I guess you just have to, um, make sure the marzipan's thin enough to, um – '

'Come on, speak up, son.'

What I wouldn't do to punch his lights out.

'Yeah, you have to make sure the marzipan isn't sticky, and it's thin enough to shagging roll out – '

Death stare from full-screw Clarke.

'Corporal,' I add in the nick of the time – best to be formal with Clarkey when you're in the shit.

Seems to do the trick 'cause he goes, 'Okay, fill yer boots,' and stomps off, leaving me to roll out the marzipan. Fuck about! What a mare. Make it too thin and it breaks, too thick and it won't look right. I settle on my third attempt – I mean, who gives a flying one if the Rupert's wedding cake looks like it came from Tesco?

Always cutting corners, eh, you useless slacker?

Fucking hell, mate, concentrate, I tell myself, *ignore your constant self-loathing and self-pity!*

I try and do just that, and start again from scratch, laying down the marzipan and rolling it into a soft smooth ball. 'Perfectly pink', they want the roses, so in goes one tiny drop of red food colouring. Looks more pukey pink than perfect. Whatever. It'll have to do. Next, I lay out the wax paper, starting to roll out very fine layers of the pink gunk between each sheet – the thinner each layer the better, to make sure the roses are delicate. Then, as precisely as possible, I cut out three circles for each rosebud petal, overlapping each one to roll it up into a cylinder. Whoah! My fingers surprise me with a massive tremble as I try to roll up the first petal. This is hardly the job for someone with the shakes, I tell ya.

I'll take you up to the highest heights,
Let's spread our wings and fly away,
Surround you with love that's pure delight,
Release your spirits, set you free.

There's that tune again. Baby D, 'Let Me Be Your Fantasy'. Wicked!

And as it continues to rumble around my head, I rack my brains to remember the last time I heard it out at a rave. Fuck, yeah! It's that last time me and Amy went to Dreamscape, with my crew back home. She and I had a stonking row, over –

Hold up. I don't want to think about that. Why did that little nugget pop up? Always freaks me out, that. How thoughts steal their way into your mind, as if some evil ghost-fuck had whispered them in your ear. So now I'm thinking about thinking. Where do our thoughts come from? And that one too. Where did that last one come from? And that, why that? Fuck about! A fella could go fucking mental if he went on like this all day.

I tune in to the *tick, tick* of the big clock on the wall instead, trying to blot out all this other shit chasing about. Don't want to look at the time, mind you – I've probably only been at it for half an hour. But yeah, you guessed it: now the 'what time is it?' seed has been planted I can't help myself. I steal a quick look. Harsh! Over an hour to go till lunch, or, put it another way – another fifty sodding rosebuds.

It's not like me to be a clock-watcher, as it goes. Hate them, in fact. I was brought up to work hard. Had to. My mum's a teacher, my dad's a copper, always pushing, pushing, pushing me to make the best of myself. Yeah, yeah, Cal's started on his life story, now you're getting mine. What did you expect – one of them books where the characters appear out of thin air?

Anyway. Right now I can't stop myself looking at the clock. I think: if I can just follow the second hand round for one tour of the clock-face without chucking up, throwing a whitey or screaming, *That's it, you got me, I'm a fucking druggie*, then I'll be alright till the end of the shift.

One. I button my lips and clench my arse cheeks together, to stop myself fainting like a girl. *Ten*. I take a few deep breaths to stop my heart from going like the clappers. In out, in out, in out. *Twenty*. The last, tiny frail rose I've made rebels, gluing to my hands. *Forty*. What's stopping me from doing one? Holding my hands up, handing myself in for drugs and fucking off back to Blighty? Fastest fucking way of signing yer papers, so they say. Answer? Fear, most probably. Don't want to leave Cal in the shit, neither. *Sixty*! Right. Times that last minute by what – seventy? – and I'll be out of here faster than a virgin jizzing over a porno.

MORE FROM MYRIAD EDITIONS

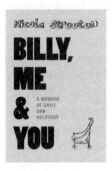

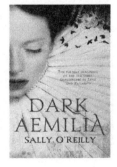

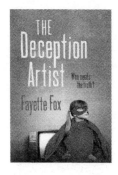

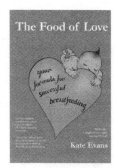

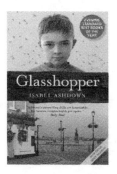

MORE FROM MYRIAD EDITIONS

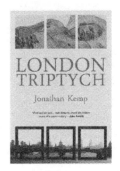

MORE FROM MYRIAD EDITIONS

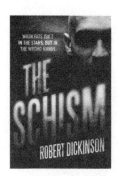

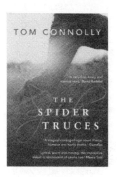

About the author

Nina de la Mer's debut novel *4 a.m.*, shortlisted for the Writer's Retreat Competition, was published in 2011 by Myriad Editions. In 2013, she received an Arts Council England Grant for the Arts to write *Layla*. Nina was born in Scotland and grew up there and in Brighton, where she now lives with her husband and two children.